THE
DEAD FISH
MUSEUM

THE
DEAD FISH
MUSEUM

Charles D'Ambrosio

ALFRED A. KNOPF   NEW YORK 2006

THIS IS A BORZOI BOOK
PUBLISHED BY ALFRED A. KNOPF

www.aaknopf.com

Knopf, Borzoi Books, and the colophon are
registered trademarks of Random House, Inc.

"The Dead Fish Museum" originally appeared in *A Public Space*
(Issue 1, Spring 2006). The following stories previously appeared
in *The New Yorker:* "Drummond & Son," "Screenwriter," "The
High Divide," "The Scheme of Things," and "Up North."

Library of Congress Cataloging-in-Publication Data
D'Ambrosio, Charles.
The dead fish museum / by Charles D'Ambrosio.— 1st ed.
p.   cm.
ISBN 1-4000-4286-0
I. Title

PS3554.A469D43 2006   813'.54—dc22   2005044672

Manufactured in the United States of America
First Edition

For Heather Larimer

The desperate man has no native land.

—ALBERT CAMUS

Contents

THE
DEAD FISH
MUSEUM

The High Divide

At the Home I'd get up early, when the Sisters were still asleep, and head to the ancient Chinese man's store. The ancient Chinese man was a brown, knotted, shriveled man who looked like a chunk of gingerroot and ran one of those tiny stores that sells grapefruits, wine, and toilet paper, and no one can ever figure out how they survive. But he survived, he figured it out. His ancient Chinese wife was a little twig of a woman who sat in a chair and never said a word. He spoke only enough English to conduct business, to say hello and goodbye, to make change, although every morning, when I came for my grapefruit, I tried to teach him some useful vocabulary.

I came out of the gray drizzle through the glass door with the old Fishback Appliance Repair sign still stenciled on it, a copper cowbell clanging above me, and the store was cold, the lights weren't even on. I went to the bin and picked through the grapefruits and found one that wasn't bad, a yellow ball, soft and square from sitting too long in the box, and then I went to the counter. The Chinese man wasn't there. His tiny branchlike wife was sitting in her chair, all bent up. I searched my pockets for show, knowing all along that I'd be a little short. I came up with twenty-seven cents, half a paper clip, a pen cap, and a ball of blue lint. I put the money in her hand and she stared at it. By the lonesome sound my nickels and pennies made when she sorted them into their slots I also knew that the till was empty. I looked behind her through the beaded curtain to the small apartment behind the shop. Next to the kitchen sink was an apple with a bite out of it, the bite turned brown like an old laugh.

I held my grapefruit, tossed it up in the air, caught it.

Where is he? I asked.

She was chewing on a slice of ginger and offered me a piece, which I accepted. In the morning, they chewed ginger instead of drinking coffee.

Husband? I said.

She blinked and spat on the floor. *Meiyou xiwang,* she said. *Meiyou xiwang.*

She folded her hands, tangling the tiny brown roots together. *Meiyou xiwang,* she said, touching her heart, and sending her hands flying apart. Her singsong voice beat an echo against the bare walls. Her hands flapped like a bat. I shook my head. *Meiyou xiwang,* she insisted. Huh? I said, but I knew we could go on forever not making any sense. She hugged herself, like she was cold. I didn't know what to say. She'd traveled all this way, she'd left China and crossed the ocean and come to Bremerton and opened a little store and put grapefruit in the bins and Mogen David on the shelves, but she'd gone too far, because now she couldn't tell anybody what was happening to her anymore.

I had two projects at the Home. I was reading the encyclopedia, working through the whole circle of learning available to man, as the introduction said. I'd started with Ignatius Loyola, because I'm named after him, and the Inquisition, and this led me right into the topic of torture.

My other project involved learning Latin so I could be an altar boy. I got the idea one morning at Sacred Heart while I was staring at the cold altar and the Cross and winking at the nailed-up Christ to see if He'd wink back. Our priest said that he didn't go for the vernacular because it was vulgar. If you were God Eternal, he said, would you want to listen to such yowling? He said that everything in the Church was a sign for something else, and a priest was a man who knew all the signs, but an altar boy knew a few of them, too. I looked around the sanctuary. With the snowy marble slab of altar, the gilt dome of the tabernacle and its tiny doors, the chalices and cruets, the fresh-cut flowers, the sparkling candlelight, the sanctuary was like a foreign country, and if I knew the language I could go there.

Several times I read the Missal as far as the Minor Elevation, the part of the Mass just after you pray for the dead. *Per omnia saecula saeculorum. Amen.* World without end. Amen. But I was trying to learn Latin with phonetics—the Missal was Latin on one side, English on the other—and, needless to say, my comprehension was zero, and I was always finding myself back at the beginning, starting over. *Per omnia saecula saeculorum, amen!*

Most of our schoolwork focused on how to get into Heaven. Sister Eulalia, the catechism nun, taught us about sin and the opportunities for salvation. She was a short, wide old woman with thick glasses and blue eyes that drifted behind them like tropical fish. She kept calling Jesus the Holy Victim and the Word Made Flesh and the Unspotted Sacrifice. She said that sacrifice didn't mean to kill but to make holy. We are made in the image of God's great mystery but through our ignorance and despair our vision is clouded. Salvation, she told us, is our presence in a bright light where we at last become the perfect image and reflection of our Creator.

We saw a slide show on the scapular. A boy was riding by a

gas station on his bicycle. A man was pumping gas and a family
was waiting in a car. Then the gas station was blowing up
and the boy was flying through the air. Everybody died but
the boy, who was wearing his scapular. Sister Eulalia passed
around blank order forms and said to fill them out and bring
$2.50 if you thought it was prudent to have a scapular for your-
self. I'd spent all my money on grapefruits, though.

At night, in bed, I practiced my prayers. We had to memo-
rize so many at the Home: Our Father, Hail Mary, Glory Be, Act
of Faith, of Hope, of Love, of Contrition. Praying either put me
to sleep or made me think of girls. Once, I passed a girl a note
during class and Sister Josephine, the discipline nun, inter-
cepted it and said someone my age doesn't know the least thing
about love and shouldn't use that word the way I did. That
kind of love is special, she said. It's a rare gift from God, it's the
consummation of a union, and it's certainly nothing for children. Sister Josephine called it The Marriage Act. It's embarrassing for me to admit, but she made me cry, she was yelling so
much. I never sent another note. Still, I attached a vague feeling of hope to different girls, a feeling of, I don't know, of
whatever, that came out, some nights, when I said prayers.

We had to learn the prayers because we prayed for everything: we prayed for food, we prayed for sleep, we prayed for
new basketballs. Three times a day, Sister Catherine, the food
nun, took us to the church cafeteria for our meals. Volunteer
ladies served us—they were all old and kind and had science-
fiction hair, clouds of blue gas, burning white-hot rocket fuel,
explosions of atomic frizz. I loved the endless stacks of white
bread and the cold slabs of butter. When the nuns said I was
underfoot, I went downstairs and studied the encyclopedias or
read Latin or went outside and shot buses with my pump gun.
Buses passed the Home every twenty-six minutes. I built up my

arm pitching rocks at a tree until a circle of pulpy white wood was exposed in the bark. One afternoon I planted a sunflower in a milk carton.

I longed to go somewhere but there wasn't anywhere good that I knew of. Then one day I found the public-school yard.

What're you doing here, you stupid shit? asked one kid, a pudgy boy with skin like a baby.

He and some other boys pushed around me in a circle.

The pudge said, Who are you?

When I didn't answer, he said, You're one of those orphan bastards, right?

The boys crowded in closer and I was afraid to speak. People could tell you were from the Home by your haircut. We were all shaved up like the Dalai Lama.

Finally I smiled and mumbled, If you say so.

What? the pudge said. I didn't hear you.

The circle of boys cinched like a knot. Their looming heads were way up in the sky.

Yeah, I said.

After that I sat below the monkey bars and chewed a butter sandwich and watched pudge-boy and his gang over by the water fountain with some girls and I knew I was going to have to kick his ass sooner or later. Everything else was new and strange but this seemed predictable and something I could rely on.

That spring the pudge had the nerve to try out for baseball. He wore brand-new cleats and threw like a fem and his mitt, also brand-new, very orange and stiff, wouldn't close. He might as well have been standing in right field with a piece of toast. He dropped everything. The second day of practice, we had an intrasquad game and I nailed him three times. I just chose places on his fat body and threw the ball at them. Eventually, pudge-boy was afraid to stand in the batter's box. The coach thought I had a control problem but I didn't. My control was perfect.

I whiffed nine guys and made the team and the pudge was cut. He walked away, crying. I ran down the hill and jumped on his back. I hit him in the face and the neck and beat on his ear over and over. You hear that? I shouted. You hear that, you fat fucker? Now that I had him alone I was insane. The pudge rolled away on the grass, holding his ear. Blood was coming out. He was bawling, and I hawked a gob of spit right into his black wailing mouth and said, You bastard.

That night, I was asleep with the encyclopedia pitched like a tent over my nose when Sister Celestine, the head nun, came in.

Why weren't you at dinner?

I could hear the polished rocks of Sister Celestine's rosary rattling as she worried them between her fingers.

She pulled the encyclopedia off my head.

Won't you talk? Sister said.

She tucked a dry, stray shaft of hair back beneath her habit. Maybe you'd feel more comfortable making a confession?

I picked at the fuzzballs on my blanket.

I just got off the phone with that boy's mother, she said.

She touched a cut on my lip and took a deep breath. She said, You called him a name. Do you know what that name means?

I shook my head.

She took off her scapular and put it around my neck. Two small pieces of brown wool hung on a cord, one in back, the other in front.

I rubbed the wool between my finger and thumb.

It's not magic, she said.

No?

More like a sign, she said, that helps guide people—she paused—like us. When you pray to it you never say amen, because the prayer is continuous. It doesn't have an end. Before I received my calling, she said, I used to be a lot like you. I felt trapped. It was like I lived in a dark little corner of my own mind. She sighed. Ignatius, do you know what the opposite of love is?

Hate, I said.

Despair, Sister said. Despair is the opposite of love.

When the pudge came to the yard, he was obviously beat-up and everybody wanted to know what happened. Before I could say anything, he came charging across the lot and said, Truce, truce. We shook hands and sat under the monkey bars, which had become my private territory.

I thought Catholics were pansies, he said.

Ignatius Loyola was a warrior, I said.

That's a weird name, the pudge said. My name's Donny.

Ignatius, I told him.

I'm sorry I called you a bastard, Donny said. He peeled a strip of red rubber off his tennis shoe and stretched and snapped it in the air. Then he put it in his mouth and chewed on it.

You should meet my dad, he said.

My dad used to race pigeons, I said. He had about a hundred of them.

Donny looked impressed. How do you race pigeons? he asked.

You just drive out to the country and let them go—they

always find their way back to the coop. You can use pigeons to send messages.

My dad ate a pigeon once, Donny said. In France.

Donny told me about the Eurekan Territory, which was something he'd made up on summer vacation. The Eurekan Territory came from Eureka, California, where he had relatives he didn't like. All they did was drink greyhounds, he said, and talk about people you didn't know. They were always slapping their knees and saying, Gosh, isn't that funny? when nothing was funny.

Donny wasn't a Catholic but I let him wear my scapular, which he kept on calling a spatula.

You should come over to our house, Donny said. It's big. My dad rakes it in.

I said, You want to go see my dad?

Donny looked at me. Where? he said.

What do you mean, where?

Isn't he dead?

Follow me, I said.

St. Jude's Hospital was a huge old brick building. A hurricane fence caged in a patio that was scattered with benches and garbage cans. We walked around the fence, plucking the cold wires with our fingers.

My dad was sitting on a bench with a loaf of bread and an orange. He wore a paper nightgown with snaps in the back. His eyes were like blown fuses, and dry white yuck made a crust around his mouth. Wind ruffled his hair. It was too cold to be outside in a paper outfit.

Don't you want a sweater? I said.

I climbed up the chain-link fence.

This is my friend Donny, I said. Donny, this is my dad, Tony Banner.

Dad was barefoot on one foot and wore a foam rubber slipper on the other. He grabbed the fence and the links shivered. He looked out west, toward the Olympic Mountains, and we looked, too. It was getting dark.

Hey, Dad?

He dropped a piece of bread through the fence, and a couple of cooing pigeons bobbed along the gutter and fought each other for it. They were ugly pigeons, dirty like a sidewalk. They were right under me and Donny's feet. I kicked one in the head. It fell over and beat the dirt with its wings.

I'm learning quite a lot of prayers at school, I said.

That got him to laugh. The cuts on his hands were healing. That last week at our house he emptied all the soup cans in the garage and kept the rusty nails in his pockets. One morning for breakfast he served me a bowl of nails with milk and then squeezed a fistful of them in his hand until blood came out. He kept saying with his voice very loud and fast, I got the nails, I got the nails right here, boy—where's my cross, eh? Now he was gentle. He pushed bread through the fence until the loaf was gone and the pigeons flew away, except the one I'd kicked.

I gotta go home and eat, Donny said to me.

Donny's gotta go home and eat, I told my dad, translating for him. I've got to go eat, too.

I turned around once, real quick, and he was gripping the fence, looking off nowhere, then Donny and I crawled through a hole in the hedge.

Donny's dad asked us, Who wants to get the hell out of here? Who wants to go hiking in the Olympics?

I'd spent most of my summer at Donny's house, so I knew his parents. Mrs. Cheetam was a beautiful woman with silver-and-gold hair. Mr. Cheetam was a traveling salesman and wasn't home much, but it was true, he raked it in. They bought Donny everything. Donny told me he had a sister who died of leukemia. He played me a cassette of her last farewell. Near the end of the tape she said, Donny? I love you, remember that. I want you to know that wherever I am, and wherever you are, I'll be watching. I'll be with you always. I love you. Do you hear me? Donny?

When she said that—I love you. Do you hear me? Donny?— I got a lonely sort of chill.

We're now leaving the Eurekan Territory! Donny said as we drove away, and I said, That's right. Goodbye, Eurekan Territory!

Mr. Cheetam listened to different tapes from a big collection he kept in a suitcase. They were old radio shows, and one I liked was called *The Shadow:* Who knows what evil lurks in the hearts of men? Mr. Cheetam and Donny knew all the words and talked right along with the tapes. The Shadow knows, they said, ha ha ha!

Later Donny woke up and asked, Where are we? Mr. Cheetam said, You see that river there, Donny? That's the Quinault River, and we're going to hike up along what's called the High Divide, and when we get to the top we'll be at the source of that river. You'll be able to skip right over it, he said, so remember how big it is now. Donny asked, What if we see the Sasquatch? I said we'd be famous, if we captured it. Or took a picture, Donny said. But I don't want to see it, he added. We parked at the ranger station and signed in. It was silent and we could hear our feet crunching the gravel. We cinched up our pack straps and looked at each other. This is it, Mr. Cheetam said. He looked up the trail. This is where we separate the men from the boys.

After about an hour, we cut off the main path and headed toward the river. This is where I buried my dad, Mr. Cheetam explained. I always visit once a year. Right beside the river was a tree, hanging over the water and shadowing everything. Initials were carved in the tree on the side facing the river. BC is Billy Cheetam, Donny said. That's my grandpa. Is he under the tree? I asked. No, no, Mr. Cheetam laughed. He was cremated and I scattered his ashes in the river. But this is the spot, he said. The river was deep and wide at that point. Mr. Cheetam asked if he and Donny could be alone to think and remember and I hiked back out to the main trail. I sat against a fallen log until Donny came back. He talks to him, Donny said. What's he say? I asked, but Donny didn't know.

Our first camp was disappointing because we could hear Boy Scouts hooting and farting around, a troop of about sixty in green uniforms with red or yellow hankies around their necks. It was like the Army, with pup tents everywhere. Mr. Cheetam said not to worry, higher up there won't be any Scouts.

We found wood and lit a campfire and made dinner—beef Stroganoff—and I sopped up all the gravy with my fingers. We washed the pots and pans with pebbles and sand in the river. Mr. Cheetam drank whiskey from a silver flask, wiping his lips and saying, Aaahhh, this is living!

The Boy Scouts sounded off with taps. Donny and I shared a smokewood stogie—a kind of gray stick you could smoke—and when it was quiet Mr. Cheetam cupped his hands around his mouth and moaned, Who stole my Golden Arm? Whoooo stooole my Goool-den Aaarm? You could hear his voice echoing in the forest. *Whoooo stooole my Goool-den Aaarm?* You did! Mr. Cheetam shouted, grabbing Donny. We crawled into our tents

and I started laughing and Donny got hysterical, too. Mr. Cheetam had a different tent and told us to shut up.

Donny whispered how he hated the Japs and never wanted
to be captured by them—they knew how to make you talk.
I told him about the Inquisition and all the tortures they'd
invented for getting confessions.

They had this one thing called the press, I said. If you were
accused of a crime and didn't make a plea, the King ordered
you to lie down. Then he piled rocks on you until you con-
fessed the truth or got crushed.

How big were the rocks? Donny asked.

I don't know.

What if you had thirty—what if you had a hundred—no,
wait, what if you had a thousand rocks on you and then you
decided to tell the truth?

You could, I said. But if you said you *didn't* do anything, the
King didn't want to hear that, and he'd just go ahead with
another rock, until you admitted you *did* do it.

Donny hesitated, and I thought I understood.

I know, I said. *I know.*

At the next camp, only two people were around, a man and a
woman, who were sitting naked on a rock in the river when we
first arrived, but kept to themselves afterward. Donny and Mr.
Cheetam fished for a while but quit after Donny's hook got
caught in the trees too many times. Mr. Cheetam said, Don't
worry about it, Donny. It's no good down here. Higher up the
water's colder and we'll catch tons of rainbows, maybe some
Dolly Varden.

We ate a great meal of dehydrated chicken tetrazzini and
pilot biscuits and chocolate for dessert. Donny and I shared

more smokewood. Now and then we added sticks to the fire and the light breathed out and made a circle around us. I love getting away from it all, Mr. Cheetam said.

He tipped back his flask and in the bright curved silver I could see the fire flaming up.

Once upon a time, Mr. Cheetam said, there was a boy and girl who were very much in love.

Where was this? Donny asked.

Oh, Mr. Cheetam said, it doesn't matter, does it? Love's the same everywhere you go, so let's just make up a place.

How about the Eurekan Territory? I said.

Okay, Mr. Cheetam said. The Eurekan Territory, that's where they were in love. It was a small place, and everybody knew everybody else, so eventually people figured out this boy and girl had a thing going. You know what a thing is, right?

Donny said he did.

Good for you, Mr. Cheetam said. Well, this thing was frowned on by everyone. People took different sides, against the boy, or against the girl, everybody blaming everybody else. But the boy and girl were madly in love and you can't stop love, not when it's the real thing.

He went to his pack and pulled out a big bottle and refilled his flask. When he came back he said, You know what that's like, to have a real thing?

Donny said, Yeah, I know.

I mean really real, Mr. Cheetam said.

How real? I said.

Mr. Cheetam ignored me. To hell with what anybody thinks, these kids, these lovers, said. So one night the boy meets the girl on the edge of town and they drive up a dark winding road to a lovers' leap. They can see everything from up there, but they're not looking. No sirree, Bob. The boy and the girl sit in the car, spooning, as we used to call it back in the days—making out, and listening to love songs on the radio, until one of the songs is interrupted by a special bulletin. A prisoner has escaped!

Does the prisoner have hooks instead of hands? I asked.

Yeah, Mr. Cheetam said, that's the guy.

How'd you know? Donny asked.

I knew because the story wasn't true. The girl hears something outside, and the boy says, Oh, baby baby, don't worry, we're way up here above everything, we're safe. The boy tries to get at the girl, and the girl keeps hearing something outside, so eventually it's no fun, and they go home. When the boy opens the door for the girl to drop her out he finds a hook clawing and banging at the door handle, just clinging there, ripped right off the prisoner's arm. Mr. Cheetam didn't scare me, but Donny was scared.

We were quiet for a minute, and then I told them about when my dad was driving in his car. The other car came out of nowhere, I said. And my dad was hanging half out the door. His foot was stuck under the clutch and his head was banging on the road. He was dragged about two hundred feet. He was in the hospital for a month. My mom died.

No one said anything, so I added, That's a true-life story.

You don't think mine was? Mr. Cheetam asked. He looked at me strangely and winked.

Well, I said, yeah, I do. I know it is. I heard about those lovers before.

Mr. Cheetam stood up, stretched, and fell down. Donny and I looked at each other, then we got in our sleeping bags.

Your dad sure enjoys whiskey, I said.

In the middle of the night, Donny said, Hey, you hear that?

Come off it, I said.

I swear I heard something.

There's nothing out there, I said, but Donny went over to sleep in his dad's tent anyway.

We reached a sign that pointed different ways: the High Divide and the Low Divide. We took the high, up and up. There were fewer trees, and we climbed on loose rock called scree, and the air was thinner. Donny had an ugly blister on his heel and complained, and Mr. Cheetam got impatient with him. Just pull yourself up and get going, he said. Don't fall behind. Finally we crossed a field full of pink and yellow wildflowers, and at the far end, where the path ended, was a lake. The surface was perfectly clear and placid and we could see ourselves.

Here we are, Mr. Cheetam said.

Skinny-dipping, Donny said.

First things first, girls, Mr. Cheetam said, so we hopped to, setting up camp and scrounging enough wood for the night.

Donny and I stripped naked and jumped off the cliffs. No one else was around, but when we swam and shouted and splashed, our voices bounced back and forth off the rocks. Ricochet, we yelled. We dove and dove. Then we lay on a hot flat rock. I noticed that Donny had hair on his balls and he probably noticed so did I. You want to smoke a stogerooni? Donny asked. Nah, later, I said. We were stretched out and quiet: blue sky, yellow sun, white mountain—everything was perfect but Donny got antsy doing nothing for so long and took another dip. He came up fast and said, A fish! I saw a fish! And he got his fishing pole and caught a rainbow, like pulling a prayer from the water.

Good work, Donny, Mr. Cheetam said.

The fish wasn't all the way dead yet and Mr. Cheetam had to slap its head against a rock. Blood came out the eyes. The knife blade sank into the skin with a ripping sound. What do we do with the guts? I asked. Toss 'em in the lake, Mr. Cheetam said. We don't want any animals coming into camp. Bears? Donny said. It's not impossible, Mr. Cheetam said, but not likely, either. Maybe the Sasquatch, Donny said. Mr. Cheetam said to shut up about that damned Sasquatch. It's time you grow up, he said, shaking Donny's arm. Jesus, Donny said, rubbing himself.

Mr. Cheetam wrapped the fillets in foil and set them on the fire. It was soft out now, not dark but not light, either. Our shadows were weak around the fire, and Mount Olympus was tinged pink and purple, and the wind died down.

Hey, I said, what about the Quinault?

Yeah, the Quinault! Donny said. You said I'd get to walk across it.

Oh crap, what was I thinking? Mr. Cheetam asked himself. You already did and I forgot, God damn it!

We ran back through the darkening wildflowers. We found a little stream about a foot wide and three inches deep that you would never think was a river but it was. There's your mighty Quinault, Donny, Mr. Cheetam said. Donny asked if we built a dam would the river dry up below and Mr. Cheetam laughed, saying, No, I'm afraid it doesn't work that way. We bent down and drank and splashed our faces in the water. We listened to the little river, trickling in a whisper. It was almost like nothing.

The fish was all burned to hell when we got back to camp. Donny was upset and kept whining. I'm sorry, Mr. Cheetam said, but things happen. What can I say? Then he offered, Tomorrow? You want to stay another day? Donny looked at me, then said, Stay! Stay! Okay, Mr. Cheetam said, I think we've got everything we need—plenty of provisions—and we'll catch some more fish.

After dinner, Mr. Cheetam drew out his flask again. His face was like my dad's had been in the last days, rough and black.

One night toward the end I'd found him, my dad, in our broom closet. He had all his Bob Dylan records out and was writing new lyrics on them with a nail. Other things happened that I prefer to keep to myself. All week his loud voice was like the echo of thoughts he'd had a long time ago. Then one morning at the very end I heard him calling me in the rain. He was on top of our house in boxer shorts, yelling. Our neighbor tried to drive him off the roof by throwing a pot of geraniums at him. My dad started ripping apart the chimney and pitching bricks down on me and everybody else on the front lawn. We had to call the authorities. For a while he thought he was Jesus in a hospital called St. Judas, but it was really St. Jude's and my dad, of course, wasn't Jesus. The same people who took him to the hospital brought me to the Home. I hadn't eaten in three days.

Nearby we saw field mice hopping around, and Mr. Cheetam said that we'd better keep our packs inside the tents tonight. He hooked his arm around Donny's neck and said, How'd you like to go to California?

Not Eureka, Donny said.

No, Mr. Cheetam said, LA.

Donny said he didn't know anything about LA. Mr. Cheetam fussed with the fire, arranging the coals. When that goes out that's it until morning, he said. He tipped back the flask. Then he capped it and said, That's it for that, too. He stretched and groaned and walked out where the firelight failed. I heard him whistling in the dark.

Son? Mr. Cheetam said.

What? Donny asked.

Come on over here a minute, Mr. Cheetam said.

They were in the shadows. I heard Donny say, What does Mom think?

That's the thing, Mr. Cheetam said. Your mother would stay.

I don't know, Donny said. How long would we be gone?

Donald, Mr. Cheetam said, don't be stupid. We're divorcing, your mom and I. You see, we won't come back—we'll live in a brand-new house there.

Donny begged, But why?

Donald, come on. You see how things are.

The two of them were quiet and staring ahead, like their next thoughts might fall out of the sky.

What can I say? Mr. Cheetam said.

Nothing, Donny said.

I love you, Donald. You know that.

I crawled inside our tent. A little while later, Donny got in his bag, buried down inside. He was crying and choking. I whispered, Donny, hey, hey Donny? Donny? I think I hear something out there. Do you hear it? Let's go look! I hugged my arm around him and he started jerking in his bag and sat up and cried to me, Here's your stupid spatula! Then he crossed over into Mr. Cheetam's tent but kept crying and begging even louder for no divorce.

Look, I heard Mr. Cheetam say, after your sister died—His voice fell apart. That's too easy, he said. I've met someone else. He was quiet a minute. That's the truth.

I thought the crying would go on forever, but eventually Donny must have fallen asleep.

I turned over and over in my sleeping bag, and then I put on Sister Celestine's scapular and grabbed the flashlight and crawled out of the tent. The fire made a hiss and I kicked the last few embers around in the bed of ash. Mr. Cheetam snorted in his sleep and I heard Donny say, Dad? and Mr. Cheetam say, What? but there was nothing after that, even though I stood outside their tent a long time, listening.

I aimed my flashlight ahead to the flat rock rim of the lake and followed the narrow beam up there. I sat, dangling my feet, and snapped off the light. I think I was feeling sorry for myself. Suddenly it felt like we'd been gone for ages. Was it Sunday? I gathered up ten rocks for a rosary, to count my prayers. I rattled them in my hands and started the Our Father but my voice was weird. I shook the rocks in my fist like dice. I threw one in the lake, and a little while later I heard the splash. Circles opened out where the stone had vanished. I thought of saying something in Latin but couldn't recall a single word, except amen. I yelled out, A-men! and heard back, Hey-men, hey-men, hey-men, smaller and smaller.

I stretched out on the rock. Sister Celestine's scapular was old, the wool worn soft from handling. Once, at the Home, I had climbed the stairs, six flights up from my room in the basement, to see where she lived. We weren't supposed to go up there. I saw why. Hosiery hung from the water pipes. Candy wrappers were crumpled on the floor. A black habit lay like an empty sack beside the bed. The bed was unmade, and I could see the hollow where Sister Celestine slept. A pale green blanket and a thin yellow top sheet had been twisted into a tight braid and kicked off the end of the mattress. The only decoration was a black wooden crucifix, nailed on the wall above the bed like a permanent shadow.

I was still lying there when Donny and Mr. Cheetam came running up the rock in their undies. Hey, what's going on? they asked. They said they'd heard me shouting and were afraid I'd got lost or seen something.

Maybe the Sasquatch, Donny said.

God damn it, Donald, there is no such thing, Mr. Cheetam said. That's just a myth.

Oh yeah, Donny said. How do you know?

Don't worry, I said. It was nothing.

You sure? Donny said.

It was nothing, I said. I'm sure.

A wind was blowing and it was a little cold on that rock. Nobody knew what to say.

See out there? Above Mount Olympus? That green star? Mr. Cheetam said, pointing. We all looked—a vague white shadow, a green light. It's not really a star. That's a planet— that's Venus, Mr. Cheetam said. The goddess of love.

That's just a *myth*, Donny said, looking at his father. Bastard.

I didn't hear you, Mr. Cheetam said. What did you say?

Nothing, Donny said.

Nothing? It didn't sound like nothing to me.

I pitched another rock in the lake, way out there, as far as possible. We all listened. Across the water a circle spread out, wider and wider. Then, shaking with cold, Donny folded his arms around himself and yelled out, Hey, and we heard back, Hey, hey, hey, and then I yelled out, Hey, and even Mr. Cheetam joined in, and we kept hearing back, Hey, hey, hey, like there were millions of us everywhere.

Drummond & Son

Drummond opened the shop every morning at seven so he and his boy could eat breakfast while the first dropoffs were coming in. The boy liked cereal and sat at the workbench in back, slurping his milk, while Drummond occasionally hustled out to the curb to help a secretary haul a cumbersome IBM from the back seat of a car. The front of the store was a showroom for refurbished machines, displayed on shelves, each with a fresh sheet of white bond rolled into the platen, while the back was a chaos of wrecked typewriters Drummond would either salvage or cannibalize for parts someday. There were two stools and two lamps at the workbench for the rare times when the son felt like joining his father, cleaning keys, but generally after breakfast the boy spent the rest of the day sitting behind Drummond in an old Naugahyde recliner, laughing to himself and saying prayers, or wandering out to the sidewalk to smoke a cigarette. That he step outside to smoke was the only major request Drummond ever made of his son.

"Next week's your birthday," Drummond said.

"Next week." The boy finished his cereal, plunking the spoon against the empty bowl. He said, "I think I'll go outside."

"How about rinsing your bowl?"

"Oh, yeah."

"It's raining pretty hard out."

"That's okay," Pete said, grabbing a broken umbrella he'd

found in the street, a batty contraption of bent spokes and torn black fabric.

A clear-plastic curtain separated the two parts of the store, and Drummond kept a careful eye on his son from the bench. Drummond had acquired sole ownership of the business after his father died of emphysema, and he still remembered those last months beside him on the bench, the faint whisper as the plastic tube fed the old man oxygen. He knew the tank was pumping air through his dad's nose and into his lungs, but day after day it sounded as though the life were leaking out of him. The elder Drummond had just cleaned his glasses with a purple shop rag and nudged them back on the bridge of his nose when he died, and it was as if, for a lingering moment, he were looking over the workbench, among a lifetime's clutter of keys and type bars, dental tools and unraveling ribbons, for his last breath.

Shortly after his dad died, Drummond had started bringing Pete to the shop, and he sometimes guessed that his wife, free of the boy for the first time in years, had discovered she liked living without the burden. She had hinted as much in a letter he recently received, postmarked from her new address in Portland, suggesting that he meet with a social worker to discuss "the future." He missed his wife tremendously when he opened the envelope and saw the beautiful loops of blue cursive running across the page. He hadn't written back yet, because he wasn't sure what to say to this woman whose absence rendered his life so strange. They had eloped during his senior year at West Seattle High, and this would have been their silver anniversary. Without her he felt lonely, but he wasn't angry, and he wondered if their marriage, after twenty-five years, had simply run its course.

The sheets of white paper in the twenty or so typewriters on display waved in unison when Pete opened the door after smoking his cigarette.

"Now is the time, now is the time, now is the time," the boy said, sweeping along the shelf and inspecting the sheets.

"You want to do some keys?" Drummond asked.

"Not now," Pete said, sitting in his brown recliner.

Drummond wore a blue smock and leaned under a bright fluorescent lamp like a jeweler or a dentist, dipping a Q-tip in solvent and dabbing inked dust off the type heads of an Olivetti Lettera 32. The machine belonged to a writer, a young man, about Pete's age, who worked next door, at La Bas Books, and was struggling to finish his first novel. The machine was a mess. Divots pocked the platen and the keys had a cranky, uneven touch, so that they punched through the paper or, on the really recalcitrant letters, the "A" or "Q," stuck midway and swung impotently at the empty air. Using so much muscle made a crescent moon of every comma, a pinprick of every period. Drummond offered to sell the young man an identical Olivetti, pristine, with case and original instruction manual, but was refused. Like a lot of writers, as Drummond had discovered, the kid believed a resident genie was housed inside his machine. He had to have this one. "Just not so totally fucked up," he'd said.

Hardly anybody used typewriters these days, but with the epochal change in clientele brought on by computers Drummond's business shifted in small ways and remained profitably intact. He had a steady stream of customers, some loyally held over from the old days, some new. Drummond was a good mechanic, and word spread among an emerging breed of hobbyist. Collectors came to him from around the city, mostly men, often retired, fussy and strange, a little contrary, who liked the smell of solvents and enjoyed talking shop and seemed to believe an unwritten life was stubbornly buried away in the dusty machines they brought in for restoration. His business had become more sociable as a growing tribe of holdouts banded together. He now kept a coffee urn and a stack of Styrofoam cups next to the register, for customers who liked to hang out. There were pockets of people who warily refused the future or the promise or whatever it was computers were offering and stuck by their typewriters. Some of them were secretaries who filled out forms, and others were writers, a sudden surge of them from all over Seattle. There were professors and poets and young women with colored hair who wrote for the local weeklies. There were aging lefties who made carbons of their correspondence or owned mimeographs and hand-cranked the ink drums and dittoed urgent newsletters that smelled of freshly laundered cotton for their dwindling coteries. Now and then, too, customers walked in off the street, a trickle of curious shoppers who simply wanted to touch the machines, tapping the keys and slapping back the carriage when the bell rang out, leaving a couple of sentences behind.

Drummond tore down the old Olivetti. While he worked, he could hear his son laughing to himself.

"What's so funny?" Drummond asked.

"Nothing," the boy said.

"You always say 'nothing,' " Drummond said, "but you keep on laughing. I'd sure like to know for once what you find so funny all the time."

The boy's face hadn't been moved by a real smile in years and he never cried. He had been quite close to Drummond's father—who doted on his only grandchild—but the boy's reaction at the funeral was unreadable: blanker and less emotional than that of a stranger, who at least might have reflected selfishly on his own death, or the death of friends, or death generally, digging up some connection.

But on the short drive from the church to the cemetary, Pete had only sat slumped in his seat, staring out at the rain-swept gray city, laughing.

"What are you laughing at?" Drummond had asked.

"Nothing."

Drummond had pressed the boy. On such a momentous day, the laughing had got to him.

"Tell me," he'd said impatiently.

"I just start to laugh when I see something sad," Pete had said.

"You think it's funny?"

"I don't think I find it funny. But I laugh anyway."

"Some of these are crooked as hell," Drummond said now, gently twisting the "T" with a pair of needle-nose pliers. "They'll never seat right in the guides, even if I could straighten them out. You see that?" He turned in his stool and showed the boy the bent type bar, just as his father had shown him ages ago. "Not with the precision you want, anyway. A good typewriter needs to work like a watch."

The boy couldn't carry his end of a conversation, not even with nods of feigned interest. His moods were a kind of unsettled weather, either wind-whipped and stormy with crazy words or becalmed by an overcasting silence. His face, blunt and drawn inward, was now and then seized by spasms, and his body, boggy and soft, was racked by jerky, purposeless movements. He wore slipshod saddle shoes that had flattened and grown wide at the toe like a clown's, collapsing under his monotonous tread. His button-down blue oxford shirt and his khakis were neatly pressed; Drummond ironed them every morning on a board built into a cupboard in the kitchen. He spritzed them as he'd seen his wife do, putting an orderly crease in slacks that were otherwise so deeply soiled with a greasy sheen that he was never able to wash the stain out.

"I think I'll go outside," Pete said.

"You sure smoke a lot," Drummond told him.

"Am I smiling?"

He wasn't, but Drummond smiled and said that he was.

"I feel like I am inside," Pete said.

It was a gray Seattle day. There was a bus stop in front of the shop, and often the people who came in and browsed among the typewriters were just trying to escape the cold. A big, boxy heater with louvred vents hung from the ceiling on threaded pipe, warmly humming, and wet kids would gather in the right spot, huddled with upturned faces under the canted currents of streaming heat. Drummond let them be. He found the familiar moods and rhythms satisfying, the tapping keys enclosed in the larger tapping of the rain. Almost everyone who entered the shop left at least a word behind—their name, some scat, a quote. Even kids who typed a line of gobbledygook managed to communicate their hunger or hurt by an anemic touch or an angry jab. The sullen strokes of a stiffly pointing finger, the frustrated, hammering fist, the tentative, tinkering notes that opened to a torrent as the feel of the machine returned to the hand—all of it was like a single line of type, a continuous sentence. As far back as Drummond could recall, he'd had typewriter parts in his pockets and ink in the crevices of his fingers and a light sheen of Remington gun oil on his skin. His own stained hands were really just a replica of his father's, a version of the original he could still see, smeared violet from handling silk ribbons, the blunt blue-black nails squeezing soft white bread as the first team of Drummond & Son, taking a lunch break, ate their baloney-and-sweet-pickle sandwiches on Saturday afternoons.

A rosary of maroon beads dangled between the boy's legs, faintly ticking, as he rocked in his recliner and kept track of the decades. A silent prayer moved his lips.

"Jesus Christ was brain-dead," Pete said. "That's what I've been thinking lately."

Drummond turned on his stool. "Sometimes your illness tells you things, Pete. You know that." The smutted skin on the boy's hands was cracked and bleeding. "You need some lotion," Drummond said. Dead flakes sloughed to the floor, and a snow of scurf whitened the boy's lap. "You like that Vaseline, don't you?"

The boy didn't answer.

"You know I worry," Drummond said.

"Especially when I talk about God."

"Yeah, especially."

"You believe."

"I do," Drummond said, although of late he wasn't sure that was true. "But that's different."

"There's only one true God," the boy said.

"I know."

"I was thinking of writing a symphony to prove it."

"You want some classical?" Drummond asked, reaching for the radio knob.

"Don't," Pete said.

"Okay, okay."

"I'd show how many ways, how many ideas all lead to one idea. God. I'd get the main structure, and jam around it. The whole thing could be a jam."

Drummond futzed with the novelist's machine while he listened to the boy. The old platen's rubber, cracked and hard as concrete, was partially responsible for chewing up the paper and shredding the ribbons. Pressing his thumbnail into a new one, Drummond found that it was properly soft and pliant, in near-mint condition, and he began pulling out the old platen. Drummond had been one of those kids who, after taking apart an old clock or a radio, actually put it back together again, and his satisfaction at the end of any job still drew on the pleasure of that original competence.

"I'd rather record on a computer," the boy continued. "Instead of a static piece of stuff, like an album, you go right to the people, right into their brain. You can do that with a computer."

"You remember about your visitor?"

"Yeah."

"Today is going to be a little different," Drummond said. "We're not going to Dunkin' Donuts right away."

"I like the Dunkin' Donuts,"Pete said.

"I know you do." Drummond took a deep breath and said firmly, "Today we're doing things just a little different from normal. You're having a visitor. She's a nice lady, and she wants to ask you some questions."

"I think I'd like to become a baker."

"What happened to being a janitor?"

"Maybe a janitor at a bakery."

"Now you're thinking." Drummond turned on his stool and looked his son in the eye. "Remember how Mom used to bake bread?"

"No," said the boy.

"No?" Drummond absently cleaned ink from a fingernail with the blade of a screwdriver. "Of course you do. She'd put a damp towel over the bowl, and you'd sing to her. She used to tell you that it was your singing that made the dough rise, remember?"

Drummond turned back to his workbench and listened to

the rain and to the boy praying and telling the beads. The wall in front of his bench was covered with pinups of writers posed beside their typewriters. Drummond wasn't particularly well read but he knew a lot about literature through the machines that made it. This knowledge was handy in selling a Royal Quiet De Luxe to an aspiring writer whose hero was Hemingway or a Hermes Baby Rocket to a Steinbeck fan. A curiosity he'd never been able to figure out was that many of these writers didn't really know how to type. They hung like vultures over their machines, clawing at the keyboard with two fingers and sometimes a thumb, and while they were often hugely prolific, they went about it desperately, hunting and pecking, as though scratching sentences out of the dirt. Given their technique, it was a miracle some of them managed to say anything. An editorialist for the *Seattle Times* told Drummond that he just sat there and hit the machine until, letter by letter, it coughed up the words he wanted. Even Michener, a man Drummond had read and esteemed highly, in part for having typed more than anyone on earth, except perhaps a few unsung women from the bygone era of the secretarial pool, was a clod at the keys.

"You had a really good voice," Drummond said.

At twenty-minute intervals, the sidewalk filled and then emptied, the shopwindow blooming with successive crops of black umbrellas as buses came and went. The hour for the appointment with the social worker approached, and Drummond found that he could no longer concentrate. He rolled two sheets of paper into the novelist's Olivetti, typing the date and a salutation to his wife, then sat with his elbows on the workbench, staring. He wondered if he should drop "Dear" and go simply with "Theresa," keeping things businesslike, a touch cold. Whenever Drummond opened a machine, he saw a life in the amphitheater of seated type bars, just as a dentist, peering into a mouth for the first time, probably understood something about the person, his age and habits and vices. Letters were gnawed and ground down like teeth, gunked up with ink and the plaque of gum erasers, stained with everything from coffee to nicotine and lipstick, but none of his knowledge helped him now. Drummond wanted to type a letter and update his wife, but the mechanic in him felt as though the soul of what he had to say just wasn't in the machine. He looked at the greeting again and noticed that the capital "T" in his wife's name was faintly blurred. That sometimes happened when the type bar struck the guide and slipped sideways on impact, indicating a slight misalignment.

Drummond had been expecting a rendition of his wife, but the woman who walked in the door shortly after noon was nothing like Theresa. She couldn't have been much older than Pete, and she wore faded jeans and a soft, sloppy V-necked sweater with the sleeves casually bunched up at her elbows. Her hair was long and her eyes were gray and her nose, though small, was bulbous. Drummond offered her a stool at the back of the shop and brought her a cup of coffee.

"So, Peter, I'm from Keystone," she said. "A halfway house in Fremont."

Pete squirmed in his recliner, rubbing his hands over the thighs of his soiled khakis.

"Nothing's been decided," Drummond assured the boy.

"Do you have many friends?" the social worker asked.

"No," Pete said.

"No one you see on a regular basis?"

The boy reached for the crumpled pack of cigarettes in his

shirt pocket and then picked up his rosary beads instead. The long chain trembled in his trembling hands, and his mouth made smacking noises, as though he were slopping down soup.

"When I talked to your father, he said you were in a day program several years ago. Did you enjoy that?"

"It was okay."

"Why did you stop going?"

"I think I'll go outside."

"No," Drummond said. "Stay here and talk to the lady. She only has a few questions, and then we're done."

The copper cowbell above the shop door clattered and the sheets of paper in the typewriters waved and rustled, giving off the slight dry whisper of skittering leaves. Drummond half listened to the tapping keys and the ringing bells and the ratchet of the returning carriage until the cowbell clanged dully a second time as the customer left. In the ensuing quiet, the sound of his boy working the polished rosary beads between his rough scaly fingers distracted Drummond from the social worker's questions. The cowbell clapped a third time. A young mother was trying to ease a tandem carriage across the threshold without waking her twin babies. Drummond excused himself and went to help lift the front axle over the bump.

"My husband would love that," the woman said. Mindful of her babies, she spoke in a soft voice. "What is it?"

"That's a Remington Streamliner," Drummond said.

"Do you mind if I give it a try?"

"No, go right ahead."

He set the machine on a desk and held a chair for the woman. Perhaps the new world of computers had taught people timidity, schooling them in the possibility or threat of losing a thing irrevocably with the slightest touch. This woman's hand pressed the "H" so tentatively that the type bar fell back with an exhausted plop before it reached the paper.

"Go ahead," Drummond said. "Give it a good, clean stroke. You won't hurt it. With a manual typewriter you want a little bounce. You can put your shoulders into it."

"Now is the time for all good men now is the time," the woman typed on the black-lacquered machine, and when the bell rang out, happily ratifying what she'd written, she squealed and clapped her hands.

"This is the most beautiful typewriter I've ever seen," she said. "It's so—so noir! It's got Hollywood written all over it."

"It's prewar," Drummond said. "WWII, I mean. What's your husband do?"

"He's a lawyer," the woman said. "But he's got that midlife thing going on and wants to try his hand at screenplays. He's got lots of stories from his days as a public defender. His birthday's coming up, and I just know he's going to be depressed."

"Hold on," Drummond said, walking back to his workbench. He pulled a photo off the wall.

"If your mind's too great for you," Pete was saying, "you should just let God take it. That's what Christ did. He was brain-dead. He never thought on his own."

"I've never heard that before," the social worker said.

Drummond took the photograph and, somewhat chagrined at the wacky course the interview was taking, returned to the showroom. "That's Raymond Chandler," he said. Chandler wore large owlish glasses and sat with a pipe clenched between his teeth, in a bungalow on the Paramount lot. A sleek gleaming Streamliner rested on his desk.

The woman ran a slender hand lovingly over the polished casing, as though it were the hood of a car. Drummond told her the price, expecting her to balk, but instead she gave the machine a pat, ticking her wedding band against the metal, and then brought out a checkbook, paying for the machine and purchasing, in addition, extra ribbons, a bottle of Wite-Out, and a foam pad. "It's just too perfect," she said. The typewriter was added like a third sleeping baby to the carriage. Drummond helped the woman over the threshold again and watched her go. All the young mothers these days were so lovely in a casual, offhand way. Drummond still dressed like his father, who had always worn a shirt and tie under his smock, as though his job were on a par, in dignity and importance, with the work of a doctor.

Drummond returned to his son and the social worker.

"If I let God take my brain, I'd be laughing. I'd know where I was going."

The woman wrote something on a clipboard, which was beginning to crawl with tiny, antlike words.

"Where would you be going?" she asked.

"I'd be going down."

"Down?"

"I'm trying to figure my brain. What it wants me to do. I think to go down, but I can't figure out what it's good for. It's too much for me."

Pete's lips smacked grotesquely, and he stood up.

"I think I just want to be a son," he said. "Not a god." His elbow jerked involuntarily. "I have to go to the bathroom."

The boy vanished into the back of the shop. Drummond turned to the social worker, whose long straight hair framed a lovely, plain face.

"Is that typical?" she asked. "That kind of talk?"

Drummond sat on his stool. "Yeah," he said.

"And the dyskinesia?"

Drummond nodded—tardive dyskinesia. Half the words he

needed to describe his son he couldn't spell, and all of them sounded as fantastic and as far away as the Mesozoic monsters he had loved so much as a child. He remembered paging through *The Big Golden Book of Dinosaurs* as if it were yesterday. The illustrations were lurid and the narrative encompassed the soupy advent and sad passing of an entire world. Now his boy was the incredible creature, and Drummond's vocabulary had become lumbering and dinosauric, plodding with polysyllables.

When the boy returned, he announced that he'd looked in the bathroom mirror and couldn't see any love in his eyes. Without saying goodbye to the social worker, he picked up his broken umbrella, tapping the chrome spike across the carpeted floor on his way outside to smoke.

"Are you a believer?" Drummond asked.

"No," the young woman said.

"He suffers," Drummond said. "The suffering—"

The woman nodded. Drummond told her how the boy saw faces disintegrate before his eyes, faces that fell to pieces, then disappeared, leaving a hole. He told her how in the early days of the illness they'd taken the beloved family dog to the pound because it was talking to Pete and could read his mind and Pete was afraid the dog would tear him apart. Two weeks ago it was the shop radio, an old Philco that had been Drummond's father's—they couldn't listen anymore. When the announcers laughed, Pete thought they were laughing at him. They would say exactly what he was thinking, predicting his thoughts. Last week the boy was so afraid that he'd only walk backward in public, convinced that someone was following him. He stumbled in reverse up the steps of the bus, and walked backward down the aisle.

Drummond said, "It's Friday, so, what—Wednesday night, I

guess—he smelled burning flesh in the house. I always check on him before I go to bed, just to make sure he's okay." He sighed. "When I went in that night, he had raw eggs all around his bed. So I thought it was time to call you."

"You said your wife is gone?"

"I think so," Drummond said. Even though he knew the interview was over, he let the matter drift because he was uncomfortable with sympathy. "If anything happened to me," he said, "I don't know—"

"That's got to have you worried," the woman said. She was very professional and understanding and Drummond realized how little conversation he'd had since his wife left. The interview, though, was a botch. When the social worker mentioned a waiting list, halfheartedly, Drummond saw that his growing need for help was exactly the thing disqualifying him for help from this woman.

"These things don't really bother me," he said feebly. "Because—because I understand him, you see."

Drummond taped a sign on the door and locked the shop. He and the boy walked in the rain to the drugstore. Pete twirled his ragged, useless umbrella over their heads.

"I decided against a halfway house," Drummond said.

"You have to forsake me," the boy said. "I see that eventually happening."

"You don't see, not if that's what you think."

"Maybe I just see better. I'm like a prophet. And you're sort of unevolved."

"Okay," Drummond said. "All right, maybe. I'm unevolved. Sure."

They picked up a bottle of hand lotion and then at the rack

by the register Pete tried on a pair of glasses. The gold-rimmed frames sat cockeyed on his nose, and the left lens was stamped with the manufacturer's name: Optivision. The large square lenses themselves were neutral, as clear as windowpanes. Pete looked longingly at himself in the mirror, blinking his green eyes. Drummond wasn't sure whether to dissuade him; from a distance the boy, bespectacled, looked oddly more balanced, his elusive deranged face suddenly pulled into focus.

"You don't really need glasses,"Drummond said.

"I do."

"Your eyes were fine last time we had them checked."

Pete said he wanted these glasses, these, with the gold frames, so that people would see the love. In the end, it was only another of the seemingly endless list of lunatic errands Drummond had grown accustomed to, and he gave up, paying for the glasses. They stepped next door and bought their usual lunch of doughnuts, of crullers and old-fashioneds, from the Greek. Drummond was still wary of the Greek, since the day, several months ago, when he'd asked Pete, rather loudly and obviously playing to an audience, if he wanted the psycho special. Drummond had been standing right beside Pete, but the Greek hadn't realized they were together. Pete's illness chipped away at the family resemblance and people often took them for strangers. The Greek had apologized, and Pete had forgotten the incident—if, indeed, he'd ever noticed it—but the day lingered in Drummond's mind, a slight defensive hitch, every time he walked through the door of Dunkin' Donuts.

"I love Seattle," Pete said, as they started back to the shop. He held the tattered umbrella in one hand and the white sack of doughnuts in the other. "I think Seattle's one of the most happening places on the face of the globe at this point in time. We're gonna determine civilization in the next century. I've never met so many movie stars—this is where it's at. Literally, one of the hot spots of the nation is Seattle, USA." He looked at his father through the rain-beaded, fogged lenses of his new glasses, which hung askew on the tip of his nose. "Just the other day, I ran into John Denver in the street. I said, 'Oh, John, I'm writing an album and mailing it to you. It's called *Donuts.*"

Drummond let the conversation blow away in the rain. He hooked his arm through his son's and hurried him on, but Pete shrugged him off. People glanced sideways at the two men as they made their strange way down Second Avenue. The boy's umbrella was a blasted tangle of snapping fabric and flailing spokes. Drummond's smock flew out behind him. He lowered his head against the wind and the rain and the faces. His fondest boyhood memories were of walking down this same street with his father, strolling and waving as if the elder Drummond were the mayor of the avenue. Now his father. was dead and he was the father, and this was his son.

"I love finding stuff in the street. Like this umbrella . . ." The boy lurched along, planting each foot directly in front of the other. "I went to a sculpture show. That's what the umbrella's all about. It didn't occur to me until I was walking up the street and it broke. I knew it was going to break, but I didn't know what I would do with it after. Then I thought, A sculpture. Of course. A sculpture. What else? I call it *Salvador.* After Salvador Allende, the city Salvador, and Salvador Dalí. It's a triumvirate piece of sculpture. Covering all three bases."

About a block from the shop, as they were crossing Bell Street, the boy knelt down in the intersection. He took up a storybook prayer posture, kneeling, his hands folded together in the shape of a candle flame and his head solemnly bowed with his lips touching the tips of his fingers. The sack of doughnuts split open in the rain and the umbrella skittered away in the wind. People paused to look down at the odd penitent praying in the crosswalk. Drummond saw a shiny patch on the asphalt turn from red to green, and then a few cars drove around, slowly. On either side of the crosswalk, a waiting crowd of pedestrians jostled one another at the curb for a view, and Drummond had a familiar passing urge to explain. It seemed the boy would never get up, but then suddenly he made the sign of the cross, rose, and resumed walking, contemplatively, toward the shop.

They had not made much progress when the boy again fell to the sidewalk, again crossing himself and praying, the whole thing repeated like a liturgical rite, as if the boy were kneeling for the Stations. A moment of prayer, the stream of people parting, the stares so blank they seemed to Drummond like pity or hatred, then the boy rising and picking his way cautiously along a fixed, narrow path, again dropping like a supplicant to the sidewalk. Drummond fell to his knees beside his son, imploring him to get up. The boy's glasses were gone and his thin, oily hair was pasted flat on his scalp. Drummond's long smock, saturated, clung darkly to his back. Pete rose again and put his foot down on a seam in the concrete and followed the cracked path and again began praying. Women in the beauty salon next to the shop watched at the window as Drummond knelt with his son in the rain. He tried to hoist him up by his armpits, but the boy was a heavy dead weight. He lugged him across the sidewalk, heaving him a few feet at a time, until they made it safely to the shop door.

Inside, Drummond snipped the twine on a new bundle of shop rags and began drying the boy off. He wiped his hair and ran the rag down his neck. He unbuttoned his shirt and toweled off his arms and chest, surprised, as always, to see the boy

DRUMMOND & SON   41

so hirsute. Drummond used to bathe him as an infant in the kitchen sink, and he remembered the yellow curtains Theresa had sewn, and the steamed window and the sill with the glossy green leaves of potted ivy. Drummond tried to bring back the feeling of those early winter twilights at the sink, he and the boy reflected in the window. He piled the wet rags, one after another, on the workbench, and when the boy was dry he said, "We're going to close up."

Pete nodded.

"Today's not working out," Drummond said. "Some days don't."

"My glasses," the boy said.

"Okay," Drummond said. "Okay." He sat the boy in the recliner and went out to the sidewalk. Someone had stepped on the glasses. Drummond stared, mystified, at the empty gold frames glinting in the rain. The lenses had popped out. Back at his workbench, he tweaked the bridge of the glasses until it returned to its symmetrical curve and then he gently pressured the right earpiece down so that it was again parallel with the left. He ran a bead of glue around the frames and inserted the lenses, wiping them clean with a cloth diaper. "That'll do you," he said, handing them to Pete. Drummond pulled out a pocket comb and neatly parted the boy's thinning hair and swept it back from his face. When the boy looked up at his father, faint stars of fluorescent light reflected off the glasses.

"Do your job now," Drummond said.

"I think I'll go outside," the boy said.

"Please," Drummond said under his breath. "Do your job first."

Pete began pulling the old paper from the typewriters. He stacked the sheets in a pile, squaring the edges with a couple of sharp taps against the counter. Then he fed blank sheets of paper into the platens, returned the carriages, and hit the tab buttons for the proper indentation, ready for a new paragraph, ready for the next day.

Drummond was nearly done with the Olivetti. He found the nameplate he needed—"Olivetti Lettera 32"—and glued it in place. He squeezed a daub of car wax on the cloth diaper and wiped down the case, drawing luster out of the old enamel. He called the bookstore and told the kid that he was closing shop but his typewriter was ready.

While Drummond waited, he straightened up his workbench. The blank letter to his wife lay there. He crumpled the empty sheet and tossed it into the wastebasket.

When the kid came over, he could hardly believe it was the same machine. He typed the words everyone typed: "now is the time for all good men to come to the aid of their—"

"Is it 'country' or 'party'?" he asked.

"I see it both ways," Drummond said.

He wrote up a sales slip while the kid tapped the keys a couple of times more and looked down doubtfully at the machine. There was something off in its rightness and precision, an old and familiar antagonism gone, a testiness his fingers wanted to feel. He missed the adversity of typing across a platen pitted like a minefield, the resistance of the querulous keys that would bunch and clog. Drummond had seen this before. The kid wasn't ready to say it yet, but half of him wanted the jalopy touch of his broken Olivetti back.

"It's different," he said.

"What's the plot of your novel?" Drummond said.

"It's hard to explain," the kid said.

"Well, is it sci-fi?" he asked. "Romance? Detective thriller?"

Somewhat snobbily, the kid said, "It doesn't really fit any of those categories."

Pete laughed. Drummond felt the entire length of the day settle in his bones. He said, "Take the machine back and monkey with it. See how it feels. Give yourself some time to get used to it."

"I don't know," the kid said.

"Look," Drummond said. "I kept all the old parts. I could restore it back to broken in ten minutes. Or if you don't like the way it works just throw it on the floor a few times. But first give it a fair chance." He pushed the handwritten bill across the counter.

"Can I pay you tomorrow? It's been a slow day."

"Sure," Drummond said. "Tomorrow."

Drummond and the boy boarded the bus and took their usual seats on the bench in back. Drummond wore an old snap-brim hat with a red feather in the band and a beige overcoat belted at the waist. He pulled a packet of salted nuts from the pocket, sharing them with the boy as the bus made its way slowly through the rush hour. His wife had taken their old green Fiat wagon, and Drummond sometimes wondered if he was supposed to feel foolish, letting her keep it. But he didn't really mind riding the bus, and during the past few months he and the boy had settled into a routine. They ate a snack and read what people had written during the day, and then, as they crossed the West Seattle Bridge, the boy would time the rest of the trip home, praying and telling the decades of his rosary.

"You want some?" Drummond asked, holding out the sort of small red box of raisins the boy liked. The boy shook his head indifferently, and Drummond slipped the box back into his pocket.

The boy pulled out the sheets of paper he'd taken from the

typewriters. For the most part the sentences were nonsensical, the random crashing of keys, or the repetitive phrases people remembered from typing classes. But some were more interesting, when people typed tantalizing bits of autobiography or quoted a passage of meaningful philosophy. The boy slumped against the window and shuffled through the fluttering sheets while Drummond, looking over his shoulder, followed along.

"Now is the time for all good men."

"The quick brown fox jumped over."

"God is Dead."

"zrtiENsoina;ldu?/ng;'a!"

"Tony chief Tony Tony."

"Now is the time now."

"Jaclyn was here."

"????????????!!!!!!!"

"That interview didn't work out so great," Drummond said. The bus rose, crossing over the Duwamish River. A ferry on the Sound, its windows as bright as ingots of gold, seemed to be carting a load of light out of the city, making for the dark headlands of Bainbridge island. Drummond wondered if the boy would like a boat ride for his birthday, or maybe even to go fishing. His father had kept his tackle as meticulously as he had kept his typewriters, and it was still stored with his cane rod in the hall closet. After a trip to Westport or a day on the Sound, his father had sharpened his barbs with a hand file and dried and waxed the spoons and aught-six treble hooks until they shone as brightly as silverware. Nobody Drummond had ever known did that. Even now, a year after the old man's death, his gear showed no sign of rusting.

Drummond opened the bottle of lotion and squeezed a dollop into his palm. The lotion was cold, and he massaged it between his hands until it warmed to the touch.

"Give me your hand," he said to the boy.

He rubbed the boy's hands, smoothing the dry, dead skin between his fingers, feeling the flaking scales soften between his own hands.

"Your birthday's Monday," Drummond said.

Pete laughed.

"Any idea what you'd like?"

"No," the boy said.

Theresa would probably call home on Pete's birthday. She'd always been good that way, calling or writing nice thank-you notes to people. For months Drummond had expected his wife to have a realization, although he was never sure what she'd realize. When they had eloped during his senior year—her sophomore—she was six months pregnant and beginning to show. She had never had a real honeymoon or even, she had told him bitterly, a real life. The boy had been a tremendous, bewildering amount of work for a girl of sixteen. Drummond supposed that at forty-one she was still a young woman. Now that she was gone, he found most of his social life at church. He was in charge of the coffee urn, and he picked up pastries from a bakery on California Avenue whose owner was an old crony of his father's. He enjoyed the hour of fellowship after Mass, mingling with people he'd known all his life, people in whose aging faces he still recognized the shortstop from Catholic Youth ball or the remnant of a former May Day queen's smile. There was one particular lady he thought he might consider asking out on a possible date when the time was right.

The rain falling against the roof of the bus and the warm amber light inside were familiar. Drummond capped the lotion and put the bottle away. He turned down the brim of his hat anxiously and, checking his watch, realized it was still early. He wanted to stop by the corner store before it closed; he

needed to pick up a frozen pizza and some pop and ice cream
for dinner. As the bus wound around Alki Point, he looked
again at his watch, a Hamilton pocket model, railroad grade,
which he wore on a silver fob slipped through his belt. Resting
in his palm, it had that satisfying heft well-made things often
have, the weight falling just right. It had been his father's, and
before that had belonged to his grandfather, an engineer for the
old Great Northern. They'd never had to change the initials on
the case, and the center wheel traveled four thousand miles,
round and round, in the course of a year. His grandfather had
told him that, and now Drummond often saw the image of the
elderly frail man as he wound the stem in the morning.

"Tomorrow's Saturday," he said. "I've got some catching up
to do.

"But Monday," he said, "I'll take the day off. How'd you like
that? We'll do something, just me and you.

"You'll be twenty-five years old.

"Twenty-five years," he said.

Almost by way of acknowledgment the boy nudged his
glasses up the bridge of his nose. Drummond fitted his old
snap-brim hat on the boy's head and looked at him. But his
face, reflected in the yellow glass, had already faded into its
cryptic and strange cloister. His heavy purple lips were shap-
ing the words to a prayer and the rosary was ticking in his lap
as the maroon beads, one by one, slipped through his fingers.

"I love you," Drummond said, expecting the boy to laugh,
but he only rested his head against the seat and looked out the
window at the gray city going by.

Screenwriter

How was I supposed to know that any mention of suicide to the phalanx of doctors making Friday rounds would warrant the loss of not only weekend-pass privileges but also the liberty to take a leak in private? My first suicidal ideations occurred to me when I was ten, eleven, twelve, something like that, and by now I was habituated to them and dreams of hurting myself (in the parlance of those places) formed a kind of lullaby I often used to rock myself to bed at night. I got into trouble when I told my p-doc I couldn't fall asleep until I'd made myself comfortable by drawing the blankets over my head and imagining I was closing the lid of my coffin. In confessing to him, I was only trying to be honest and accurate, a good patient, deserving. But no dice: the head p-doc put me on Maximum Observation and immediately I was being trailed around by a sober ex-athlete who, introducing himself, put a fatherly hand on my shoulder and squeezed and told me not to worry, he was a screenwriter, too—not as successful or rich as me, sure, but a screenwriter nonetheless. He said that his name was Bob and he let it be known that he'd taken this position on the mental ward only to gather material for his next script. Half the reason I was in the ward was to get away from the movies, but my whole time with Bob I kept wondering, Is this, or that, or this or that, or this, or this, or this going to be in a *movie*? Everywhere I went, he went, creeping along a few sedate paces back in soft-soled shoes, a shadow that gave off a disturbing susurrus like the maddening sibilance settling dust must make to the ears of ants.

One morning I was lying on my mattress, flipping through women's magazines, but after a while Bob started scratching his ankle, so I got up and went to the bathroom. Bob stood right behind me and in my state of excited self-consciousness the splashing of piss against the urinal cake was deafening, a cataract so loud it was like I'd managed, somehow, to urinate directly into my own ear. After that I watched a television show about a guy with massive arms but no legs climbing a mountain; with a system of pulleys and ropes he managed to belay himself up the slope like a load of bananas. He planted an American flag on the summit. This ruined man's struggle and eventual triumph moved me; in fact I began to cry. To calm myself I listened to the languorous *pick-pock* of two heavily medicated patients thwacking a Ping-Pong ball in the rec room, but there was a final *phut* and then that unnerving nothing, nothing at all, and finally an attack of the fantods drove me out to the patio. Where I sat, Bob sat, and pretty soon the patio started making me crazy, too. Sitting still—just sitting!—was like an equestrian feat. But if I stood up, if I walked in circles, then Bob would have to stand up and walk in circles with me.

The patio was perched high above the FDR and the East River and caged in with chain-link fencing. Concrete benches were scattered around like cuttlebone, and there were potted shrubs in each corner. Scavenging pigeons and seagulls flocked overhead, vaguely white and whirling in the wind. I crushed saltines in their cellophane packets and poured the crumbs in the lap of my paper gown and fed the pieces to the birds.

Bob said, "Are you gonna get better?"

I looked up from my lap and said, "This isn't very interesting, is it?"

"I didn't say that."

"I know you want to write a movie. You're looking for material. But this— It's not a thriller, that's for sure."

"And it's not a whodunit because, like, you're not doing anything."

A young woman known on the ward as the ballerina was dancing across the patio. By the way she kept her hair twisted into a prim, tight bun, and by her body, which seemed to have a memory separate from her mind, a strict memory of its own, you immediately guessed she was a dancer. Her grandparents were with her, two hunched-up people in colossal overcoats and tiny black shoes, people I assumed were immigrants or refugees, because their clothes were so out-of-date, like from the nineteenth century, and because, all bent over, they looked wary and vigilant, as though they were ducking. Lumpen, I kept thinking, or *Lumpenproletariat*—when I probably meant just plain lumpy. Every evening they came to visit their granddaughter, and now they sat on a bench and watched as she swooped like a bird through the lengthening shadows. The old man smoked an unfiltered cigarette, working his tongue in a lizardy fashion to free the flecks of tobacco lodged in his teeth. The old lady sat with her knuckle-like face rapt, a Kleenex balled in her fist. She was crying for the beauty of her granddaughter, and in motion the girl *was* beautiful, she was ecstatic. She wore a sacklike standard-issue paper gown the same as me and she was barefoot. Her arms floated away from her body as though she were trying to balance a feather on the tip of each finger. Then she jumped around, modern and spasmodic, as if the whole point of dance were to leap free of your skin. She raced from one end of the patio to the other, flew up, twirling and soaring, clawing the fence with her fingers and setting the links to shiver. But as soon as her grandparents left, *blam,* the dance in her died. She went cataleptic.

I clapped, and said, "That was nice. *Brava, brava. Bravissima!"*

"Got a smoke?" she said.

I rose to hand her a cigarette and my lighter and to look into her strange blue eyes. "You're really a good dancer," I said.

"No I'm not," she said.

Her voice had no affect and its deadness sat me right back down on the bench. She turned away and flicked the wheel of the lighter, cupping the cigarette out of the wind. A paper plate rolled as if chased, around and around the patio, like a child's game without the child. A white moth fell like a flower petal from the sky, dropped through a link in the fence, and came to light on my hand. The cooling night wind raised gooseflesh on my arms, and a cloud of smoke ripped into the air. The girl's gown was smoldering. A leading edge of orange flame was chewing up the hem. I rose from my seat to tell the ballerina she was on fire. The moth flew from my hand, a gust fanned the flames, there was a flash, and the girl ignited, lighting up like a paper lantern. She was cloaked in fire. The heat moved in waves across my face, and I had to squint against the brightness. The ballerina spread her arms and levitated, *sur les pointes,* leaving the patio as her legs, ass, and back emerged phoenix-like out of this paper chrysalis, rising up until finally the gown sloughed from her shoulders and sailed away, a tattered black ghost ascending in a column of smoke and ash, and she lowered back down, naked and white, standing there, pretty much unfazed, in first position.

After a month on the p-ward you don't get telegrams or get-well cards or stuffed animals anymore, and the petals fall off your flowers and curl like dead skin on the dresser top while the stems go soft and rot in their vases. That's a bad stretch, that Sargasso in the psych ward when the last winds of your old life die out. In the real world I was still legally married—my wife was a film producer, but she'd left me for a more glamorous opportunity, the star of our most recent movie. The script I'd written was somewhat autobiographical and the character he played was modeled after my dead father. So now my wife was banging Dad's doppelgänger and I hadn't talked to her in I don't know how long. In between therapy sessions and the administration of the usual battery of tests (Thematic Apperception, Rorschach, MMPI), as well as blood-draws and vitals, I sat on the sofa in the lounge, hoping for a certain zazen zeroness—serene and stupid—but mostly getting hung up on cravings for tobacco. One night after dinner I sat on the sofa and moved my finger to different locations around my head—below the ear, right in the ear, above the eyeball, against the roof of my mouth—experimenting with places to put the gun. I tried filling the dreary hours with poetry—my first love—but I'd been a script doctor too long. I hadn't futzed with an iamb in ages, and the words just dog-paddled around the page, senselessly. I was desperate enough for a nicotine high to harvest some of the more smokable butts out of the Folgers coffee cans the staff filled with kitty litter and set out on the patio. The pickings were slim, though; in the p-ward people tend to smoke their cigarettes ravenously. You look around, and everybody's got burnt, scabby fingers just like the Devil.

Finally I worked up the nerve to bum a smoke from Carmen,

an operatic Italian woman who was my next-door neighbor on the ward. She tapped one free of her pack. It looked like a sterile, all-white, hospital-issue ciggie that would never do anything bad, such as give you cancer. I drew it under my nose, giving it a sniff in the manner of a man with a fine cigar.

"You saved my life," I said. "Could I bother you for a match?"

"You know," she said, "I grew up a only child and was chased by every kid in my school! Teased all my life, my mom's dressin' me didn't help! I was the school clown, I can never remember being happy as a child, sexually abused from eleven to fourteen, then I started to run away at sixteen, raped several times, tried suicide several times . . . then I met a thirty-five-year-old man, got pregnant, married him, suffered beatings for seven years, left him, alone, had nowhere to go, three kids, I collapsed, went for the sixth time into the hospital . . . came out, nowhere to go, so I stayed with this guy, a friend, we started to mess around, I had my fourth child, now when I look back at it all, phew, I never had love, I hate my life, I wish I was never born, I get days when I feel so stupid that taking a bath takes two hours 'cause I can't think!"

Man, on the p-ward you asked for a match and people told you stuff. After a week on the ward you knew everybody's etiology. Illness was our lingua franca. Patients announced their worst infirmities right off, but no one dared talked about normal life. Oh, no—that was shameful and embarrassing, a botch you didn't bring up in polite conversation. Fearing I might blow my chance for a pass if I hung around Carmen, I grabbed a book of matches from a table in the Ping-Pong room and stepped out onto the patio. But the ballerina was out there, dancing.

"Got an extra smoke?" she asked.

"I don't want any encore of the last time," I said. "Besides, I only got this one. I'll share it if you want."

She sat beside the bench. Her skin smelled of ointments and steroid creams.

I said, "Are you a professional?"

"Professional nutcase," she said.

"No really."

"I've been in here and uptown at Columbia for like a donkey's year."

"I meant are you a dancer."

"Not with this body."

"Why do you say that?"

"Do you have a knife?"

"I haven't worn pants in five weeks."

"What's that supposed to mean?"

"Nothing. I just don't have any pockets. No wallet, no keys, no spare change, no lint, no rabbit's foot, and no knife. It's emasculating. Why do you want a knife anyway?"

"Never mind."

Her nose was fat and fruitlike, a nose for pratfalls and slapstick, not jetés and pirouettes and pliés and whatnot. But her lips were lovely, the color of cold meat, and her eyes, sunk deep in their sockets, were clear blue. When you looked into them, you half-expected to see fish swimming around at the back of her head, shy ones.

"All I ever wanted to do was dance, all I've ever done is dance, and I grew up into a linebacker."

"Yeah, well, I wanted to be a screenwriter, and guess what? I am one. That's the other tragedy in life." I eased back against the fence. "Anyway, you got nice legs. I don't know what you're talking about."

"My thighs, stupid!"

From the patio you could see the red gondolas rising over the East River, pendant and swaying as they made their way to Roosevelt Island. The sun was setting and I thought it would be so calm and beautiful to be hanging in a bucket way above everything, especially if they could just ride you out over the river and suspend you there, bobbing around, twilight for all time, the sun never going down, the glass forever warm, just hanging out in a lovely red bucket with that senile light dusting your cheeks.

"Calm down." I lit the cigarette and passed it to her. "Your legs are fine."

She smiled. "Well, thank you," she said. Then she puckered her lips, made a loud wet smack, sucked down a single deep drag, exhaled, and drove the cigarette into her thigh. She twisted and snubbed and jammed the coal against her skin, staring at the burn, red and flecked with ash, until the last live cinder dried out.

"You ought to quit smoking," I said.

Bob followed us back to her room where she applied some kind of topical anodyne or steroid, smoothing the white cream into her wound, dreamy as a lover, and crawled into bed.

"Why'd you do that?"

"If I knew, I wouldn't be here, now would I?"

"Sure you might. You might know exactly why you did it but you might not be able to stop yourself anyway."

I leaned over her bed and tried to kiss her but she put a hand to my lips.

After that, I came to see her every night. I totally dug her broken bohemian thing, it was so the opposite of my trajectory, my silly success. I'd made a million dollars each of the last four years running and never felt worse in my life. I'm not whining—I'm not one of those whiners. One of those affluent crybabies. But I'd lost the plot and was afraid that if my life improved any more I'd vanish. By contrast a woman setting herself on fire seemed very real; on doctor's orders, she was strapped in at nine o'clock sharp, pinned to the flat board of her bed like a specimen. At first it was unnerving to talk to a woman who was lashed to her bed with a contraption of leather belts and heavy brass buckles, so I angled my seat away from her face and spoke to her knees, which looked, in the faint blue light, as though they'd been carved by water from a bar of soap.

"How are you?" I said.

She seesawed her wrist, *comme ci, comme ça,* beneath a band of heavy saddle leather. The leather was burnished to a rich gloss by the straining of a thousand sweaty wrists on a thousand other agonized nights.

"Would you grab me an orange?"

I fetched an orange from a basket and peeled it; it was especially fragrant in the semidark. Bob was sitting in a chair in the hallway and I could hear the dry scratch of his pencil as he took notes. I didn't care. The ballerina's window was open and in the breeze the heavy curtains swept aside and the hospital courtyard, with its scalloped pattern of cobblestones, its wet bare trees and February emptiness, seemed like a scene recollected from an expatriate life in Paris that I'd never lived, a moment out of some tawdry romance I'd never had in my youth.

"Make sure you peel as much of the yuck off as possible," she said. "I hate the yuck."

"I hate the yuck, too," I said, and held a jeweled segment over her mouth. Her lips spread and her tongue slid forward. It had been ages since I'd fed anyone. It was excellent the way, when I held the crescent of orange there, poised above her blue lips, her mouth just opened. I dangled another piece and watched her mouth open like a little starveling bird's and then I pulled the piece away and watched her mouth close. Then I gave it to her.

"You don't have a match, do you?" I put a cigarette in my mouth. "A pyro like yourself."

"I'd love a smoke."

"I bet you would. Why do you burn yourself?"

"My doctor's theory is it puts the pain in a place I can find it. On the outside."

"I know exactly what he means. I thought making movies was going to be that way. Now I'd just rather be crucified."

"I don't like your mind."

"Yeah, well, I'm not here for a pedicure."

"Untie me," she whispered.

"No can do," I said.

"Please."

"Can't."

"We'll just smoke that cig and then you can buckle me right back up."

"I don't have any matches."

She smiled. "I do."

She told me to lift the table lamp and underneath it I found a cache of contraband matches. Each individual match had been ripped from the book and mustered in a neat, soldierly line, and the strip of striking was there, too, the whole kit flat enough to hide beneath the green felt base.

"Great, but I'll just hold the cig to your lips. I'm going to leave you strapped in for now."

We worked the cig down to a nub, fanning the smoke out the window, and then she yanked at the sides of her gown. A couple of the snaps popped open, and she pulled aside the paper. It made a rustling like the thin parchment pages of a Bible.

"This was the first time, after an audition for the Albany Ballet," she said, using her finger to trace a faint cicatrix the size of a postage stamp. "I wanted a sharp blade, I just had the idea. I had a disposable razor for shaving my legs, so I put that in my mouth. I bit down on it real hard, trying to crack the plastic so I could get the blade free. But I couldn't get it. It wouldn't come out. I was so frustrated. I started crying. I lit a cigarette. I had no idea what that hand with the cigarette would do—it was like it was somebody else's.

"Sometimes, like this, I'm just tense," she said, pointing out an ellipsis of brown dots down the length of her belly, marks the size of moles she'd made by extinguishing stick matches against her skin. All along her body, a palimpsest of older lesions darkened beneath the rawer, more recent burns. Her arms were crosshatched with brands she'd seared into her skin with a coat hanger heated over a gas stove.

"Can I touch?" I asked.

She nodded.

I put my finger against a dark, hard burl on her outer thigh, an elevated lump as smooth as a chestnut. I ran the flat of my hand over her hip and down her leg. Whatever I touched prompted a story, some account: auditions, classes, Tuesday nights, phone calls, weddings. I'd been horny, but now I felt detached. This display of her body wasn't sexy, the way a tour of a battlefield isn't bloody.

In the p-hosp, of course, it was seriously against the rules to touch another patient, and being under Bob's constant surveillance didn't make it easy for us. In line at the cafeteria I'd palm my food tray with one hand and feel her solid balletic rump with the other. Or I'd play footsie with her under the table at Friday-night bingo. Or I'd grope her up in the little gymnasium where, for RT, we played some of the sorriest games of volleyball you can imagine. In the typical draft that goes on against the fence at school, you know who the athletes are, who the sissies are, who to crib from in a history exam and avoid on the kickball team, but up on psych choosing a squad of decent players was primarily a pharmacological matter, something where, really, you wanted to consult the *DSM-IV* before you made your first selection. Choosing an appropriate sexual partner in a mental hospital was probably supposed to work along similar lines. You needed records!

With her malady, the ballerina wasn't really into fooling around, but I hoped her new medication, Manerix, which was supposed to dampen some of her desire to burn herself, might also lead by inverse ratio to an upsurge in her passion for old-fashioned sex. After a week, two weeks, I was getting frustrated. Most of the contact we made, skin to skin, was glancing and accidental, hardly more than what passes acceptably between strangers on the street. She had this terrific body, so looking and fantasizing was fine—for a while. But of course about this time I discovered that I couldn't whack off. My medication was giving me erectile hassles, plus Bob outside my open door didn't help. In anticipation of the day when the ballerina's Manerix would kick in I started pitching my cocktail of bupropion and lithium and clonazepam out the window.

But the ballerina made such great progress on her new meds that by the end of February her p-doc wanted her to practice sleeping through the night without restraints. After dinner we'd sit outside, on the patio, and watch the sun go down, knowing she was about to be released. And one morning, sure enough, I saw her dragging a wicker basket and a pillowcase full of clothes to the nurses' station. Departures on the psych ward were a big deal. People always swore they'd come back and visit but they never did. By the time you were a ward veteran like myself a little bit of your hope left with them and never fully returned. I expected I'd never see her again. She was cured, and that was tantamount to being gone, gone off to reside in some unfamiliar land. Her grandparents met her in the lounge with their hopeless, past-tense faces and their old leafy clothes; standing beside them in a gauzy spring dress, the ballerina seemed a mere puff of self, passing like a spirit out of their heavy Old World sadness, whatever it was about. She told me that as soon as I managed to wrangle my first pass she wanted to see me. She used a red felt pen to write her name and number across the hem of my gown, and we shook hands, but after she was gone and I took up my station on the sofa, I felt certain I wouldn't rise again until some angel came by and blew a trumpet.

It was maybe a couple weeks later, and I was no longer on Maximum Observation. Bob was gone and I was on my own. My window was open and little things stirred as they had in my childhood, so that the clothes scattered on the floor were once again the bodies of dead men. When I was a boy, my father and his six brothers seined for salmon out of Ilwaco, Washington, and every couple years one or another of them would wash up in the frog water around Chehalis Slough, drowned. The funerals seemed to last days, weeks, even months, as the remaining brothers gathered nightly in the Riptide bar and stared drunkenly into each other's eyes like dazed, speechless toads. Left at home, sleepless and alone—I have a mother somewhere, but I never knew her—I imagined that each shirt on the floor was a dead uncle and I could not leave the tipsy life raft of my bed, waiting out those long nights when the ocean fog was cool and full of premonitions and the beacon at the end of the break-water threw green shadows against the walls of my room. Now I drew the blanket over my head. "Our Father who art in heaven . . . etc. . . . etc. . . . now and at the hour of our death amen!" When the coffin thing didn't put me to sleep I peeked over the satiny selvage of my blanket and stared at the ceiling and listened to the tedious complaints of patients as they wept into the pay phone across the hall: (8:02) . . . *My parents had a bad marriage, then divorced and married worse people . . .* (8:07) . . . *I'll show you what's the matter with me. Then I get my razor. I cut down sharp and quick. I scream and go out onto the court and bleed all over . . .* (8:47) . . . *It's hard to kill yourself by taking Tylenol. You die from liver failure, which takes a long time . . .*

This kind of serial conversation went on night after night, a litany of complaint and outrage, right outside my door. People were hospitalized when their feelings reached an acute phase, but if you eavesdropped on all the jabbering, all the lonely, late-night calls, the whole long history of pain and madness fused into a single humdrum story, without much drama. It went flat. I'd been revolving in and out of various mental wards my whole life and previously had always considered myself touched and unique. I was kind of snobby about it—like a war vet, bitter and proud—but now I flipped the covers to the floor and queued up with all the other lunatics, waiting my turn.

"Look," I said, "can I come see you?"

"You can get out?" the ballerina asked.

"What're you saying?"

"Are you better?"

"No," I said. "Not really. But I'm off MO."

She didn't say anything. On the p-ward you often found the phone swaying from the end of its metal cord like the pendulum of a clock, no one in sight. People just drifted away from conversations, too frazzled and forgetful to end the call or maybe too medicated and lethargic to hang up. That's what I was imagining when the ballerina went silent, the dangling phone.

"Okay?" I said, finally.

"Okay," she said.

I hung up and crawled back into bed and stared at the ceiling and listened: (9:31) . . . *I swear I spent sixty percent of my life puking* . . . (9:33) . . . *Then can you explain to me why every time I got in my car to go somewhere "Mr. Bojangles" was playing?* . . . (9:45) . . . *I started keeping a journal almost two years ago. I used to write only when I was happy. Then I realized that I'd look back and think that my whole life was happy, so I started only writing when I was depressed. And I realized that I wasn't always depressed, so I started to write every day. Now I calculate I'm fifty percent happy and fifty percent depressed so I don't see the point of writing at all anymore* . . . (10:07) . . . *It hurts.*

I used my very first pass to visit the ballerina. With three hours before lockdown, I caught a cab, stopped for a bottle of wine, then hustled over to her place, a small apartment just off Varick. She showed me around with exactly three gestures. "Kitchen," she said. "Bedroom. Bathroom." We uncorked the wine and toasted my new freedom.

After being abstemious for so long, I was drunk in no time. I bent and gave the ballerina a kiss on the tip of her big old nose and crossed the room in that deliberate way of drunks. Her bathroom was a frilly gift that one girl might give to another, an assortment of powders, soaps, oils, lotions, perfumes, sea sponges, lava stones, and so on. There were yellow candles set at the corners of the tub. Bath beads in translucent capsules sat in jars like sapphires. A fragrant potpourri filled a blue glass bottle and there was a bar of brown soap with chunks of something abrasive, like sawdust, embedded in it. The whole place was stockpiled with not just your boring brand-name products but all these totally recherché and esoteric potions searched out in faraway quarters of the city. I opened the medicine cabinet and fingered through the shelves, reading. A jar of astringent lotion said that it would rid your skin of the toxins that are an inescapable part of modern life. I didn't believe it, of course, and yet who doesn't want to "revive" and "replenish," who doesn't love the words "pure" and "essential"? My p-doc hadn't been using any of this uplifting language, and after a couple months on the ward the exotica listed on the backs of these bottles—olive, kukui, Saint-John's-wort, wild yam— sounded good to me, sounded like the fruits of some heavenly place, an island off somewhere in the blue future. Hadn't Columbus set sail in search of these very ingredients?

Mixed in with all that humbug were the serious amber bottles of medication: Effexor, Paxil, Wellbutrin, Prozac, Zoloft, the whole starting roster of antidepressants. The ballerina couldn't have been taking them in combination, so what was the history here? I lined the bottles up according to the date the script had been filled at the pharmacy but the time line gave out about a month before she entered the psych ward. No refill for Manerix in sight. What was the deal? In a back row of the medicine chest she kept the scrubs and utility players, and I popped a few Tuinals, washing them down with water from the faucet, and then tapped a couple Xanax and Valium into my palm, to save for a rainy day. I took a leak and flushed the toilet and stared at myself in the mirror. My eyes were dark pits and my gums had turned a pulpy red. I seemed to be looking at the portrait of a man who hadn't eaten a piece of fruit in years.

When I came out she said, "Lots of medications, huh?"

"You got the whole library in there," I said.

"You were snooping around, trying to get a read on me. I know, so don't even bother saying you weren't."

"I said I was looking."

"I don't care. I always look, too. It's okay."

I shrugged. "What's up with the Manerix?"

"That new antidepressant that's supposed to depress my depression better than the old antidepressants did?"

"Yeah, that one."

"I ditched it."

"Is that a good idea? How's it going, without meds?"

"I feel like burning myself, if that's what you mean."

For ten years I'd been dutiful and hardworking, cranking out those big-time Hollywood screenplays in order to bankroll a lifestyle that broke the sillymeter. Now it was like, Bring on the degradation! Let's break through the bullshit and get real! I wished I'd brought another bottle of wine, to help lower me back into the bohemian hopes I'd had at twenty-five— literature and pussy. Baudelaire and women that stank like Gruyère! I'd never really wanted to write screenplays. I'd wanted to be a poet. And here I was, in poetry central. There were candles on the shelves, on the floor, fat and thin candles, tall and short, red and green and all the gradients of soft pastel, scented with the sweet and cloying flavors of guava, pomegranate, mango. Everything here was *luxe, calme,* and *volupté,* all right. In his Tahitian diary Gauguin wrote, "Life being what it is, we dream of revenge," a phrase whose ruthlessness used to be right up my alley. But what kind of revenge did I need when last year I'd managed to enjoy three summers, two springs, and four falls—one in Moscow, another in Florence, two more in Cairo and Burma? I was a touch manic, and after I walked off the set of my last movie, winter just didn't make it onto the itinerary. I was like a god, laughing at the weather. Who needed Gauguin and his gaudy painted paradise? For me, now, the most extreme, remote, Polynesian corner of the globe was inside the ballerina's skull.

She crawled across the floor on her hands and knees and the front of her dress gaped open and showed her breasts just hanging in that lovely, lovely way, guavaish and weighty, ready for plucking. I reached in and pinched a nipple. She shrank back and told me she didn't feel like being touched tonight.

"You don't?"

"Not really," she said. "You look scared. Are you scared?"

"Scared?" I looked up at her. "I don't know. I don't even know who I am right now. I'm all bottomed out. I'm down here with the basal ganglia and the halibuts."

"Did you take any of my pills?"

"You bet."

"You liar! You did, too."

"I said I did, you goofy bitch!"

That started the ballerina pacing, head erect, back swayed, tense. Her heels pounded the floor like a ball-peen hammer. She marched over to her dresser and rearranged some objects. I heard glass clinking and jars slamming down. She jerked a chair away from the window and set it by the door. She slapped shut a book that had been lying open beside a cereal bowl on the table. She disappeared into the kitchen alcove. She stomped back in with a cup of ice in her hand. She chewed the ice and the broken shards fell out of her mouth to the floor. She grabbed the chair at the door and returned it to its original place by the window. Her whole total animal thing took over, while for me, thanks to the downers, all memory of the upright life was gone. I would never again walk into a room and shake someone's hand. I could barely turn my head to keep track of the ballerina. Some words came out of her mouth but I don't know where in the room they went. I never heard them.

Her dress dropped to the floor and she sat on the bed. Her panties were black, webby things; it looked as if a huge hairy spider had clamped itself onto her. Beside her she had a pack of cigarettes and a candle and a green knitting needle I wasn't too crazy about. She lifted the candle and lit the cigarette and drained some of the hot wax on her thigh. All the while she watched me, and after a few minutes she had me hooked, I was mesmerized, charmed, I was down way deep into that blue pool where the fish shyly waited. She took a drag of the cigarette, exhaled, then turned the hot coal around and twirled the ash off against her nipple. Another drag, and she turned her attention to the other nipple. Pretty soon both aureoles were ashy smudges. Her eyes remained wide open and, I guess, fixed on me, but they were blue and unfocused, and the pain was miles away.

I watched her, but something had gone wrong. Her torment wasn't turning me on. I didn't feel a thing. Obviously the drugs I'd snatched from her medicine cabinet weren't elevating my mood, and the thought of all those sundries in her bathroom was bringing me down, hard. Every last sad soap in that utopian toilet was bumming me out. They were all part of a repertoire of hope I'd already lived through. I'd already washed myself with that crap. I'd taken those pills. I'd tried to feel loose and relaxed in a tub of hot water, beneath that shadowy candlelight. It all seemed so familiar. Her paisley sheets and the fan of peacock feathers above the futon and the tasseled lampshade screamed *boudoir*. The tiny shells and rocks and twigs italicized *a special moment long ago*. In the little syncretic boutiquey spiritual figurines lined up on the windowsill and the crystal prisms strung from the ceiling on threads of monofilament I saw the very same occult trinkets that had decorated every bedroom I'd ever been in. My anticipation was gone, I couldn't lust or desire.

All this intense specialness, along with the way she was effortfully trying to turn her pain to pleasure, was ending up as a very dull result in my brain. I heard the tindery snap, the kindling crackle of burning hair. She was burning herself, *là-bas*. The whole room stank. As she closed in on a climax, soot washed down her thigh like the aftermath of a calamity when the uncaring rain begins to carry it all out to sea . . .

"Here," she said, passing me the cigarette.

"No, thanks," I said.

"Burn me."

I'm a screenwriter and my movies gross millions and when I write "THE CAR BLOWS UP" there's a pretty good chance a real car will indeed blow up, but I wasn't particularly keen on the idea of roasting this woman's cunt over a hot coal. I can't even say the word "cunt" convincingly. The Frenchy sangfroid I'd felt leaving the psych ward was completely gone now. I wasn't Henry Miller, I wasn't Eugène-Henri-Paul Gauguin, I wasn't any of those expat guys. My career as a sexual adventurer was about half an hour old, and it was over already. I've read Baudelaire but I wouldn't want to have his big ugly forehead. I was known among my friends as a major cork dork and the wine I'd bought I wouldn't even have cooked with at home, fricasseeing stew meat for the dog. When I left the ballerina, if I chose, I could check myself out of the hospital and into the Plaza, stay a month, order room service, conduct business through my agent, while I watched other people out the window, real lunatics, splashing in the fountain, singing holy songs, dancing and shouting hosannas into the sky until the police came and tasered them back into submission. When I squared up my tab at the p-hosp it would run me about thirty-five grand and at that rate the Plaza would be a bargain.

I needed air. I managed to stand and make it to the window and was swinging a foot onto the fire escape when a wet gob of something hit with a splat on the back of my neck. I thought for sure it was bird shit. I looked up. A blue rain was falling through the streetlamps and at the Korean deli on the corner a crippled man leaned on a wooden cane, picking through a pyramid of oranges. An old Korean woman sat on a white bucket, cutting the stems on peonies, huge lion-headed flowers with pink petals that shook loose in the wind and were pasted to the wet sidewalk like découpage. Everything seemed to have been given a new coat of varnish sometime in the night. Every wire and railing glistened, and the air was clean and cool. Above the intersection a traffic signal turned green. Several cars went by, their sleepy wipers blinking away the drizzle. Down at the deli the cripple reached into his pocket and paid for the orange, and the old woman went back to cutting her peonies. How could so much peace and calm reign between two people? I balanced on the windowsill and looked back at the ballerina.

She was a mess, ghoulish with a plastering of soot and ash. Her body, crisscrossed with brandings and burned by match heads, looked fully clothed. She'd never be naked again, not with the textile weave of her scars, the plaids and polka dots she'd made of her skin.

She said, "What?"

I hadn't said anything. "Isn't there anything else you like to do?"

"I don't know."

"It's raining out."

"Why?"

"Why?" I said. "Why is it raining?"

The air in the room was stale and hot as a kiln, the motion baked out of it. I opened another window in the kitchen alcove. Instantly a sort of pulmonary breeze blew a green curtain into the room, expanding the space. I saw a forgotten slice of bread in the chrome slot of her toaster and a used tea bag set to rest on the edge of her sink, the stub of a cigarette going soggy inside it. When I returned to the bedroom the ballerina hadn't moved. She'd sleep in these ashes, like some black-feathered bird. Her back was to me, and I went to her, but the burns covering her body—how would you even hold such a woman? Where exactly do you put your hands on somebody who hurts everywhere? I stopped short. I'd never seen her back before, and it was pristine. The skin was flawless, a cold hibernal blue where her blood flowed beneath. I blew on my fingers, warming them, and then laid my hand between her shoulder blades, lightly, as though to press too hard would leave a print.

"How about cleaning up?" I said.

"Oh," she sniffled. "I don't know."

In the bathroom I plugged the drain with a dry cracked stopper and dialed the spigots until the water running over my wrist was hot and tropical. I looked around at all the ingredients. The stuff in jars looked like penny candy, and I spilled some of that in. The beaded things were especially pretty, and I tossed a combination of yellow and green gelcaps in the tub, followed by a pill that effervesced and changed the color of the water to a pale Caribbean blue. I gave up on any idea of alchemy and just went wild. Pine Forest, Prairie Grass, Mountain Snow, Ocean Breeze. Once I got into it, I saw no reason to stop—juniper, vanilla, cranberry. A capful of almond oil, a splash of *bain moussant,* some pink and blue flakes from a box that turned out to be ordinary bubble bath.

"Okay," I said, closing the bathroom door to trap the steam. She hadn't budged from her place on the bed. I hooked her arm over my shoulder. For a ballerina she had pretty much zero *ballon* at this point. Her feet dragged across the floor like the last two dodoes. I was afraid that when I lowered her into the tub she'd sink to the bottom. I made her sit upright. With steam curling down from above and a heady lather of bubble bath rising over the edge of the tub, the bathroom was now one massive cumulus cloud.

"A candle," she said.

I snapped the chain on a bare bulb above the sink. "No more candles tonight."

I grabbed a soft white cloth from the shelf and sat beside the tub, in a pillow of suds.

"My life is so simple a one-year-old could live it," she said.

"You're just having one of those days," I said. I wrung the washcloth and let the warm water dribble down her chest. "What's up with those old people? Your grandparents?"

"They emigrated here after my mom died."

"Where'd they come from?"

"Yugoslavia," she said. "Bosnia, Herzegovina, Croatia, Serbia, Slovenia, Macedonia, that whole thing."

"You speak their language?"

"Mala količina."

I soaped her shoulders and neck, rinsed the cloth and ran it slowly along the length of her arm, studying the scars. I was

stupidly surprised when the wounds didn't wash away. A siren
passed in the street. Her startled fingers took off in flight, fluttering up from the sea of foam and sailing through the fragrant
steam, darting here and there.

"What's *wrong* with you?" she asked.

"I don't know," I said.

"You must have a diagnosis. Everyone has a diagnosis."

"Well, just before I came to the hospital I spent three hundred dollars on Astro Turf and PVC pipe, trying to build a
driving range in my dining room."

"It's your dining room," she said. "You can do what you
want."

"I've never owned a golf club in my life."

"Oh."

"Travel brochures are a bad sign, too, but you know what's
the worst? Messing with the medications. Like lithium—it
makes my hands shake and I can't walk steadily. So I decide to
back the lithium off a little and titrate up on something like
BuSpar or Lamictal. My hands stop shaking but I can't remember anything or I start eating like a pig. I keep trying, you
know, making all these little adjustments, but it's like— I don't
know. I don't know what it's like."

"It's not *like* anything," she said.

"Eventually I can't move. I'll have the thought, Oh, I want to
go out, so I put on my hat and stare at the door. Right about
then I check into the hospital, they fix me up, send me back
out. I kick ass for a while and then collapse."

"You know your diagnosis," she said.

"Whatever—bipolar II, Fruit Of The Loom IV, it doesn't
make a difference."

"We'll never get out," she said.

"*Au contraire*—I'm getting myself discharged AMA, first
thing tomorrow."

"But at least we have our own language."

"Yeah, Greek."

"In grade school," she said, "I wrote a report about how a myth was a female moth. We were studying the Greeks."

"You have a beautiful mouth," I said. "I'd like to crawl in it and die."

"I'm twenty-nine years old," she said. "My mouth is full of dead boys." She blew me a kiss. "Sometimes your mind gives me a feeling of great tiredness. Aren't you exhausted?"

"My curfew," I said feebly.

"The fires are going out, it's true." She sank down in the tub and submerged so that only her knees, her small dancer's breasts, her big nose, her lovely mouth and blue eyes, these isolated islands of herself, rose above the darkening water. Flecks of ash floated over the surface. "Here's my idea for your next screenplay," she said. "Sirens are going everywhere. People are weeping. It doesn't really matter where you are, it's all black. You can't open your eyes anyway."

"What are you saying?"

"And there's a donkey marooned on an island in the middle of the ocean. A volcano is erupting on the island and rivers of hot lava are flowing toward the donkey. In addition, all around the small island is a ring of fire. What would you do?"

I considered the possibilities. "I don't know."

Smiling, she said, "The donkey doesn't know, either."

"That's a good one."

She poked at the remaining bubbles with her finger, popping them. I checked my watch. It was midnight on the nose and all that awaited me back at the p-ward was another morning and a long walk down a putty-colored corridor and, at the end of it, a paper cup full of pills. And in a month or a year the ballerina would touch a scar on her breast and tell a rather pointless story about a screenwriter she'd met in the psych ward. Waves of dirty water lapped against the sides of the tub, and her skin, moist and gleaming, was fragrant with wild yam and almond. Then everything went briefly quiet in one of those strange becalmed moments where it's hard to believe you're still in Manhattan.

Up North

We angled our heads back and opened our mouths like fledgling birds. Smoke gave the cool air a faintly burned flavor, an aftertaste of ash. A single flake lit on my wife's eyelash, a stellar crystal, cold and intricate. I blew a warm breath over her face, melting the snow.

"It's been falling since Saginaw," I said.

"Listen," she said.

The flight from New York had been rough, and my ears were still blocked, but somewhere in the distance, beyond the immediate silence of the falling snow and the thick woods, I heard the muffled echo of rifle shots.

"Deer season," Caroline said.

"Your father go out?"

"He usually goes," she said. "He and the boys. And now you. Now you'll be one of the boys."

Caroline brushed her hair free of a few tangles and clipped it back in a ponytail that made her look a decade younger—say, twenty years old, taking her back to a time before I'd met her. Perhaps in reflex I remembered the sensation I'd had the first night we slept together, thinking how beautiful she was, how from every angle and in every light she was flawless, like some kind of figurine. Now she examined herself in the small round mirror she'd pulled from her purse, grimacing. The shallow cup of the compact looked to be holding a kind of flesh dust, a spare skin. She dabbed powder around her cheeks, the set line of her jaw. She took a thick brush and stroked a line on either side of her face, magically lifting her cheekbones. She traced her lips lightly with a subdued shade of red and suddenly she was smiling.

"Up a ways there's a fork," she said. "You want to stay right."

Before I could start the car again, two men in orange caps crossed in front of us, rifles slung over their shoulders. They stopped in the road and waved, the ears beneath their caps like pink blossoms in the raw cold, and then they bumbled into the woods. I stared at their fresh footprints in the snow.

"You know them?" I asked.

"No," she said.

At the cabin, we ate a late lunch without the men, who were out on a mission that was, it seemed, top secret. Caroline's mother, Lucy, had been kept in the dark, and so had Sandy Rababy, whose husband, Steve, was a partner in the accounting firm founded by Caroline's father. We ate tuna sandwiches and potato chips on paper plates that had been gnawed by mice. Lucy set out a plastic tray of carrots and celery sticks and black olives. We drank mulled wine in Dixie cups, from which I nervously nibbled the wax coating.

"They took their guns and vests and packed peanut-butter sandwiches and a half gallon of Scotch," Sandy said. "Now, where do you think they're going?"

"We heard guns on the drive in," I said.

"Isn't it awful?" Lucy said.

"What's worse," Sandy said, "the toilet's busted."

"It froze," Lucy said, "and the bowl cracked. Or the pipes broke or something. We're using the outhouse."

She pointed, and through the window I saw a rickety leaning structure, and a dirty trough of footprints in the snow where people had traipsed back and forth.

"You need to wear a fluorescent hat out there," Sandy said, "so you don't get shot trying to relieve yourself."

The cabin was open and cozy, a single large room with a high ceiling, and although I'd never been there before, it struck me as familiar. It was rustic and unpretentious, with that haphazardly curatorial décor that accumulates in old family haunts. At one end was a large fireplace constructed of smooth stones hauled up from the lakeshore, and at the other end were the log bunks where we'd all sleep. Everything that had ever happened here was, in a way, still happening: the smell of wet woollens steaming by the stove, of dry leather gathering dust, of iodine and burned logs and Coppertone—all of it lingered in the air. Two persistent grayling, long extinct in Michigan, surfaced in the wash of light above the back windows, and even the mounted deer and elk heads flanking the fireplace suggested souvenirs from some gone, legendary time. It was exactly the kind of abiding paradise people create for their kids just so that, long after the last summer, the past will live on.

"Caroline, you're quiet," Lucy said to her daughter, my wife, who sat with her legs crossed at the head of the table. The minute we arrived, Caroline had gone directly to an old gouged dresser and, from the bottom drawer, pulled out a man's bulky sweater, which she wore now—it was green and moth-eaten and voluminous, belonging to her father, whose girth was still a ghostly, orotund presence in the stiff wool. As soon as she sank into the sweater, it was as if she were officially home, and no longer had to explain herself. She took a bite of her sandwich, and her silver earrings shivered against her neck, catching the light. They were a gift, I imagined, from SJ, the man whose initials now coded her journal and date book. She bunched a sleeve of the sweater above her elbow and said, "Tell me the news."

"You know Lindstrom's wife passed away?" Lucy said.

Caroline said, "Poor Lindy."

"He's very depressed, especially coming up here," Sandy said. "This is the first Thanksgiving without her."

I'd met Lindy and his wife, Beth Ann, on several occasions when the whole group had come to New York for a weekend of theater. They, like Sandy and Steve Rababy, were lifelong friends of the Jansens. They'd all met in college, when the men were brothers at the Phi Delt fraternity in Ann Arbor, and now, years later, the group remained intact and inseparable except for this death.

"Hey, Daly, what about these lips?" Sandy said, sliding the torn page of a magazine toward me. She'd had cheek implants and was currently in the market for new lips. I was meant to offer a proxy opinion for all men. The woman in the magazine was pouting sadly or seductively, it was hard to tell, and she was looking confused or far off into the distance, also hard to tell.

"Those are Caroline's lips," I said. Sandy held the page to her nose, and then looked at Caroline, who modeled a little moue.

"You're right, they are," Sandy said. "I want your lips."

"They're spoken for," my wife said, touching my knee under the table, quaintly.

Caroline heard the men come up the tote road around nine o'clock. I went outside and watched as her father horsed the truck over a hillock of snow, rocking it back and forth and stubbornly and finally into the yard.

"Where's my little girl?" Robert Jansen said as soon as he

saw me. His voice boomed, a deep bass that echoed away, bounding into the woods. He looked past me toward the lighted door of the cabin, where Caroline stood, her long blue shadow thrown on the snow.

"Hi, Daddy," she said.

"How'd it go?" Sandy shouted from the kitchen.

It was obvious as the men stood warming their hands at the fire that part of what had been top secret about their day involved a bar. Their cheeks flushed red and their eyes sparked wetly and none of them was able to stand perfectly still—they looked like a trio of overweight crooners, swaying boozily in the soft light for a last song.

Lucy rattled a plastic jar of aspirin and set it out on the table with a pitcher of ice water.

"So?" she said.

Lindy lifted a log into the fire, raking the bed of coals with an iron, and wiped his hands.

"No luck," Steve said.

"But you found the bar all right," Lucy said.

"Huh—yeah," Sandy said. "The bar wasn't running through the woods."

"Tomorrow," Mr. Jansen offered. He was a large man, so large he always struck me as unfinished, the rough framing of a man who would never fully occupy the space he'd annexed. He had a flat owlish face and arched gray eyebrows and a pounding, theatrical voice. It was he, more than anyone else, who had encouraged my wife in her acting career. "And Daly'll come along."

I knew better than to object, although I'd fired a gun only twice in my life, and both times I'd missed the can. There was no romance for me in weapons, and I found it effortful to be around men who liked to shoot. I always had, beginning with my father, who was an avid gun collector and fancied himself a marksman. In an act of adolescent defiance, I'd become an equally avid birder, a member of the local Audubon, and a preachy vegetarian, turning the table into a pulpit while my father, ignoring me, packed it away, head bent over his plate. Now I stared at the men, looking them in the eye, one by one— I had rehearsed this moment for weeks—but learned nothing when, to my surprise, each of them averted his eyes.

"How about fixing the damn toilet instead?" Sandy said.

"What's wrong with the outhouse?" her husband countered.

"The forest is full of drunks with guns," Sandy said. "Girls don't like that."

When I thought I was the only one awake, I reached for Caroline's thigh, sliding my hand inside her nightgown. In the cold cabin, she was like the discovery of buried warmth, of hibernating life. I heard the fire pop and hiss, the crumbling sound as the pile of logs collapsed and settled. Stirred by the noise, Lindy rose and stoked the fire, adding a few logs and some split-cedar shakes. Steve snored loudly, and Sandy whispered something to him, and I heard them both grunt and turn over in bed. With the fire rekindled, a cobweb fluttered in the waves of rising heat, and the thin gray filament threw a shadow that wound and unwound, snaking along the far wall. I moved my hand up Caroline's thigh until I felt the rough edge of pubic hair curling out from beneath the elastic band of her G-string. I slipped a finger under the band, and then I reached for myself. Caroline rose up, startled, and said, "What, what," but I don't think she ever fully woke. She stared around herself, still safely in her dream, and then she lay back down, balling up beneath the comforter with her back to me.

My wife was raped the summer she turned eighteen. She told me this after we'd been together for a year, on a night when I'd once again caught her crying for no apparent reason. I felt instantly that I'd known all along. An entire history and sensibility suddenly pulled into focus, and there was Caroline, my wife, the blur of herself resolved into something sharp and clear. Our whole time together, I sensed that I had been tracing the contours of that moment, describing and defining its shape. This was, I thought, the elusive thing I'd been trying to put my hands on.

For months afterward, I found myself drifting away from conversations as I rehearsed the scenario in my mind. What I imagined was horrible for me—the rain and the bushes, a black man, a knife. I saw things. I saw the underpants she'd have to pull on again when he was done, I saw her walk home in a world suddenly gone strange, I saw the mud she'd have to wash off the backs of her thighs and the way the stream of gray would circle the drain, I saw pebbles embedded in her knees, I saw her days later, alone and crying, dropping the knife the first time she cut into a tomato, I saw the halved red fruit on the white cutting board the next morning, the spilled seeds now dried to the plastic. I saw these things, I imagined them. Our life together took on a second intention, and a sock on the floor would stop me cold. My eyes would lose focus and I'd daydream, trying to capture the moment and make it less strange, trying to inhabit the past, intervening. I wanted to be there, and, failing, I developed instead a tendency to ascribe every dip and depression to the rape, organizing our shared life around it, carrying it forward into our future like a germ.

I now understand that rape is more often than not a domestic matter, but I had been deeply confused when, after pressuring my wife relentlessly, she told me that the rapist was a close friend of her father's. I had staked all my understanding on increasingly elaborate and far-fetched horrors, but the dark stranger I had been improvising was a grotesque cliché. She had been raped here, in this cabin, on her annual trip up north. My desire to know more—I wanted his name, I wanted her to say it—was met with a steady resistance, an intricate system of refusals, with the result that, constantly sparring, skirmishing, denying, we were never very deeply honest with each other. Caroline was resolute. She wouldn't talk about it, except to say that the truth would kill her father. "He wouldn't be able to take it," she said. I had never been up north, refusing until now to make the annual trip.

This is not easy for me to say, so I'll start with the clinical by saying that Caroline was anorgasmic: she'd never had a climax, not with me or anyone else, not even by herself. Like many other men before me, I believed that I would remedy that problem, that it was merely a matter of prowess and patience, of a deeper love and a greater persistence, but no matter what we did—the books, the scents, the oils, all the hoodoo of love—none of it changed a thing. With time, my conceit broke down. In defeat I came to feel weak and ashamed. In some way, her lack of sexual fulfillment accounted for her promiscuity: what she missed in intensity she made up for in scope. She had never been a faithful lover, either before or after our marriage; she preferred sex with strangers, which I could never be, not again. It was as if she were determined to revisit, over and over, that original moment of absolute strangeness. And yet she continued to need the scrim of familiarity I offered, so that the world would fill more sharply with the unfamiliar. Daily I lost more and more of my status as a stranger, and our marriage was like a constant halving of the distance, without ever arriving at the moment in time where, utterly familiar, I'd vanish.

Caroline was currently having an affair with a talent agent, a man from London who, roughly a month ago, had begun to make regular appearances in her diary and date book as SJ. In her Filofax: "Lunch w/ SJ"; "SJ for drinks." A page with his home number, then his address scribbled on the square for October 23. (Before SJ, there'd been an M, a D, a G. She always used initials, some nicety of convention she must have come across in adolescence.) I had, of course, taken to reading her diary, hoping it contained some sort of truth. I'd read the most recent entry as I read all of them, at three in the morning, crouched on the side of the tub in our tiny bathroom, in terror of being discovered, my skin blue and bloodless under the frank fluorescent light. In that entry she considers whether she should go with SJ, the week after Thanksgiving, to his house in Vermont, telling me—what? she wonders. That she's landed a part in a commercial shoot that will take her overnight to Boston? What part? And what commercial? she asks herself, plotting for the plausible, the approximate, some arrangement of words that would deceive and soothe and sound, recognizably, like our life.

The truck was loaded and we were off before dawn, while the women still slept. The sky was slate blue and brittle, and at one point I saw the green flare of a meteor burn out above a line of trees. It happened so fast that I doubted myself in the very moment of wonder, and, feeling sleepy and uncertain, decided not to mention it to anybody. I imagined that a kind of fraternal ridicule kept this group cohesive, and I didn't want to become the scapegoat who helped them bond.

Mr. Jansen stopped for coffee at a filling station, where trucks and cars idled in the raw air, their headlamps lighting the tiny lot. Hunters were already heading back to the city with their kills. Nearly every car was tricked out with a carcass—a six-point buck strapped to the roof of a yellow Cadillac, the head of a doe lolling beneath the lid of a half-closed trunk.

Steve reached into his pocket and pulled out a pack of cigarettes. He tapped a few loose and, turning to me, said, "Smoke?"

"Can't you wait?" Lindy said.

"I'll crack the window."

"Fuck, just wait."

"No, thanks," I said, waving away the offer.

Steve had been the first up that morning, and he'd taken the time to shave. His red jowly face was smooth and smelled of lime. Below his ear a spot of blood had dried where he'd nicked himself. I've never really liked men on whom I can smell cosmetic products, and it was that morning, in the truck, so close to Steve, that I realized it had nothing to do with the particular soap or aftershave but with the proximity. If I could smell a man, he was too close. Now Steve lit a cigarette and inhaled with a grimace, relishing the pain.

"How's things in insurance?" he asked.

"Good enough," I said.

"You're an adjuster, right? Claims?"

I nodded.

Mr. Jansen returned with the coffee. He poured a cup from the thermos, and we passed it around, heading up the highway.

We turned onto a narrow rutted road, which ended in a blinding expanse of white. A dirty beige Pontiac was parked next to a rotted fence—dark leaning posts from which coils of rusted barbed wire ran like stitching through the quilted fields of snow. We got out of the truck.

"Hey, Tennessee," Mr. Jansen said. The man in the car rolled down his window. A cigarette hung from his lip and toast crumbs flecked his beard. He had hard blue eyes and a red scar along the side of his nose. A little girl slept next to him, wrapped in a blanket.

"Boys," he said, with a faint nod. He gazed through the windshield, his eyes fixed on something distant and still. "Cleared off a patch in the snow and put down corn."

Steve reached for his wallet. It was fat with credit cards, and an accordion of brittle plastic held photos of his wife and two kids. He leaned through the window.

"C-note?" he said.

Tennessee nodded.

"That's a costly turkey," Steve said.

Tennessee swallowed. "You only get one, I guess it might be." He continued to stare through the windshield. He didn't seem unfriendly, just far away, preserving his distance, as if he weren't really a party to this. Next to him, his little girl turned in her sleep, and he adjusted the blanket over her bare legs. Steve handed him the money. Tennessee put the folded bill in his shirt pocket without looking at it and slipped the car into gear, easing through the dry snow.

When he was gone, Steve said, "Hard-up fucking hillbilly."

Mr. Jansen was unracking the guns and gathering our packs. We wore bulky camouflage snowsuits, each the same pattern—dark branches on a white background. We had only three guns, and so I carried the decoy, a brown plastic hen with galvanized-steel legs. Thinking of Tennessee, I wondered if we were trespassing. I guessed that baiting was illegal but kept quiet. Despite myself, I was looking forward to the hunt, and I hurried along in step with the others, through the deep drifted snow until, at the edge of the field, we came to the blind.

"Jesus," Steve said, after we'd crowded in. He pulled out a monogrammed silver flask and poured us each a jigger of Scotch, as "an eye-opener," he said. He winked at me, and said, "Sitting all day in a blind with a bunch of liberals."

"I think you'll survive," Mr. Jansen told him.

"If we got stuck here, I'd eat you. I'd have no problem with that."

The blind was a small dark hut with a flat tarpaper roof and a packed-dirt floor and two rectangular holes cut in the weathered boards. It sheltered us from the wind, and our huddled bodies seemed to warm it somewhat.

"Ben Franklin wanted the turkey for the national symbol," Lindy said.

"Smart birds, no doubt about that," Steve said. "Wily."

Mr. Jansen brought out the thermos of coffee.

"How about a toast?" he said.

My own silence was making me increasingly self-conscious, and I felt an old inadequacy, not joining in on the banter.

"Whose property is this?" I asked.

"Some union big shot in Detroit," Mr. Jansen said. "Tennessee's the caretaker."

"You wouldn't think a couple of Democrats would go in for poaching," Steve said. "But I guess turkey hunts make for strange bedfellows. Like politics."

I couldn't follow the drift of his political beliefs, the precise arrangement of bigotries that he used to sort the world, but I raised my cup with everyone else.

Lindy said, "To a big fat tom."

The coffee and the Scotch parted ways immediately, one warming my stomach, the other rising in a vapor to my head.

"Daly," Mr. Jansen said, "why don't you set the decoy?"

"Sure," I said, glad for something to do, a small role.

Outside the blind, the snow spun like shifting sand. I

planted the decoy off to the left of the corn, driving the steel legs into the frozen ground. I squinted across the white moving expanse, and my eyes ached. Everything was either black or white, flat or upright, reduced to the stark lines of winter. I couldn't believe this plastic turkey had a prayer, it looked so obviously counterfeit. I looked back to the blind, wondering if my snowsuit disguised me at this distance. Steve Rababy's head was squarely framed in the window. His face was round and ruddy, blown up in some beefy sated English way. In the asperity of early winter, he seemed grossly overfed.

"Who wants to call?" Lindy asked as I was crawling back in.

"More important," Steve said, "who gets first crack at him?"

"I thought we'd let Daly have the honor," Mr. Jansen said.

"I think we should draw lots," Steve said. "That's tradition."

Before I could say "Leave me out of it," Mr. Jansen said, "Okay, choose a number between one and ten."

"Five," Lindy said.

"Three," Steve said.

I chose nine, and Mr. Jansen said, "Nine it is."

"Fuck you it's nine," Steve said.

Mr. Jansen laughed heartily while Steve removed his mittens and worked the call, rubbing the wooden slat over the box. A dry squawking was carried downwind from the blind. He waited a short while and then, leaning one ear to the instrument, like a violinist, gave the call another grating, followed by a couple of percussive clucks. The call was faint, unequal to the wind, the gusting snow. It sounded lost and weak, too plaintive, and it was hard to imagine the sort of hunger that would mishear these false notes.

"With steel shot," Lindy said, "you've really got to call them in. Killing range isn't the same as lead."

"Use my gun," Steve said. He blew on his freckled red

hands. "I've got some old lead shot in there. I packed a couple of those babies last night."

"I don't know about a ten-gauge," Lindy said. "You get some extra distance, but you pay for it in recoil."

"I don't like to be undergunned," Steve said.

Lindy said, "Choke matters more."

"That's full," Steve said. "Pretty tight. The pattern density's fine at forty yards. I just tested it."

"What Steve's doing," Mr. Jansen explained, "he's trying to imitate a hen and draw a gobbler out of the trees. He'll keep calling until he gets an answer."

Steve said, "Right now I'm telling him there's a chance for poon out here, so he'd better get his ass out of the woods while the gettin's good." He looked away from his post to see if I was listening. "After we spot him—way out there on the edge of the field—I'll space out the calls. That's my style. I like to let the silence draw the bird in. Turkeys are skittish—they've got amazing hearing and eyesight—but they're curious, too, and that's their doom."

"Killing range is anywhere inside forty yards," Mr. Jansen continued, "but let's try to hold off until Steve gets him to more like twenty."

"You'll probably feel a little hot," Steve explained, "and your face'll flush. That's turkey fever. But just recognize it and relax and breathe deep and blow out and squeeze. You don't want to do what most guys do, you don't want to flock shoot. Aim—aim for the neck and head, not the turkey."

Mr. Jansen lit a cigarette. He said, "You want to kill it without pumping the meat full of lead."

Steve coaxed a steady confab of calls out of the box, playing the wooden tongue back and forth. To my ears, the sound remained ugly and discordant, certainly not musical and harmonious in the way of the passerine birds, like finches or warblers, with their contralto trilling in spring. Mr. Jansen seemed content to be out early, away from the women, with a drink in his hand and plenty more in the flask. Lindy was crouched in the corner, sunk into himself. He'd shown no real animation since we'd arrived.

"It wouldn't do to eat the national symbol," I said, trying to pick up the conversation where Lindy had left off. I felt instantly that I'd made an awkward, pointless comment. "Taboo," I added, trying to cover myself.

"Daly here is an RC," Mr. Jansen said.

"You eat your Saviour every Sunday," Steve said. "Isn't that what those crackers are?"

"Beth Ann was Catholic," Lindy said. He ran his finger in the dirt floor, drawing a cross. He pinched some of the dirt and threw it at the walls of the blind. "She wanted a Catholic funeral, and that's what she got."

Steve Rababy and Mr. Jansen averted their eyes, staring vacantly at different walls, as if trying to keep the separate lines of vision from tangling. Lindy looked at each of us, a soft well of tears pooling in his eyes. He rubbed a thick mitten across his face.

"I never converted," he said, in a very small voice. "At the funeral, it was like a foreign language. They were saying goodbye to my wife, using words I didn't understand."

"Get over it," Steve said. He had stopped working the call, but now he leaned out the window, scraping the wooden tongue over the box.

"That's a little cold," I said.

"Well," Steve said, "we've heard all this. We heard it yesterday and the day before and the day before that. We drove up goddam I-75 singing this song." He aimed a hard stare at Lindy. "It was almost a year ago. It's just sentimental bullshit at this point. It's fucking weak."

"Take it easy, Steve," Mr. Jansen said. He helped himself to another cup of hot coffee, cooling it with a measure of Scotch. "Everybody has their own time, Lindy most of all."

"She knew everything about me," Lindy continued, as if he hadn't heard Steve. "Everything." Tears streaked shamelessly down a face that crying contorted and turned ugly, a squalling baby's face that was not sympathetic in a grown man. "Now no one does."

"No one ever does," Steve said. "You know, here's your goddam marriage. All right? Okay? Let me recap. For thirty-five fucking years I listened to you bitch and moan about Beth Ann. All right? Every afternoon at the bar, starting the day after you came back from your honeymoon. Five o'clock and I could fucking count on it. How she didn't give it up enough, how she wouldn't swallow, how she didn't look young anymore, blah blah blah"—with each "blah," he swiped a strident cluck from the call—"on and on and on. And now she's dead and it's like, mamma mia, she's some kind of fucking saint."

"Lucy knows everything about me," Mr. Jansen offered. It seemed a silly, conciliatory remark, not at all the kind of thing my wife's father believed.

Steve called him on it. "Yeah, right—I know more about you than she ever will."

Steve continued to scrape the call, but the wind had blown the horizon blank and there was no sign of a bird.

"And both of you know a fuck of a lot more about me than Sandy does," he said. "The way I see our marriage is, like, finally, after thirty-nine years, we understand we don't understand each other. We finally got that cleared up.

"Give me another drink," he said, beating senselessly on. "She could give a rat's ass about hunting—sitting out here in this box would seem stupid to her.

"Forget the turkey," he said. "I have a mind to shoot myself."

"Go ahead," I said.

Steve barked a frantic, nearly hysterical call, working the tongue rapidly, like honing a knife against a whetstone.

"You don't like me, do you? You got a problem with me."

"Jesus, how'd we end up here?" Mr. Jansen said. "Let's just everybody shut up for a minute."

Steve said, "There's key shit Sandy doesn't know and never will. Stuff about Katrina, and that whole saga, right?" He sniffed, then spat through the window. "And yeah, every Friday about eleven, twelve o'clock you could always find Lindy's car parked outside the massage parlor on Warren. Those Oriental girls, they look like teenagers until they're forty, eh Lindy? And you," he said, turning on my father-in-law. "You—"

"That's enough, Steve."

"Hey," Lindy said.

"And you," Steve said to me. "You obviously got some kind of fucked-up agenda—"

"Look," Lindy said.

"Where?" Steve said.

Moving against a low sea current of snow, a turkey, its narrow neck bent, came toward us, following the call. Lindy grabbed a spotting scope from one of the packs, adjusting the focus. "It's got a beard and a half," he said, passing me the scope. I slipped off my mittens. Steve worked the wooden slat in a new rhythm, as if mating the tempo to his excitement, locating the music of his desire. I looked through the scope and saw the turkey, its long straggling beard and chocolate-brown feathers and its beady black eyes, narrowed in a heavy-lidded squint against the blowing snow. I passed the scope to Mr. Jansen and he slid the gun into my hand.

We were all silent now, and even the smallest sounds—Lindy's labored breathing or Mr. Jansen absently rubbing his thigh—seemed a gross and fatal intrusion. Steve let the call fall silent for a moment, and then resumed, and when he did we could hear for the first time the low guttural of the old tom's response. The turkey drummed and strutted in what seemed to me like hesitation, and then, in a sudden dash, hurried straight toward the decoy.

The gun had a satisfying heft, a weight in my hand that was exactly right. I raised the stock to my shoulder and looked with one eye down the barrel, arranging the red wattle neatly within the notched iron sight. In this snow the dark-brown bird was exposed, and I had a vague sense of understanding the risk it took, the declaration it was making. The tom's beard blew in the wind, and he began to circle the hen, spreading his wings and fanning his tail. The bird puffed up to three times its size. It was a terrific display, cocky and proud and blustery and, I thought, soon to be irrelevant; my father-in-law gave a nod and I drew a breath and my mind went blank and I let go of the breath as I squeezed the trigger and nothing, nothing at all, happened. I went cold and, confused, stopped sighting the bird. Lindy said, "The fucking safety." He grabbed the gun, raised it to his shoulder, and fired. A deep blast echoed and unrolled, just as the tom seemed to know it had been fooled. Instantly, the fan of feathers folded and the turkey collapsed.

We rushed from the blind and gathered in a circle over the bird. The shot had been a good one; the turkey's head was gone, and its neck was now hardly more than a hose filling a hole in the snow with blood. No one bent to touch it, as if this were the scene of a crime and we were waiting for some other, final authority to arrive. At last, Steve Rababy lit a cigarette and, covering his heart with his hat, gave the bird a brief eulogy.

"He was looking for pussy and now he's dead. Let that be a lesson to you liars."

Lindy offered a sentimental rephrasing, managing to work a trace of irony into his voice: "He died for love."

"Dinner," Mr. Jansen said, putting his vast appetite where it belonged, before all.

The shell had detonated inches from my ear. I worked a finger in it to clear the ringing.

Lindy said to me, "I had to take your shot."

"I didn't know about the safety," I said.

"That's my fault," Mr. Jansen said.

"Let's agree on a story," Steve said.

"Fine by me," Lindy said.

They looked at Mr. Jansen for ratification, and then he said, "Okay, we'll say it was Daly."

After the high of the hunt, the rest of the afternoon had the long, languid feel of a Sunday. People kept up a compensatory busyness. Mr. Jansen plucked the bird in the garage and brazed the remaining nubs with a blowtorch. He wore an orange watch cap with a comical fur ball dangling from a string, and drank steadily from a cache of beers he'd buried in a mound of snow. Sandy Rababy worked a wooden spoon in a big pink bowl, and Lindy sat on the couch reading the newspaper. Caroline and Lucy discussed acting careers, my wife's in particular, although now and then my mother-in-law offered an item of gossip she'd gleaned from the tabloids, restating fantasy and rumor as if they were fact. I listened, not so much to the content as to the lilt in my wife's voice, the English phrasing in some of her sentences, a strange cadence that rose up, seeming to free itself, now and then, from her flat Michigan accent. She had an actor's gift for mimicry, a hunger for imitation, absorbing the speech of others unself-consciously, and on

several occasions in the past her affairs had chillingly registered for me first in a new sound, a surprising word in her
vocabulary, a foreign inflection in her voice.

Late in the afternoon, in guest mode, with no specific chore,
I went for a walk. The trail I took led through a stand of white
pine, ending at the lake behind the Jansens' cabin. A diving
raft was beached on the icy shore, and a string of rental boats
was chained to a tree, each boat filled with snow, its gunwales
whelmed by deep drifts. I felt as though I were seeing a sculp-
tor's rendition of my wife's memories, a summer dream hacked
into ice. The lake was fairly large, the surface sealed shut as
though paraffin had been poured over it. I walked to the end of
the dock. Below the ice, a blue sand pail and a yellow shovel
from summer had sunk into the murk. Then I saw my wife out
on the lake, perhaps half a mile from the dock, bundled in a
shapeless red snowsuit. Her progress over the ice was painfully
slow, as though she feared falling through, but then she was
gone, and I heard a loon and tilted my good ear toward its call.
A loon's cry makes a haunting music on summer evenings, a
tremolo you hear in the dark—eerie, because the two alternat-
ing notes mimic the sound of an echo, a call going out and then
returning unanswered, a prayerful lament without a response.
It was very late in the season to be migrating. The black bird
was standing on the ice. Loons are ungainly, barely able to
walk, achieving flight only after a long awkward struggle. In
the air, they're graceful and capable of flying sixty miles an
hour. I watched until the bird rose up and the black speck,
clearing the trees, dissolved like a drop of tint in the darkening sky.

Trussed and displayed, our bird seemed to have been sitting on
the table for ages, waiting for a banquet to begin. On either side

of it, tall white candles flickered in a crosscurrent of the cabin's many drafts, sending uncertain shadows over the table and lending a layer of depth to the setting. McIntosh apples were mounded in a bowl lined with yellow and brown satin leaves, and a wicker cornucopia at the opposite end of the table had been filled with Indian corn, along with acorns and walnuts and filberts, gourds, sprigs of dried sweet william, figs, a pomegranate—the open mouth of it overflowing with the stuff of harvest. A basket of warm glazed buns was wrapped in a white cloth, and a rich, earthy stuffing, steaming like a bog, was kept hot in a glass-lidded serving dish. China and silver settings had been brought north from Detroit, and there were goblets for both wine and water. With the pipes broken, water was the scarcer commodity. But there was wine. Two bottles had been uncorked and were breathing on the table, and six more sat on a sideboard, above which, on the wall, a large ornately framed mirror, slightly canted, held the whole scene like a still life.

Mr. Jansen poured wine for everyone, and then, as people settled into their seats, stood at the head of the table, flipping open the brass latches of a wooden box and pulling his carving knife and fork from a bed of red crushed velvet. He scraped the knife against a hone, crossing them above his head like a swashbuckler, and then, asking for silence, cleanly cut a first slice of white meat and placed it ceremoniously on my plate. The others clapped and cheered and stomped their feet, and I felt that my face must have reddened. I looked into the mirror and was able to see, as if I were hovering above the table, everyone but myself.

"To Daly, after all these years," Lucy said.

"Hear! Hear!" Steve and Lindy and Mr. Jansen all said together.

The toast's concluding ring of crystal rang dully in my

right ear, still numb from the shotgun blast. We all drank in
my honor, and then drank again when Steve, winking my
way, rose to salute the turkey I'd shot.

"I'm surprised," Caroline said. "It doesn't seem like you,
Daly."

A gravy boat came down the line, and I ladled a thick,
brown, floury paste over everything.

"Yeah," Lucy said.

"Well . . ." I didn't know what to say.

Mr. Jansen jumped in. "Why not, Lucille? What, may I
ask, is your idea of him?"

"I don't know."

Sandy answered. "More passive—not passive but, like,
more a pacifist, I mean, a pacifist, not a killer."

"Oh, no," Lindy said. "Not the killer conversation again."

"Hunting," Steve said, cluing me in, somewhat vaguely, as
he had with his politics. His assumption that we shared something unspoken only sharpened my resentment of him.

"You eat, you can't complain," Mr. Jansen said.

"But it's true," my wife said. "He's a major bird-watcher. He
keeps this stupid little book— I'm sorry, I don't mean stupid. I
mean . . . you know what I mean." She paused, patting my fore-
arm, and then, covering the awkward silence, continued. "You
should have seen how excited he was the day he saw a pileated
woodpecker in Central Park."

"I'll show you a pileated woodpecker," Steve said.

"Oh, God, not that pecker conversation again," Sandy
yelled.

"What's the point of that, anyway, Daly?" Mr. Jansen asked,
steering the conversation off the subject of sex. For a pleasure-
loving, hard-drinking barfly, my wife's father was surprisingly
prudish. His face was flushed. He'd tucked a corner of his

napkin into his shirtfront, like a little boy. As the discussion jumped around, he swiveled his head from side to side, slashing his knife and fork in the air, as if he were trying to stab a word out of the conversation and eat it. "And what's a pileated? That needs to be cleared up."

"What's the point of what?" I asked stiffly. I was seated at the far end of the table, with everyone to my right, and I couldn't keep pace with the conversation. I was beginning to think my eardrum was punctured. A warm fluid seemed to be leaking from it.

"Watching birds." Between the sound of his booming voice and my comprehension, there was a distracting lag, and the only replies I could make were serious and plodding, out of sync with the rising hilarity.

"A pileum," I said, "is the top of a bird's head."

"Don't all birds have tops to their heads?"

"Some birds are topless," Lindy said.

All this badinage was just crashing and piling up in front of me. It seemed really cornball and canned, but I couldn't quite catch the tone and join in. I reached for my water and held the glass in my palm, cool against my skin.

"Come again," I said.

"What?" Lindy said. "Huh?"

"What—" I began, and then everyone at the table started in.

"What? What?"

"What? What? What?"

"What?"

"I'm sorry," I said. "I can't hear."

"Ah," Steve said, "from the shotgun."

"Just in my right," I said.

Steve stood beside me with his plate and utensils in hand.

"Trade places," he said.

"That's okay."

"No, come on. You still got one good ear, right? Let's switch. It's no problem."

Stubbornly insisting on my seat would only have caused a scene at this point.

"Maybe he doesn't want to hear," Lindy said.

Sandy laughed. "Lord knows, he's better off."

"Switch over," Mr. Jansen said with a preemptive wave of his knife. By the time I was seated again, the entire conversation had moved on. Caroline was playing with her food, and I wondered what she was thinking. The silver earrings SJ had given her caught the firelight and flickered as she brought her hand to her lips. Something dropped on her plate, tinging loudly enough for all of us to hear.

Her mother said, "I got one, too."

"Lead?" Mr. Jansen asked.

"Me, too. That's lead?" Sandy turned to her husband. "Isn't lead illegal? That's what you told me."

"Baiting turkey itself is illegal," Steve said. "So whether or not we used a little lead didn't seem to matter much." Sandy looked at me, and I made an exaggerated shrug, absolving myself of any accessory role in the crime.

"There's nothing really wrong with it," Steve said.

"Except it causes brain damage," Lucy said.

"Well, don't swallow any," Steve said.

Lucy said, "But won't it taint the meat around it, too?"

Sandy said, "The whole bird is poisoned!"

"Goddam," Steve said.

"I don't like being reminded of this dead thing that was alive," Sandy said. "That's my other point. I for sure don't like biting into the bullets that killed it during dinner."

"Those aren't bullets, for fuck's sake," her husband said. "It's just shot, number-six shot."

Sandy said, "I like to make believe my turkey was grown on a tree or bush."

"Yeah, well, it wasn't," Mr. Jansen said.

"You liked that fancy squab in Paris plenty," Steve said to his wife, working the hypocrisy angle that always seemed to crop up at the end of these discussions. It was as if the interminable debate—men on one side, women on the other—would end only when it swallowed its own tail.

"You owed me that squab," Sandy said. She was drunker than the rest of us, or less capable of hiding it. "You owed me that squab for fucking Katrina."

"Sandy," my wife's mother said.

"Ten years. Ten goddamn years."

Sandy reached for one of the bottles of wine that had been left to breathe on the sideboard. She rose from her chair and said, "You all just go out and hunt and sit around and swap stories. You all think it's funny." She walked unsteadily around the table. "And no one's ever hurt and it's all just stories. Ha ha. Oh, yeah." She bent as if to kiss her husband on the ear. "I hate guns," she said. "I hate guns. I hate guns." She straightened up and looked over the table as if waiting for applause, and when none came she filled her glass, and then poured the rest of the bottle of wine over her husband's head. His knife and fork were poised above his plate, and he smiled patiently as the wine dripped down his face. When the bottle was empty, he put a piece of meat in his mouth and chewed it slowly, then swallowed.

No one said anything.

"I could tell some stories," Sandy said.

"We can clean up tomorrow," Lucy said.

"There's others," Sandy said.

Lucy insisted. "It's bedtime for you."

Sandy put on a red union suit and climbed the ladder into

her bunk, and we tried to resume dinner, but soon she was leaning over the edge of the bed, shouting down at us.

"That's the difference," she said.

"Go to bed, dear," Steve said.

"I want to tell you the difference!"

"Okay," Steve said. "What's the difference?"

"You all have stories," Sandy said. "And we have secrets."

"Good night," Mr. Jansen said.

"That's the difference," she said.

Before bed, I walked across the Jansens' drive and stood under the awning of the garage. It was snowing lightly. Firelight lit the cabin windows, and I could see my wife, standing at the kitchen sink, framed in an oval of frost where the glass was too warm to freeze. I fumbled with a book of matches as I watched her, this lovely woman carved like a cameo against the window. I was about to head back inside when Mr. Jansen joined me. "You want a light?" he asked, and suddenly the flame from a lighter flared in my face. He lit a cigarette and said, "What's your problem with Steve?"

My father-in-law's face was gray with stubble, as if the long day had aged him. He looked tired and uncertain, and I wondered how he'd react if he knew the truth about his friends. This old man could be shattered with a sentence, but in the blind I had begun to lose my grip on the clarity of my dreams. I could no longer imagine the shape of my revenge, the loss I was trying to recoup, the pain I was trying to stop—Caroline's, or mine. I had been jarred by the end of dinner, sad for Steve, which surprised me, and sad for Sandy—especially Sandy, the way she lived with the rankling knowledge that she existed in her husband's affections as a thin anecdote, an illustration of his mediocre griefs. I didn't want to become the sort of man Steve was, and I honestly believed at that moment, as I watched the snow curl around the cabin windows, that I would never tell my wife's story, that her secret, what little of it I knew, was safe with me.

Mr. Jansen watched his daughter in the window, her face blurring behind a cloud of steam as she poured boiled water into the sink and began washing the dinner dishes.

"It's a tough haul, acting," he said. "But she's good, isn't she?"

"Better than you know," I said.

"I wouldn't be so sure. I used to do some acting. That's where her talent comes from. Someday she'll be famous. She'll be well known."

"You're drunk," I said.

For a moment, he seemed to vacate his own face, leaving behind the hollowed eyes and nose and mouth of a mask. He stubbed his smoke in the snow and stumbled across the icy drive back to the cabin. A little while later, I came in and climbed the ladder to our bunk. I lay awake, listening to the subdued voices below. I remember only that my wife used the word "wanker," and then for a while low whispers were skimming the surface of my sleep until, late in the night, toward dawn, really, I woke and found myself alone.

My heart was racing, pounding with a familiar fear—that Caroline was gone and I would never find her. I hurried down the ladder and opened the cabin door. The temperature had dropped and the snow had glazed over with a sheen of ice. The thin crust cracked underfoot with a distinct breaking sound. I walked along the trampled path, shortening my stride to fit my feet into the frozen mold of previous footprints, losing myself in concentration. At the outhouse, I stood for a moment, listening.

I called her name.

There was no response, and I panicked, as you might in a dream where all your assumptions are not exactly wrong but irrelevant. Far off in the woods, a coyote yipped and howled, and others answered. I leaned my head back and watched the breath stream from my mouth and disappear. The bare winter branches of the alders tangled above my head like a web. Then some black thing raced into the trees in front of me, and I jumped. It crashed through the underbrush and was gone.

The ground was pocked with fallen leaves and pine needles. Bare grass showed in the small circles of warmth beneath the sagging branches of fir trees. Everything that had moved in the woods over the past few days had left a record of its passing; the snow was marked with the tracks of hunters and birds and squirrels and deer and dogs, all the trails crisscrossing and weaving and intersecting, so that, if time were collapsed, you could imagine nothing but hapless collisions, a kind of antic vaudeville.

Caroline opened the outhouse door. She wore only her nightgown. Her feet were bare.

"You must be cold."

"Not really," she said. "I mean, I am, but I'm going in."

We looked back through the woods to the cabin. A rope of gray smoke curled up through the chimney, rising, it struck me, out of my simplistic imagination.

"You didn't shoot that turkey," she said.

"How do you know?"

She smiled and shook her head. "It's just not you."

"I guess," I said, although I resented the comment, the assumed familiarity. "I'd like to leave early tomorrow."

"I'm already packed," she said. "I've got a big week coming up."

I held my breath and waited for the scripted words.

"I got a part," she said. "A detergent commercial, Monday. We're shooting in Boston."

She was a good liar. She knew to look me directly in the eye. You can no more make someone tell the truth than you can force someone to love you. So that she wouldn't have to pretend anymore, I nodded, releasing her gaze.

"Who did?" she asked.

"Did what?"

"Shoot the turkey."

"Lindy," I said.

"I'm freezing," my wife said. "I'm going in now."

I grabbed her by the shoulder, turning her toward me. She tried to shrug free, and I dug my fingers into her shoulders. "Tell me," I said, tightening my grip until I felt bone roll beneath my thumbs. Her teeth were chattering, and she bit a crease of white in her lower lip, trying to stop them. She was trembling, and her frailty in the cold enraged me. I pulled her in close and then abruptly pushed her away, shaking and shoving until she fell back, breaking through the crust of ice the way children do, making angels. The deep powder closed over her face and her mouth was stopped with snow, and she lay still, her dark eyes staring vacantly up. She tried to rise, flailing her arms, and then, dreamily, she stretched out her hand, reaching for mine.

I walked away, now trembling myself, but for some reason I turned, and when I did she called my name. I didn't answer. She was standing by the outhouse, sunk to her knees in the broken drift, her hands clasping her shoulders so that she seemed to be embracing herself. Wind separated the ragged wisp of smoke from the chimney into several twining strands. Her long blond hair held the moonlight. Her nightgown billowed out, fluttering behind her, and she appeared to be hovering, almost drifting, as through water.

The Scheme of Things

Lance vanished behind the white door of the men's room and when he came out a few minutes later he was utterly changed. Gone was the tangled nest of thinning black hair, gone was the shadow of beard, gone, too, was the grime on his hands, the crescents of black beneath his blunt, chewed nails. Shaving had sharpened the lines of his jaw and revealed the face of a younger man. His shirt was tucked neatly into his trousers and buttoned up to his throat. He looked as clean and bland as an evangelist. He bowed to Kirsten with a stagy sweep of his hand and entered the gas station. All business, he returned immediately with the attendant in tow, a kid of sixteen, seventeen.

"This here's my wife, Kirsten," Lance said.

Kirsten smiled.

"Pleased," the kid said. He crawled under the chassis of the car and inspected the tailpipe.

"Your whole underside's rusted to hell," he said, standing up, wiping his hands clean of red dust. "I'm surprised you haven't fallen through."

"I don't know much about cars," Lance said.

"Well," the kid said, his face bright with expertise, "you should replace everything, right up to the manifold. It's a big job. It'll take a day, and it'll cost you."

"You can do it?" Kirsten asked.

"Sure," the kid said. "No problem."

Lance squinted at the oval patch above the boy's shirt pocket. "Randy," he said, "what's the least we can do?"

"My name's Bill,"the kid said "Randy's a guy used to work here."

"So, Bill, what's the least we can get away with?"

"Strap it up, I suppose. It'll probably hold until you get where you're going. Loud as hell, though."

The kid looked at Kirsten. His clear blue eyes lingered on her chest.

"We represent a charity." Lance handed the kid one of the printed pamphlets, watching his eyes skim back and forth as he took in the information. "Outside of immediate and necessary expenses, we don't have much money."

"Things are sure going to hell," the kid said. He shook his head, returning the pamphlet to Lance.

"Seems that way," Lance said.

The kid hurried into the station and brought back a coil of pipe strap. While he was under the car, Lance sat on the warm hood, listening to the wind rustle in the corn. Brown clouds of soil rose from the fields and gave the air a sepia tint. Harvest dust settled over the leaves of a few dying elms, over the windows of a cinder-block building, over the trailers in the courtyard across the street. One of the trailer doors swung open. Two Indians and a cowgirl climbed down the wooden steps. It was Halloween.

"You got a phone?" Lance asked.

"Inside," the kid said.

Lance looked down and saw the soles of the kid's work boots beneath the car, a patch of dirty sock visible through the hole widening in one of them. He walked away, into the station.

———

The kid hadn't charged them a cent, and they now sat at an intersection, trying to decide on a direction. The idle was rough. The car detonated like a bomb.

"Here's your gum," Lance said.

He emptied his front and back pockets and pulled the cuff of his pants up his leg and reached under the elastic band of his gym socks. Pink and green and blue and red packages of gum piled up in Kirsten's lap. He pulled a candy bar from his shirt pocket and began sucking away at the chocolate coating.

"One pack would've been fine," Kirsten said. "A gumball would have been fine."

"Land of plenty, sweetheart," he said.

Kirsten softened up a piece of pink gum and blew a large round bubble until it burst and the gum hung like flesh from her nose.

"Without money, we're just trying to open a can of beans with a cucumber," Lance said. "It doesn't matter how hungry we are, how desirous of those beans we are—without the right tools, those beans might as well be on the moon." Lance laughed to himself. "Moon beans," he said.

Kirsten got out of the car. The day was turning cold, turning to night. She leaned through the open window, smelling the warm air that was wafting unpleasantly with the mixed scent of chocolate and diesel.

"What's your gut feel?" Lance asked.

"I don't know, Lance."

She walked toward the intersection. Ghosts and witches crossed from house to house, holding paper sacks and pillowcases. The street lights sputtered nervously in the fading twilight. With the cold wind cutting through her T-shirt, Kirsten felt her nipples harden. She was small-breasted and sensitive and the clasp on her only bra had broken. She untucked the shirt and hunched her shoulders forward so that the nipples wouldn't show, but still the dark circles pressed against the white cotton. The casual clothes that Lance had bought her in Key Biscayne, Florida, had come to seem like a costume and were now especially flimsy and ridiculous here in Tiffin, Iowa.

A young girl crossed the road, and Kirsten followed her. She thought she might befriend the girl and take her home, a gambit, playing on the gratitude of the worried parents that Kirsten always imagined when she saw a child alone. The pavement gave way to gravel and the gravel to dirt, and finally a narrow path in the weeds dipped through a dragline ditch and vanished into a cornfield. The girl was gone. Kirsten waited at the edge of the field, listening to the wind, until she caught a glimpse of the little girl again, far down one of the rows, sitting and secretly eating candy from her sack.

"You'll spoil your dinner," Kirsten said.

The girl clutched the neck of her sack and shook her head. Entering the field felt to Kirsten like wading from shore and finding herself, with one fatal step, out to sea. She sat in the dirt, facing the girl. The corn rose over their heads and blew in waves, bending with the wind.

"Aren't you cold?" Kirsten said. "I'm cold."

"Are you a stranger?" the girl asked.

"What's a stranger?"

"Somebody that kills you."

"No, then, I'm not a stranger."

Kirsten picked a strand of silk that hung in the little girl's hair.

"I'm your friend," she said. "Why are you hiding?"

"I'm not hiding. I'm going home."

"Through this field?" Kirsten said.

"I know my way," the little girl said. The girl was dressed in a calico frock and dirty pink pumps, but Kirsten wasn't quite sure it was a costume. A rim of red lipstick distorted the girl's mouth grotesquely, and blue moons of eyeshadow gave her face an unseeing vagueness.

"What are you supposed to be?" Kirsten asked.

The girl squeezed a caramel from its cellophane wrapper, and said, "A grown-up."

"It's getting dark," Kirsten said." You aren't scared?"

The little girl shrugged and chewed the caramel slowly. Juice dribbled down her chin.

"Let me take you back home."

"No," the girl said.

"You can't stay out here all by yourself."

The girl recoiled when Kirsten grabbed her hand. "Let me go," she screamed, her thin body jolting away. "Let me go!" The fury in her voice shocked Kirsten, and she felt the small fingers slip like feathers from her hand. When the girl ran off through the rows of corn, it was as if the wind had taken her away. Instantly, she was nowhere and everywhere. In every direction, the stalks swayed and the dry leaves turned as if the little girl, passing by, had just brushed against them.

When Kirsten finally found her way out of the field, she was in another part of town. She walked the length of the street, looking for signs, deciding at last on a two-story house in the middle of the block. A trike lay tipped over in the rutted grass, and a plastic pool of water held a scum of leaves. Clay pots with dead marigolds—woolly brown swabs on bent, withered stalks—lined the steps. A family of carved pumpkins sat on the porch rail, smiling toothy candle-lit grins that flickered to black, guttering in laughter with every gust of wind. On the porch, newspapers curled beside a milk crate. Warm yellow light lit the downstairs and a woman's shadow flitted across a steam-clouded kitchen window.

Kirsten heard a radio playing. She knocked on the door.

The woman answered. Her hair was knotted up on her head with a blue rubber band, a few fugitive strands dangling down over her ears, one graying wisp curling around her eye. A smudge of flour dusted her cheek.

"Yes?" the woman said.

"Evening, ma'am." Kirsten handed the woman a pamphlet. "I'm with BAD," she said. "Babies Addicted to Drugs. Are you busy?"

The woman switched on the porch light and held the printed flyer close to her face. Closing one eye, she studied the bold-red statistics on the front of the page and then flipped it over and looked into the face of the dark, shriveled baby on the back.

"Doesn't hardly look human, does it?" Kirsten said.

"No, I can't say it does," the woman said.

"That's what's happening out there, ma'am. That, and worse." Kirsten looked off down the road, east to where the town ended and the world opened up to cornfields and darkening sky. She thought of the little girl.

"Smells nice inside," Kirsten said.

"Cookies," the woman said.

"You mind if I come in?"

The woman looked quickly down the road and, seeing nothing there, said, "Sure. For a minute."

Kirsten sat in a Naugahyde recliner that had been angled to face the television. Across from her was a couch covered with a clear plastic sheet. The woman returned with a plate of cookies. She set them in front of Kirsten and slipped a coaster under a coffee cup full of milk.

"My partner and me have been assigned to the Midwest territory," Kirsten said. "I got into this when I was living in New Jersey and saw it all with my own eyes and couldn't stand by and do nothing. Those babies were just calling out to me for help."

"I've got three children myself," the woman said.

"That's what the cookies are for," Kirsten said. She bit into one and tasted the warm chocolate.

"Homemade," the woman said. "But the kids like store-bought. All they want is Wing Dings or what have you."

"They'll appreciate it later, ma'am. I know they will. They'll remember it and love you."

In the low light, Kirsten again noticed the spectral smudge of flour on the woman's cheek—she had reached to touch herself in a still, private moment as she thought of something she couldn't quite recall, a doubt too weak to claim a place in the clamor of her day.

"That baby on the flyer isn't getting any homemade cookies. That baby was born addicted to drugs. There's women I've personally met who would do anything to get their drugs and don't care what-all happens to their kids. There's babies getting pitched out windows and dumped in trash cans and born in public lavatories."

"Things are terrible, I'm sure, but I can't give you any money. I worked all day making the kids' Halloween costumes—they want store-bought, of course, but they can't have them, not this year."

"What're they going to be?"

"Janie's a farmer, Randall's a ghost. Kenny's costume was the hardest. He's a devil with a cape and hood and a tail." If she could coax five dollars out of this woman, Kirsten thought, she could buy a cheap bra out of a bin at the dime store. Her breasts ached. When she'd seen the trike on the lawn out front, she'd assumed that this woman would reach immediately for her pocketbook.

"With a ten-dollar donation, you get your choice of two magazine subscriptions, free of charge for a year." Kirsten showed the woman the list of magazines *"Cosmo,"* she said. *"Vogue, Redbook,* all them."

"I'm sorry," the woman said.

The front window washed with white light.

"You had better go." The woman stood up. "I don't have any use for your magazines."

On the porch, they met a man, his face darkened with the same brown dirt and dust that had rolled through and clouded the sky that day. Spikes of straw stabbed his hair and the pale gray molt of a barn swallow clung to his plaid shirt. A silent look passed between the man and the woman, and Kirsten hurried away, down the steps.

"I thought she was trick-or-treating," the woman said as she shut the door.

"Nothing?" Lance said. "Nothing?"

Kirsten tore the wrapping from another piece of gum. They had driven to the outskirts of town, where the light ended and the pavement gave way to gravel and the road, rutted like a washboard, snaked off toward a defile choked with cottonwoods. Every street out of town seemed to dead-end in farmland, and here a lighted combine swept back and forth over the field, rising and falling like a ship over high seas. The combine's engine roared as it moved past them, crushing a path through the dry corn.

"A man came home," Kirsten said.

"So?"

"So the lady got all nervous and said I had to go."

"Should've worked the man," Lance said. He ran his finger along the outline of her breasts, as if he were drawing a cartoon bust. "We've talked about that. A man'll give money just to be a man about things."

"I'm too skinny," Kirsten said.

"You're filling out, I've noticed. You're getting some shape to you."

Lance smiled his smile, a wide, white grin with a hole in the middle of it. Two of his teeth had fallen out, owing to a weakness for sweets. He worried his tongue in the empty space, slithering it in and out along the bare gum.

"I wish I had a fix right now," Kirsten said. She hugged herself to stop a chill radiating from her spine. The ghost of her habit trailed after her.

Again the voracious growling of the combine came near. Kirsten watched the golden kernels spray into the holding bin. A man sat up front in a glass booth, smoking a pipe, a yellow cap tilted back on his head.

"My cowboy brain's about dead," Lance said. "What do you think?"

Kirsten had died once, and had made the mistake, before she understood how superstitious he was, of telling Lance about it. Her heart had stopped and she had drifted toward a white light that rose away from her like a windblown sheet, hovering over what she recognized as her cluttered living room. She was placid and smiling into the faces of people she had never seen before, people she realized instantly were relatives, aunts and uncles, cousins, the mother she had never known. Kirsten had grown up in foster care, but now this true mother reached toward her from within the source of light, her pale pink hands fluttering like the wings of a bird. A sense of calm told Kirsten that this was the afterlife, where brand-new rules obtained.

She woke in a Key Biscayne hospital, her foster mother in a metal chair beside the bed, two uniformed cops standing at the door, ready to read Kirsten her rights.

"Don't always ask me," Kirsten said.

"Just close your eyes, honey. Close 'em and tell me the first thing you see."

With her eyes closed, she saw the little girl, alone, running, lost in the corn.

"Let's get out of here," she said.

"That's what you saw?"

"Start the car, Okay? I can't explain everything I see."

She had met him in Florida, in her second year of detention. Her special problem was heroin, his was methamphetamine. They lived in a compound of low pink cinder-block buildings situated maddeningly close to a thoroughfare with a strip of shops, out beyond a chain-link fence and a greenbelt. At night, neon lights lit up the swaying palm fronds and banana plants, fringing the tangled jungle with exotic highlights of pink and blue. They'd climbed the fence together, running through the greenbelt, disappearing into the fantastic jungle. A year passed in a blur of stupid jobs—for Lance, stints driving a cab, delivering flowers, and, for Kirsten, tearing movie tickets in half as a stream of happy dreamers clicked through the turnstiles, then sweeping debris from the floors in the dead-still hours when the decent world slept. Lance, dressed in a white uniform, worked a second job deep-frying doughnuts in blackened vats of oil.

But *this*, Lance had said, *this* would allow them to turn their backs on that year, on everything they'd done for survival. A regular at the doughnut shop had set them up with their kit— the picture ID, the magazine subscriptions, the pamphlets. Although the deal worked like a pyramid scheme, it wasn't entirely a scam; a thin layer of legality existed, and ten percent of the money collected actually went to the babies. Another ten percent was skimmed by collectors in the field and the remainder was mailed to a PO box in Key Biscayne. Of that, the recruiters took a percentage, and the recruiters of the recruiters took an even bigger cut. That's the way it was supposed to work, but when Lance and Kirsten left Florida the tenuous sense of obligation weakened and finally vanished, and Lance was no longer sending any money to the PO box. They were renegade now; they kept everything.

Lance got out of the car. He tried to break the dragging tailpipe free, but it wouldn't budge. He wiped his hands. Down the road the yellow lights of a farmhouse glowed like portals. A dog barked and the wind soughing through the corn called hoarsely.

"The worst they can do is say no," Lance said.

"They won't," Kirsten said.

Lance grabbed his ledger and a sheaf of pamphlets and his ID. They left the car and walked down the road in the milky light of a gibbous moon that lit the feathery edges of a high, isolated cloud. The house was white, and seemed illuminated, as did the ghostly white fence and the silver silo. When they opened the gate, the dog barked wildly and charged them, quickly using up its length of chain; its neck snapped and the barking stopped, and when the dog regained its feet it followed them in a semicircle, as if tracing a path drawn by a compass.

Before they could knock, an old woman answered, holding a bowl of candy. Her hair was thin and white, more the memory or suggestion of hair than the thing itself. Her eyes were blue and the lines of her creased face held the image of the land around her, worn and furrowed. Her housedress drifted vaguely around her body like a fog.

"Evening, ma'am," Lance said.

When he was done delivering his introduction on the evils of drugs, he turned to Kirsten for her part, but she said nothing, letting the silence become a burden. The whole of the night—the last crickets chirring in the cold, the brown moths beating against the yellow light, the moon shadows and the quiet that came, faintly humming, from the land itself—pressed in close, weighing on the woman.

Finally Kirsten said, "If you could give us a place to stay for the night, we'd be grateful."

Lance said, "Now, honey, we can't impose."

"I'm tired and I'm cold," Kirsten said.

Again the silence accumulated around them like a world filling with water.

"My husband's gone up to bed," the woman said at last. "I hate to wake Effie."

"No need," Kirsten said. "If we could just sleep tonight in your girl's room, we'll be gone in the morning."

"My girl?"

"That's a lovely picture she drew," Kirsten said, "and it's wonderful that you hang it in the living room. You must have loved her very much."

A quelling hand went to the woman's lips. She backed away from the door—not so much a welcome as a surrender, a ceding of the space—and Kirsten and Lance entered. Years of sunlight had slowly paled the wallpaper in the living room and drained the red from the plastic roses on the sill. A familiar path was padded into the carpet and a pair of suede slippers waited at their place by the sofa. The air in the house was warm and still and faintly stale like a held breath.

———

In the morning, Kirsten woke feeling queasy and sat up on the cramped child's mattress. She pulled aside the curtain. The old couple were in the backyard. The wife was hanging a load of wash on a line, socks, a bra, underwear, linens that unfurled like flags in the wind. The husband hoed weeds from a thinning garden of gaunt cornstalks, black-stemmed tomato plants, and a few last, lopsided pumpkins that sat sad-faced on the ground, saved from rot by a bedding of straw. A cane swung from a belt loop in his dungarees.

"Any dreams?" Lance said. He reached for Kirsten, squeezing her thigh.

"Who needs dreams?" Kirsten said, letting the curtain fall back.

"Bitter, bitter," Lance said. "Don't be bitter."

He picked his slacks off the floor and shook out the pockets, unfolding the crumpled bills and arranging the coins in separate stacks on his stomach.

"Let's see where we're at," he said. Lance grabbed his notebook from the floor and thumbed the foxed, dirty pages in which he kept a meticulous tally of their finances.

"You don't need a pencil and paper," Kirsten said.

"Discipline is important," he said. "When we strike it rich, we don't want to be all stupid and clueless. Can you see them old folks out there?"

"They're out there."

"It must be something to live in a place like this," Lance said. He put down the notebook and peered out the window. "Just go out and get yourself some corn when you're hungry." He pressed his hand flat against the glass. In the field to the east, the corn had been gathered, the ground laid bare. "It looks weird out there."

Kirsten had noticed it also. "It looks too late," she said.

"That's the whole problem with the seventies."

"It's 1989, Lance."

"Well, then, high time we do some something about it." He pulled the curtain closed. "I'm sick and tired of washing my crotch in sinks."

"I'll go out and talk to them," Kirsten said.

"Where'd you go last night?" Lance asked. "After the gas station."

She didn't want to say, and said, "Nowhere."

"Get a look at yourself in that mirror there," he said.

Kirsten sat in a child's chair, looking at herself in the mirror of a vanity that had doubled as a desk at one time—beside the perfume bottles and a hairbrush and a box of costume jewelry were cups of crayons and pens and pencils and a yellowed writing tablet. Kirsten leaned her head to the side and began to brush her hair, combing the leaves and dirt out of it.

"Lance," she said.

"Yeah?"

"Don't take anything from these people."

"You can't hide anything from me," he said, with an assured, tolerant smile.

Kirsten set down the brush and walked out into the yard, where the old woman was stretched on her toes, struggling to hang a last billowing sheet.

"Lend me a hand here," she said. "The wind's blowing so—"

Kirsten held an end and helped fasten the sheet. Dust clung to the wet cotton.

"I probably shouldn't even bother hanging out the wash, this time of year," the old woman said. She pronounced it "warsh."

The swallowing mouth of a combine opened a path along the fence. The old woman shuddered and turned away.

"You have a beautiful place," Kirsten said. "All this land yours?"

"We got two sections. Daddy's too old to work it now, so we lease everything to a commercial outfit in Kalona."

"You must eat a lot of corn."

"Oh, hon, that's not sweet corn. That corn's for hogs. It's feed."

"Oh," she said.

"That blue Rabbit up the road yours?" The old man walked with an injured stoop, punting himself forward with the cane. He introduced himself—Effie Bowen, Effie and his wife, Gen. He was short of breath and gritted his teeth as if biting the difficult air. A rime of salt stained the brim of his red cap.

"That's us, I'm sorry to say."

He tipped the hat back, bringing his eyes out of the shade.

"Momma thinks I can tow you with the tractor," he said." I say she's right. I went and looked at it this morning."

"I'm not sure we can afford any major repairs," Kirsten said.

"You work for a children's charity," the old woman said.

"That's right."

"We'll get you going," the man said.

"Up to the Mennonites, right, Momma?"

The old woman nodded. "I put towels out. You kids help yourselves to a hot shower, and meanwhile Daddy and me'll tow your car up to the plain people and then we'll just see."

"We'd like to go into town," Kirsten said "If that's okay."

"Sure," the old woman said. She looked at her husband. "Yeah?"

"Of course, yes. Yes."

Main Street was wide and empty, the storefronts colorless in the flat light. A traffic signal swaying over the only intersection ticked like a clock in the quiet. Feeling faint, her stomach cramping, Kirsten sat on the curb. A hand-lettered sign on a sheet of unpainted plywood leaned against a low stucco building, advertising Fresh Eggs, Milk, Broccoli, Cherries, Bread, Potatoes, Watermelon, Strawberries, Root Beer, Antiques.

"No corn," Lance observed, pitching a rock at the sign. "So, you gonna tell me?"

She shook her head. "I just went for a walk, Lance. Nowhere," she said, pressing a print of her hand in the dust. She was wary of Lance, knowing that if she let him he would tap her every mood. He believed that a rich and deserved life ran parallel to theirs, a life that she alone could see, and he would probe her dreams for directions and tease her premonitions for meanings, as if her nightmares and moods gave her access to a world of utter certainty, when in fact Kirsten knew the truth—that every dream was a reservoir of doubt. A life spent revolving through institutions had taught her that. Foster care, detox, detention—even the woman she called Mother was an institution, a fumbling scheme. Kristen's improvised family of shifting faces sat together in common rooms furnished with donated sofas and burned lampshades and ashtrays of cut green glass, in lounges that were more home to her than home ever was, the inmates more family than she'd ever known.

It was in those lounges, on mornings that never began, through nights that wouldn't end, that Kirsten had elaborated her sense of the other world. She had stripped her diet of the staples of institutional life—the starches, the endless urns of coffee and the sugar cubes and creamers, the cigarettes. She'd cropped her hair short and stopped wearing jewelry, and one afternoon, while the janitor mopped the hallway, she'd slipped the watch from her wrist and dumped it into his bucket of dingy water. She'd cleaned her room and kept it spare, and she was considered a model inmate, neat and quiet and nearly invisible. By experimenting, she discovered that the only deeply quiet time on the ward was in the dark hour before dawn, and so she'd begun to wake at 4 a. m., first with an alarm clock, then automatically, easing from sleep into a stillness that was as spacious and as close to freedom as anything inside detention could be. Then she would pull a candle from her dresser drawer, melt it to her bedpost, sit in her chair, and stare at the mirror bolted to her wall. For weeks, she waited for something to appear in the clear depth, looking into the glass as if into a great distance. An instinct told her she was trying too hard, but one morning her arms lost life and went leaden, her hands curled, and the mirror turned cloudy, her face fading as if it had sunk below the surface of the glass, and her true mother's fingers reached toward hers. The next morning, she learned that guiding the images made them go away, and she spent another disconsolate hour staring at herself. Eventually she was able to sit without panic as her image sank and vanished, and often she emerged from her trances with her own hand stretched to meet the hand in the mirror.

Early in her detention, a social worker had advised Kirsten that the only thing better than heroin was a future, and that had been Lance's gift, a restlessness that seemed focused on tomorrow, a desire that made the days seem available. But he was impatient, and his sense of her gift was profane and depleting, with every half thought and reverie expected to strike pay dirt.

"Okay, fine," Lance said. "Let's hit the trailer court."

"I'm tired of those smelly trailers."

"We've talked about this I don't know how many times."

"I want the nice houses. Those people have the money."

"They have the money," he said, "because they don't fall for bullshit like ours."

They started up the steps of the biggest and nicest house on the street. With its wide and deep veranda, it seemed to have been built with a different prospect in mind, a more expansive view. Kirsten knocked and wiped her feet on the welcome mat and shuffled through her pamphlets and forms. Dressed in overalls, stuffed with straw, a scarecrow slumped on a porch swing, its head a forlorn sack knotted at the neck with a red kerchief. Kirsten knocked again, and then once more, but no one answered.

"See?" Lance said.

"See nothing," Kirsten said. She marched across the lawn to the neighbor's door. Lance sat on the curb, picking apart a leaf. No one answered her knock. She shuffled through her materials, stalling.

"Time to hit the trailer trash," Lance said.

Kirsten ran to the next house. A ghost hung from the awning, and the family name, Strand, was engraved on a wooden plaque above the door. She drew a deep breath and knocked. For some time now, she'd done things Lance's way. She'd solicited only the homes where she found signs of a shoddy slide—a car on blocks, a windowpane repaired with tape, some loss of contour in the slouching house itself—fissures in somebody else's hope that she and Lance could crawl through.

But what had happened? They'd become sad little children, petty thieves and liars, swiping things that no one would miss—five dollars here, ten dollars there—and laying siege to it with large plans, intricate calculations. Lance had his theories, but lately it had occurred to Kirsten that he was conducting his life with folklore. He had a knack for discovering the reverse of everything—the good were bad, the rich were poor, the great were low and mean—and it was no surprise that they were now living lives that were upside down.

A little girl pulled the door open a crack, peering shyly up at Kirsten.

"Is your momma home?"

"Momma!"

The woman who came to the door, wiping her hands on a dish towel, was a fuller version of the little girl, with the same blond hair and blue eyes. Kirsten offered her one of the brochures.

The little girl clung to her mother's leg. She wore one yellow sock and one green, orange dance tights, a purple skirt, a red turtleneck.

Kirsten said, "Did you get dressed all by yourself this morning?"

The little girl nodded and buried her face in the folds of her mother's skirt.

The mother smiled. "Cuts down on the fighting, right, April? We have a deal. She dresses herself, then she has to eat all her breakfast." She handed Kirsten the pamphlet. "I just made some coffee," she said.

Kirsten sat in a faded green chair by the window and leaned forward to watch Lance aimlessly tossing rocks and sticks in the street.

The woman brought two cups of coffee and a plate with Pop-Tarts, toasted and cut in thirds, fanned around the edges.

"You'd be surprised how many around here get into drugs," she said.

"I'm not sure it would surprise me, ma'am," Kirsten said. "Everywhere I go I hear stories from people who have been touched by this thing." She sipped her coffee. "This tragedy."

"I worry about this little one," the woman said.

Kirsten bit a corner of a Pop-Tart, feeling the hot cinnamon glaze on the roof of her mouth. On the mantel above the fireplace was a collection of ceramic owls. They stared steadily into the room with eyes so wide open and unblinking they looked blind.

"My owls," the woman said. "I don't know how it is you start collecting. It just happens innocently, you think one is cute, then all of a sudden"—she waved her hand in the air—"you've got dumb owls all over the place."

"Keep them busy," Kirsten said.

"What's that?"

"April, here—and all kids—if they have something to do they won't have time for drugs."

"That makes sense."

"People think of addicts as these lazy, do-nothing sort of people, but really it's a full-time job. Most of them work at it harder than these farmers I seen in these cornfields. It takes their entire life."

The woman cupped her hands over her knees, then clasped them together. Either her wedding band was on the sill above the kitchen sink, left there after some chore, or she was divorced. Kirsten felt a rush of new words rise in her throat.

"You know what it's like to be pregnant, so I don't have to tell you what it means to have that life in you—and then just imagine feeding your baby poison all day. A baby like that one on the pamphlet, if they're born at all, they just cry all the time. You can't get them quiet."

It was a chaotic purse, and the woman had to burrow down through wadded Kleenex, key rings, and doll clothes before she pulled out a checkbook.

"I never knew my own mother," Kirsten said.

The woman's pen was poised above the check, but she set it

down to look at Kirsten. It was a look Kirsten had lived with all her life and felt ashamed of, seeing something so small and frail and helpless at the heart of other people's sympathy. They meant well and it meant nothing.

"And I never really get away from this feeling," she went on. "Sadness, you could call it. My mother—my true mother, I mean—is out there, but I'll never know her. I sometimes get a feeling like she's watching me in the dark, but that's about it. You know that sense you get, where you think something's there and you turn around and, you know, there's nothing there?"

The woman did, she did, with nods of encouragement.

"When I think about it, though, I'm better off than these babies. Just look at that little one's dark face, his shriveled head. He looks drowned."

Then the woman filled in an amount and signed her name.

"I wish I was invisible," Lance said. "I'd just walk into these houses and they wouldn't even know."

"And do what?"

"Right now I'd make some toast."

"Hungry?"

"A little."

"Wouldn't they see the bread floating around?"

"Invisible bread."

"You get that idea from your cowboy brain?"

"Don't make fun of the cowboy brain," Lance said. "It got us out of that goddamn detention. It got us over that fence."

"We're ghosts to these people, Lance. They already don't see us."

"I'd like to kill someone. That'd make them see. They'd believe then."

"You're just talking," Kirsten said. "I think I'm getting my period."

"Great," Lance said. "All we need."

"Fuck you," Kirsten said. "I haven't had a period in two years."

She turned over one of the pamphlets.

Seeing the baby's inconsolable face reminded Kirsten of a song her foster mother used to sing, but while the melody remained, the lyrics were dead to her, because merely thinking of this mother meant collaborating in a lie and everything in it was somehow corrupted. Words to songs never returned to Kirsten readily—she had to think hard just to recall a Christmas carol.

"Little babies like that one," she said, "they'll scream all the time. Their little hands are jittery. They have terrible fits where they keep squeezing their hands real tight and grabbing the air. They can't stop shaking, but when you try to hold them they turn stiff as a board."

"To be perfectly honest," Lance said, "I don't really give a fuck about those babies."

"I know."

"We just need money for gas."

"I know."

At the next house, a man answered, and immediately Kirsten smelled the sour odor of settledness through the screen door. A television played in the cramped front room. A spider plant sat on a stereo speaker, still in its plastic pot, the soil dry and hard yet with a pale shoot thriving, growing down to the shag carpet, as if it might find a way to root in the fibers. Pans in the sink he scrubbed as needed, coffee grounds and macaroni on the floor, pennies and dimes caught in clots of dog hair. A somber, unmoving light in rooms where the windows were never opened, the curtains always closed.

"Some got to be addicted," the man said, after Kirsten explained herself. "They never go away."

"That may be so," Kirsten admitted. "I've thought the same myself."

He went to the kitchen and opened the fridge.

"You want a beer?"

"No thanks."

The blue air around the television was its own atmosphere, and when the man sank back in his chair it was as if he'd gone there to breathe. He looked at Kirsten's breasts, then down at her feet, and finally at his own hands, which were clumsy and large, curling tightly around the bottle.

"Where you staying?"

"About a mile out of town," she said. She handed the man a pamphlet. "I've had that same despair you're talking about. When you feel nothing's going to change enough to wipe out all the problem."

"Bunch of niggers, mostly."

"Did you look at the one there?"

"Tar baby."

"That kid's white," Kirsten said. She had no idea if this was true.

He didn't say anything.

Kirsten nodded at the television. "Who's winning?"

"Who's playing?" the man said. He was using a coat hanger for an aerial. "The blue ones, I guess."

"But isn't it enough? If you can save one baby from this life of hell, isn't that okay?"

"Doesn't matter much," he said. "In the scheme of things."

"It would mean everything," Kirsten said, "if it was you."

"But," he said, "it's not me." The blur of the television interested him more. "Where?"

"Where what?"

"Where'd you say you were staying?"

"With these old people, Effie, Effie and his wife, Gen."

He dropped the pamphlet on the floor and pushed himself out of the chair. He swayed and stared dumbly into a wallet full of receipts.

"Well, tonight you say hi to them for me. You tell Effie and Gen Johnny says hi." When he looked at Kirsten, his eyes had gone neutral. "You tell them I'm sorry, and you give them this," he said, leaning toward Kirsten. Then his lips were gone from her mouth, and he was handing her the last five from his billfold.

When they returned to the farmhouse, their car was sitting in the drive and dinner was cooking. The kitchen windows were steamed, and the moist air, warm and fragrant, settled like a perfume on Kirsten's skin. She ran hot water and lathered her hands. The ball of soap was as smooth and worn as an old bone, a mosaic assembled from remnants, small pieces thriftily saved and then softened and clumped together. Everything in the house seemed to have that same quality, softened by the touch of hands—hands that had rubbed the brass plating from the doorknobs, hands that had worn the painted handles of spoons and ladles down to bare wood. Kirsten rinsed the soap away, and Gen offered her a towel.

"You don't have any other clothes, do you?" the old woman asked.

"No, ma'am," she said.

"Let's go pull some stuff out of the attic," Gen said. She

drew a level line from the top of her head to the top of Kirsten's." We're about the same size, I figure. You won't win any fashion awards—it's just old funny things, some wool pants, a jacket, a couple cardigan sweaters. But you aren't dressed for Iowa." She pronounced it "Ioway."

"I'd appreciate that, ma'am."

"Doing the kind of work you do, I don't imagine you can afford the extras," the old woman said, as they climbed a set of steps off the upstairs hallway. "But in this country we don't consider a coat extra."

She tugged a string and a bare bulb lit the attic. In the sudden glare, the room seemed at first to house nothing but a jumble of shadows." I've held on to everything," she said.

"I met a man in town today," Kirsten said. "He said he knew you and Effie."

The old woman slit the tape on a box with her thumbnail and handed Kirsten a sweater that smelled faintly of dust and camphor.

Kirsten held the woman still and kissed her on the lips. "He said to give you that."

"Johnny?" Gen said. "He won't come out here."

Kirsten slipped into the sweater, a cardigan with black leather buttons like a baby's withered navel, a hardened ball of Kleenex in the pocket. She had never known a world of such economy, where things were saved and a room in a house could be set aside for storage. This woman had lived to pass her things on, but now there was no one to take them.

"It was a combine," Kirsten said. "It was this time of year."

The old woman nodded.

"Your little girl doesn't know she's dead. She's still out there."

"How do I know you know all this?"

"I saw her," Kirsten said. "And when me and Lance come to the door last night we never knocked."

From a rack against the wall, the old woman took down a wool overcoat.

"You were waiting up for her. You wait every year."

Gen stepped in front of a cheval mirror and held the coat against her body, modeling it for a moment.

"It wasn't Effie's fault," Kristen said.

"He feels the guilt all the same," the old woman said.

"He had to."

"Had to what?"

"Live," Kristen said. "He had to live his life, just the same as me and you."

They set four places with the good plates and silver and flowery napkins in the dining room. There was a ham pricked with cloves and ringed around with pineapple and black olives and green beans and salad and bread. Effie fussed over his wife as if he'd never had dinner with her, passing dishes and offering extra helpings, which she refused each time, saying, "Help yourself." Kirsten eventually caught on, seeing that this solicitude was the old man's sly way of offering a compliment and serving himself a little more at the same time. The food was good; it all glistened, the juices from the ham, the butter running off the beans, the oil on the salad. Gen spent most of the meal up on her feet, offering, spooning, heating, filling.

Effie's conversation made a wide, wandering tour of the land. Jesse James used to hide out in this country, he said. Then he was talking about no-till planting, soil that wasn't disked or plowed.

"You got corn in just about everything," he said. "In gasoline, sparkplugs, crayons, toothpaste, disposable diapers—"

"No, really?" Lance said.

"You bet," the old man went on, "and paint, beer, whiskey.
You name it." He said one out of four hogs produced in this
country came from Iowa—which he, too, pronounced "Ioway."
Hogs till Hell wouldn't have it, he said, thundering the words.
The topic of hogs led to a story he'd read about Fidel Castro
roasting a pig in a hotel room in New York, and then he told
about their travels, a trip to Ireland and another to Hawaii,
which he pronounced "Hoy."

After dinner, there was pumpkin pie—prize-winning, Effie
announced, as the pie tin took center stage on the cleared table.

It was delicious, the filling warm with a buttery vanishing
feel on Kirsten's tongue. "What's in it?" she asked.

"Oh," Gen said, "cinnamon, ginger, nutmeg, allspice,
vanilla—but real pumpkin's the key." Gen, satisfied with the
satisfaction at her table, smiled at her husband, who gravely
put down his fork.

"When you come," Effie said, "Momma said you mentioned
our little girl."

The old man looked across the table at his wife, checking her
eyes, or the turn of her mouth, for subtle signs, searching for
agreement. It was as if he found what he needed in the space
between them, and spoke aloud only to verify that it was there,
that someone else had seen it.

"Our little girl," Gen said.

"Your daughter," Kirsten said.

"I wondered if you were an old friend. Maybe from school.
Most of them have grown and gone away. I used to see—
it would have been so long ago, but . . ." He trailed off, his
pale blue eyes sparkling in the weak, splintered light of the
chandelier.

Lance said, "Kirsten's been to the other side. She's seen it."

"I would believe you," Effie said. "Some around here don't credit dowsers, but we always have. We never had reason not to. We always had plenty of water." He cleared his throat. "I'd pay anything if you could tell us—something."

"There's the babies," Lance said.

"I'll help with those babies of yours. I'll donate to your cause. Where you going after this?"

"We're aiming west," Lance said.

Effie squared his fork with the edge of the table. "Well?"

Kirsten was about to speak when she felt a hand slide over her knee, the fingers feeling their way until they rested warmly in her hand, holding it tight. She glanced at the old woman.

"It was only that picture on your wall," she said to Effie.

The picture was the one every child drew a hundred times—the house, the leafy tree, the sun in one corner, the birds overhead, the walkway widening like a river as it flows out from the front door, the family standing on the green grass, a brother, a sister, a mother with her triangle dress, the father twice as big as everybody, the stick fingers overlapping—and that no one ever saved.

"It was just that picture," Kirsten said. "I wish I could say it was more, but it wasn't."

Effie picked up his fork and pressed it against the crumbs of piecrust still on his plate, gathering them. He looked as though he had another question in mind.

"That was the last picture," the old woman said.

"She just drawn it at school," he said. "She put me and Gen in, her and her brother."

"Stephanie," Kirsten said, "and Johnny."

The old man glanced at his wife.

"She spelled all the names on the picture," Kirsten said.

Gen whispered yes, but it was Effie who had to speak up. "I

never breathed right or walked right after," he said. "Never farmed, neither, except for my little garden out back."

"That was the best pie I ever had," Kirsten said.

"Show your ribbons, Momma," Effie said.

"Oh, no," Gen said, waving her hand, shooing away the approach, the temptation of something immodest.

"Well, that's right," Effie said. "The pie's right here, huh?" He looked around the table. "The pie's right here."

Kirsten hovered above the field and could hear the rumble of an engine and the crushed stalks snapping, a crackling noise that spread and came from everywhere at once, like fire. The stalks flailed and broke and dust and chaff flew up, and then, ahead, she saw the little girl running down the rows, lost in the maze, unable to search out a safe direction. Suddenly the girl sat on the ground, her stillness an instinct, looking up through the leaves, waiting for the noise to pass. Kirsten saw her there—a little girl being good, quiet, obedient—but when the sound came closer she flattened herself against the dirt, as if the moment might pass her by. When it was too late, she kicked her feet, trying to escape, and was swallowed up. The noise faded, and a scroll of dirt and stover curved over the fields like handwriting. Then it was gone, and Kirsten saw her own reflection floating in the gray haze of the vanity.

"Lance," she said.

"What?"

"We're leaving," she said.

"Why, what?"

Kirsten gathered the old woman's clothes in a garbage sack and had Lance carry them to the car. She made the bed and fluffed the thin pillows. The house was quiet.

She sat at the small painted vanity, taking a blue crayon from the cup, and wrote a thank-you note. She wrote to the old woman that one second of love is all the love in the world, that one moment is all of them; she wrote that she'd really liked the pumpkin pie, and meant it when she'd said it was the best she'd ever had, adding that she never expected to taste better; she thanked her for the hospitality and for fixing the car; and then she copied down the words to the song the woman she called Mother had sung:

Where are you going, my little one, little one?
Where are you going, my baby, my own?
Turn around and you're two, turn around and you're four.
Turn around and you're a young girl going out of the door.

Lance was gone for a long time, and Kirsten, looking over the note, considered tearing it up each time she read it. As she sat and waited, she felt a sudden warmth and reached under the elastic of her underpants. When Lance finally returned, he was covered in dry leaves and strings of tassel, as if he'd been out working in the fields. They went outside and pushed the car down the gravel drive, out to the road. It started up, beautifully quiet.

"Wait here," Kirsten said.

She walked back to the yard. It was cool, and the damp night air released a rich smell of dung and soil and straw, a smell Kirsten was sure belonged only to Iowa, and only at certain hours. She pulled her T-shirt over her head. She was reaching for the clothespin that held the old woman's bra when something made her look up. The old woman was standing at the upstairs window, her hand pressed flat against the glass. Kirsten took the bra from the line and slipped the straps over her shoulders. She fastened the clasp and leaned forward, settling her breasts in the small white cups. The women looked at each other for what seemed like an eternity, and then Kirsten pulled on her shirt and ran back to Lance.

Under the moonlight, they drove down mazy roads cut through the fields.

"Goddam, the Lord sure hath provideth the corn around here," Lance said. He imitated the old man compulsively. "I'll be plenty glad to get out of this Ioway. Ioway! Christ Almighty. I'm sorry, but those people were corny. And that old guy, jawing on about Castro's fucking pigs in the bathtub. What'd he say, they cooked a hog in that hotel room? What the hell." Lance was taking charge, his mind hard, forging connections. He was feeling good, he was feeling certain. "And goddam I hate ham! Smells like piss!" He rolled down the window and yelled, "Goodbye, fucking Ioway!" He brushed corn silk from his sleeve and shook bits of leaves from his hair.

"Here's something for you." He reached in his pocket and handed her a long heavy chain. "Looks to me like gold with emeralds and rubies mixed in," he said.

"That's costume jewelry, Lance."

"We'll get it appraised, and you'll see. It's real," he said, bullying the truth, hating its disadvantages. "They won't miss it, Kirsten. They're old, honey. They're gonna die and they got no heirs, so don't you worry." He grinned widely and said, "I got something out of the deal, too."

He waited. Kirsten just stared at the cheap, gaudy chain, pouring it like water from one hand to the other.

Lance said, "Look in back."

When she turned around, all she saw through the rear window was a trail of dust turning red in the tail lights.

"Under the blanket," Lance said.

Kirsten reached behind her and pulled away the blanket. The rear seat was overflowing with ears of corn. Lance had turned the whole back of the car into a crib.

"Ioway corn," he said. "Makes me hungry just thinking about it."

The Dead Fish Museum

"This key isn't working," Ramage said.

Behind a thick sheet of acrylic, the desk clerk's face rushed up at him; it spread and blurred, white and without features, but never seemed to reach the surface. Ramage leaned forward and looked through a circle in the slab of glass, cut like a hole in ice. On the counter was a dinner plate with chicken bones and a few grains of rice hardening in brown gravy, and next to the plate was the splayed and broken spine of a romance. The clerk had been working over the chicken, cracking the bones and sucking the marrow. Her hair was thin and her teeth were leaning gray ruins in her lipless mouth. Her blue eyes were milky and vague, the pupils tiny beads of black. Ramage could not imagine a youth for her—it was if she'd been born fully ruined. She licked her fingers and swiveled heavily on her stool, unhooking a new key from a pegboard on the wall.

"Off season," she said. She seemed suspicious of him.

"I'm here for a job," Ramage explained. "A movie."

"Oh." A hand flew up to the crimped little mouth. The eyelids batted. "Who's in it? Anybody famous?"

"No one," Ramage said. "No one famous."

"A movie, really?" she said. "You an actor?"

"Yes," Ramage said, lagging, caught in the confusing overlap of questions. "No." He tapped his new key on the counter. "Hope this works," he said.

Ramage went back to no. 7 and this time the door unlocked. He set his canvas tool sack in one corner and draped his coat over a doorknob and instantly they seemed to have been there forever. He changed out of his shirt and splashed cold water in his face. Next door, he heard a man and a woman laughing, perhaps making love. He'd gained weight in the hospital—two sedentary months chain-smoking in the dayroom, drugged and without true hunger, yet an emptiness had kept him eating constantly. The food was institutional, flavorless, all of it boiled and pale, except for a bounty of fruit that arrived on the ward in pretty wicker gift baskets that no one wanted. One day a month into his stay, the vibrancy of an apple had started him crying. He'd been alone in the dining room and it was quiet except for the rumbling of the dumbwaiter dropping down to the basement and the singsong of black scullions rising up the shaft from the kitchen. A red apple rested on the windowsill in a beam of white morning light. Waxed and glowing, it was painfully vivid. It was perfect, he remembered thinking, but too far away to eat.

Ramage put on his coat and lingered in the doorway, trying to decide if he should carry his canvas tool sack with him. In it was everything, his tools, a change of underwear, a clean shirt, a pair of jeans. Buried at the bottom of the sack, wrapped in a purple shop rag, was the gun that he had believed, for the past year, would kill him. The gun was his constant adversary, like a drug, a deep secret that he kept from others, but it was also his passion, a theater where he poured out his lonely ardor, rehearsing scenarios, playing with possibilities. Over time the gun had become a talisman with the power and primitive comfort of a child's blanket. It would horrify him to lose it. Ramage hid the canvas sack beneath the bed. He locked the door and checked it. Halfway across the parking lot, stricken with doubt, he returned to his room and tested the handle once more, making sure.

Ramage immediately went and stole an apple and a brick of cheese at a convenience store. The woman behind the cash register sucked on a whip of red licorice and read through a beauty magazine while a tinny radio wept sentimental favorites. As he was leaving, the woman gave Ramage the eye. She knew what he'd done, he was sure, but her stake in the scheme of things didn't warrant hassling shoplifters. Had she confronted him, he would have handed over the apple and cheese as obediently as a schoolboy. He wouldn't have run away, he wouldn't have become violent, he wouldn't have elaborated a lie. He'd have felt deep shame. Maybe the cashier understood that, maybe she thought he was ridiculous.

Back in his room, Ramage took a hacksaw blade from his tool sack and sliced up his apple, fanning the pieces out on the nightstand. He cut the brick of cheese and paired up a dozen openfaced sandwiches. Next door, a baby cried, and then a man yelled, telling it to shut the fuck up. A woman shouted, "For christsake, it's just a baby. It might be hungry or something." Ramage turned on his TV and blotted out the noise. He felt evil around young children; he avoided them on buses, in waiting rooms, in city parks. The night of his release, he'd been seated in a restaurant next to a family with a baby, not six months old. The child was dressed snugly in blue footed pyjamas, gurgling and burping a white liquid all over itself. After a few minutes, Ramage moved his steak knife to the other side of his plate. Something wildly uncentered in his mind had told him he was going to stab the baby in the eye.

The memory made him shudder, and he stepped outside

for fresh air. The tourists were gone, and everything in town—
the souvenir vendors, the picture postcard shops, the ice-
cream parlors and arcades—had been closed for the season.
Bits of popcorn blew across the highway; paper cones that had
once held wigs of blue and pink cotton candy lay dirty and
trampled flat in the parking lot. Ramage drew a deep breath
and smelled sage or basil—something cooking in the spice factory down the street. A single stranded palm tree and the
motel's blue vacancy sign stood at the edge of the lot. Toilet
paper fluttered from the fender of his neighbor's car, a few
crushed tin cans were strung from the bumper, and a Burma-
Shave heart, pierced by an arrow, dripped from the rear
window.

"This is the back road to Hollywood," Greenfield said, early the
next morning.

A steady procession of people moved from the van to the
warehouse: a woman with a face pierced with pins, a punk
with a hackle of red hair, a man with the shaved blue skull of a
prisoner. They hauled trunks, hoisted lights and cameras, carried canisters of film, slung coils of cable over their shoulders.
Best boys, key grips, gaffers—titles Ramage knew from his old
habit of sitting in theaters, after the end, watching the scroll of
credits bubble up from the bottom of the screen like a movie's
last breath.

"Who am I kidding?" Greenfield said. "This doesn't go anywhere near Hollywood."

"You got lots of company," Ramage said.

"Everybody wants a little stardust to fall on them."

"Success could be all over your face next week," Ramage
said.

"Sure," Greenfield said. He took a deep breath. "This town stinks."

"There's a spice factory a few blocks over," Ramage explained.

A blond woman lifted a travel bag from the van. Greenfield nodded at her.

"My star," he said.

To Ramage, she looked like a rough outline for someone's idea of a woman, the main points greatly exaggerated.

Greenfield fumbled in his pocket and drew out a box of colored Shermans; he lit a pink one. He'd already put the box away when Ramage asked if he could bum a smoke. A cigarette might cut the gnawing in his stomach. Greenfield took a deep drag, and said, "Finish this one."

Ramage smoked. "You still pay in cash?" he asked.

"*Bien sûr.*" Greenfield lovingly patted a black shoulder bag at his side.

"How about an advance?"

"I can't do that," Greenfield said. "I've had people run out on me."

"Would it matter if I said I was broke?"

"Not much," Greenfield said. "How broke are you?"

"We've known each other a long time," Ramage said.

"I heard you were in the bin."

Ramage nodded.

"What's the least you need?" Greenfield said.

It was clear that asking for the full thousand would only bring derision. Ramage said, "Half."

Greenfield reached in his bag and separated two crisp bills from a bound stack. "Here's two hundred," he said. He held the two bills toward Ramage, then drew them back. "This doesn't mean I trust you."

Greenfield was wearing his signature black shirt and black pants; his cowboy boots were made of green snakeskin, buffed and shiny except where fine lines of dust had settled between the scales. Ramage had worked with him off and on for twelve years, beginning shortly after he'd moved to New York. Before his hospitalization, Ramage had been rehabbing the homes of the rich, but he was still loosely connected to an underground of carpenters and waitresses and bookstore clerks who, in successive waves, struggled to make films. Greenfield had been a rising star ten years ago; porn was only supposed to occupy the space of an anecdote, a moment of amusement as he looked back, a dark tint in an otherwise bright career. Ditto for Ramage: he'd scripted the movie that established Greenfield's promise a decade ago.

They walked into the building and rode the freight elevator upstairs. "First thing you do," Greenfield said, "is board up all the windows. This is a nonunion job."

"A union for porn?" Ramage said.

"Erotica," Greenfield corrected him. "There's a street tax we're not paying."

"What's the plot of this one?" Ramage asked.

Greenfield lowered his glasses and looked at him over the rims as if he were stupid.

"Boy meets girl," he said.

Ramage ran the carpentry crew. They'd boarded shut the windows and now, with fumes of fresh paint filling the warehouse, Ramage felt woozy; as a precaution, he set his hammer down and stepped off the ladder and waited for the room to resolve back into focus. With a pry bar he yanked the nails from a sheet of plywood over one of the windows; the board crashed to the floor and the air rushed in. He was slightly winded by the effort. He took off his shirt and squatted against the wall and drank from a quart of warm beer and lit his last cigarette. He crushed the empty pack, feeling weak and isolated and craven; already he was dreading the next wave of desire. There would be no one in the crew to borrow from. RB smoked snowballs that tasted medicinal and Rigo didn't smoke at all.

Rigo was in the next room rolling red paint over the walls. He was a short, stocky man with a broad, flat plate of a face whose perfect roundness was carried out thematically in his dark eyes and in the purple fleshy pouches encircling them and then again in the two wide discs of his jutting ears. These redundant open circles gave Rigo's face a spacious, uncrowded look that people routinely mistook for simplemindedness.

RB, the other carpenter, had watched Ramage step down from the ladder, and saw this as a cue to take another break.

"What-say, Spooky?" he said, sitting beside Ramage. He took a swig from the quart and swished the beer around in his mouth. "You see the ladies out there this morning?" He held his hands out in front of him to suggest breasts. He shook his head in disbelief. He looked at his empty hands and said, "I saw that blonde do a midget once. She's famous."

Ramage nodded neutrally.

"This little itty-bitty midget," RB said. "But he had the pecker of a full-grown man. About as long as his arm. Hey Rigoberto, how about pecker? You know what a pecker is?"

Rigo paused and held his roller aloft and red paint dribbled like blood between his fingers and down his arm. He had been a lieutenant in the army in El Salvador and his bearing was military; one could still sense in him the faint trace of his training at the hands of US advisors. He never fully relaxed and he held to odd protocols—after a day's work he cleaned and organized Ramage's tools and insisted on carrying the canvas sack for him, moving the bag to and from the job like a bellhop. Leftist rebels had raided his house on the outskirts of San Salvador and shot his brother, who'd been spending the night, and sleeping in Rigo's bed. The bullet had been meant for Rigo, who'd skipped the funeral and fled El Salvador with his family, deserting the army and leaving the civil war behind. Now a jackleg carpenter who spoke only a crude, cobbled English, he worked with indefatigable energy, compensating for RB's tendency to goldbrick. He lacked a green card and preferred the clarity of labor, no matter how arduous, to the vagaries of talking in a language where even the simplest notion plunged him into loss and confusion. He was still learning the names of the tools he was using.

"Pecker?" Rigo said.

"Like dong, dink, dick," RB said. He spread his legs and pointed at his crotch. "Penis."

Rigo allowed a thin smile of recognition.

"Little guy doesn't know where he's at," RB said. He fingered a scar that cut across the base of his throat. The original wound had been stitched together without much concern for cosmetics; against his oily black skin, the tissue was red and smooth and protuberant, like a worm. "We watched fuck-flicks all the time in reform school."

"You were in reform school?" Ramage asked.

"You don't believe me?"

"You've never mentioned it before. How'd you end up there?"

"I got crossed by a guy I sold some chain saws to."

"Seems to me they wouldn't allow porn."

"Shit," RB said. "Everything was allowed."

"You finish taping?"

"No."

"I guess you got that disease again."

"What disease?"

"That sit-around-on-your-ass disease."

"Oh, you're kidding. I get it."

"I'm not kidding, RB. You hardly did jack today."

"Ah, Spooky."

"Why are you calling me Spooky?"

RB looked at Ramage, then shrugged. "That cartoon," he said. He turned to Rigo and shouted, "Hey Rigoberto, take a break. Stop. No paint."

"He's not deaf," Ramage said.

"He sure don't understand." RB beat on the floor with his fist. "Rigoberto, here, sit. Sit. Sit down. Down, man."

Rigo grabbed a wrinkled brown lunch sack he'd stashed behind a stack of Sheetrock. The sack had been folded and saved and used repeatedly. His clothes showed the same habitual thrift. He wore neatly creased khakis and a crimson T-shirt, the HARVARD nearly washed away.

"You ever killed a man?" RB said.

Rigo scraped flecks of red paint from his arm and didn't answer.

"Me, I don't have the heart to kill a man. You got to have heart to kill somebody."

Using his thumb Rigo made an inconspicuous sign of the cross on his knee and silently said grace and then made the same small cross again before unwrapping the waxed paper from his sandwich.

"That must be some good-ass sandwich," RB said. "I hope it is. I sure hope to fucking God it's not baloney again."

Rigo lifted a corner of the sandwich.

"More baloney!" RB screamed, grabbing Rigo's sack and sandwich. "Jesus Christ, I swear, you're just like all them refugees." Then, as if they were co-conspirators, he said to Ramage, "See how it works, they all get together and send a man over, and he gets his shit together, eatin' baloney every damn day and savin' up his money. Never go to a movie or buy ice cream or nothing. Just baloney and baloney and more baloney. Then he sends back money so the whole family can book out of Pago Pago and come over and they all live together, nine of them to one room, everybody eatin' baloney every minute!" RB lobbed the lunch sack out the window and, his tone lowered and confidential, addressed Rigo again. "America's so wide open, see, with you people coming here, I call you refugees."

"America's so wide open," Ramage said, "it seems to have filled up with shitheads. Go get his sack."

"Spooky, man, you can't have a grown man praying for baloney. Not in America! It ain't right, I'm sorry. Now Harvard, quit praying for that shit."

"Go get it."

"Every job we do," RB said, "every week, he eats five days of straight baloney. Not even fried! Give the baloney a break, Harvard. You understand? FUCK. THE. BALONEY."

Rigo was gazing into the inscrutable square of black sky, out the empty window where his baloney sandwich had flown.

RB clattered down the fire escape and came back a minute later.

"The baloney got a little dirty," he said. He reached for his billfold. "Buy yourself something good to eat, Harvard. My treat. Something special. Get yourself a cheeseburger."

Greenfield looked about the warehouse, making no mention of the work that had been completed; it was as if the merest kindness might collapse the hierarchy. He stared up at the ceiling, inspecting a large skylight.

"I like that," Greenfield said. "I might use that."

Greenfield moved directly under the skylight, where a waning moon was visible like an amulet in the bottom of a black velvet box.

"I might quote *Citizen Kane*," he said. "What do you think? We'll crane up over the warehouse and drop down through the skylight." He lit a long red Sherman. It moved obscenely like the tongue of a lizard between his lips. "What do you think of that? Huh?" He was asking RB. "Quoting *Citizen Kane*? What's your opinion?"

RB shrugged. "Whatever gets you off."

Ramage said, "You don't have a crane."

"So?" Greenfield said.

"So you need a crane to quote *Citizen Kane*."

"I'll call the movie 'Citizen Cunt,' " Greenfield said. He pointed to Rigo and said, "You like that? Would you buy a movie with that title?"

"Certainly," he said.

"The title's important," Greenfield said. "The title's everything."

Ramage felt a tightening at his temples. Impatient, he asked, "You got any more work for us?"

"Finish painting," Greenfield said. "I want that black room glossy, like a mirror. Rub some polish on the paint after it dries. Buff it out so we can see our reflections."

RB spoke up. "Greenwad, how about putting me in the movie?"

"It's not as easy as it looks," Greenfield said.

"I can handle it," RB said. "I popped my first cherry when I was eleven, just a little spike."

"Bullshit," Ramage said.

"Ask my sister if you don't believe me."

Greenfield looked him over. "You endowed?"

"Shit," RB said, reaching for his belt buckle.

"Please," Greenfield said. He made his face into a face expressive of distaste. He looked at RB again and said, "Although, it might be a kick."

The carpentry job was straightforward: build three boxes, paint them in three colors—one red, one black, one white. With the paint still drying, Ramage had Rigo and RB help him arrange a few pieces of rented furniture—chairs, tables, lamps—and now, nearly finished, they all sat down in one of the rooms they'd built, on the bed. RB propped a pillow beneath his head and leaned back. Ramage felt RB's cool, moist skin rub against his; he inched away from the contact.

Rigo opened a beer and lofted the bottle above his head; it shone like a torch, golden in the dim light, as bubbles streamed to the surface. The outside world might have vanished, the warehouse was so suddenly quiet.

"You might be part nigger," RB said to Rigo.

Rigo sipped his beer; his face was freckled with paint.

"Spooky, don't he look like a nigger?"

RB's initials stood for nothing. "Just RB," he'd explained, when Ramage asked about his name, "straight up southern."

"Drink your beer," Ramage said.

"Look at his nappy head," RB continued. "Nigger hair. Me and Rigo could be brothers."

"I am Salvadoran," Rigo said, a little cold, prideful.

"Used to be, but now you in the U.S. of A., Jack."

"Drink," Ramage said.

RB drank, then asked, "When they start shooting?"

"Call's for seven tomorrow morning," Ramage said.

"You're all invited to my debut," RB said. "Those ladies are fine. They know all sorts a special tricks, too. You get with one of them, you'll be spoiled for life. I had this one old girlfriend that used to call me the wonder-log."

"Referring to what?"

"Hell, Spooky—"

"Why do you keep calling me Spooky?"

RB shrugged. "Just do," he said. "It's from that cartoon."

"Let's get out of here," Ramage said.

The head full of paint fumes, the numbness in the arms, the reluctant knees, the rigid back—the body's memory: Ramage felt this, and no one else moved from the bed, as if the day's work had brought them to a poise. Outside, there was nothing but the separateness of feeling used and spent, of rundown bones and sore muscles and another day and at the narrow end of it a tub of tepid water that would instantly turn tea-brown and drain away, leaving a ring of crud around the porcelain. His first day of work in two months had exhausted Ramage; he was spacey with fatigue; they all were, and for a moment Ramage wished that they might rest and sleep and dream together on this bed until morning.

Back at the motel, Ramage washed his hands and face at the sink, listening to the baby cry next door. He sponged his chest and armpits and put on his clean shirt.

Standing outside, he heard the baby, still crying, and knocked on the door. No one answered. He pushed the door open slowly and saw the baby alone in the room; a crib had been squeezed between the bed and the sliding doors of a closet. Clothes were scattered on the floor, over the nightstand, flung across the TV screen. An empty bottle of strawberry wine with its cap resealed lay in the wastebasket along with a condom wrapper and a plastic straw and a nest of black hair someone had cleaned from a comb. A calendar hung on the wall, but no one had bothered to turn the page since the end of summer.

The baby shrieked. Its tiny hands reached through the slatted cage of the crib, opening and then closing into tight fists. Ramage saw the pacifier that had fallen to the carpet. He picked it up and rinsed the hair and grit away under the faucet. He set the pacifier in the baby's hand and the baby pitched it back to the floor. Ramage cleaned it off again, and this time stuck the rubber nipple in the baby's mouth. The baby's eyes softened and it sucked contentedly. The baby was maybe a year old. It was naked. It wasn't even diapered. Ramage touched it; he pressed his thumb into the soft skin.

Outside, he saw Rigo working his way up from the beach, over the sand, past a lifeguard station that had been knocked down for the winter. He waited for him to cross the highway.

"Buy you a drink?" Ramage asked.

"Certainly," Rigo said.

Certainly: it was one of Rigo's words, a magniloquence in his otherwise lean vocabulary. Ramage ushered him into the bar. Sawdust had been strewn about the floor; oyster shells broke like bones underfoot. A few other people sat at the scattered tables. Ramage saw a man and a woman he thought might be his neighbors at the motel. They were bending into the yellow light of the jukebox, looking for a good song.

Ramage saluted Rigo with a nod of his bottle and they drank down their beers in unison.

"RB, he talk too much," Rigo said.

"That's just RB," Ramage said. "He's having fun, he's goofing."

"In Jersey City," Rigo said, "outside my apartment, there is a telephone. All night, the niggers out there. They play their music, they talk their talk. I call police—nothing."

Rigo finished his beer, ordered another round. Ramage insisted on paying; he considered it part of his position as foreman of the crew, a way of building esprit de corps.

"So I take care of business myself, as a man must," Rigo said. "I chase them with a baseball bat. I chase them every night. They always come back."

"You're going to get yourself killed," Ramage said.

"RB is nigger, not me."

"Don't call him that. Not to his face, anyway."

"He calls that to us, to our face."

"What were you doing on the beach?" Ramage asked, changing the subject, although he knew the answer: Rigo was sleeping down there, saving the expense of a motel room, pocketing the modest per diem. RB's riff on refugees had not been far off. Rigo wired a remittance every month to an uncle exiled in Honduras.

"I love the ocean, Ramage." Rigo looked at his dirty hands, a little embarrassed. Then he said, "When I first come with my family to Jersey City, every day I fish. Every morning I go with my bucket to the park where I have a view of the *Estatua*— *Estatua de la Libertad*. They are cleaning her, she is—all everywhere—they put—"

"Scaffolding?" Ramage guessed.

"Scaffolding," Rigo repeated, reciting the lesson. "I catch many fish. I bring fish home I do not know the name of." Rigo broke off. He seemed bewildered, recalling the beginning, before names. "My wife, she no say the word 'refrigerator' so good. She just learning. She say it, 'the dead fish museum.' "

"I like that," Ramage said. "The dead fish museum."

"We can no eat all that I catch."

"I'm surprised you ate any of it," Ramage said.

The bar door opened, and the blond star took up a stool near the register. Her drink came in a goblet and the bartender had produced a faded paper parasol, cocked over the frosted rim of the glass. It was a summer garnish, but in the dim slow bar the parasol failed to add much in the way of gaiety.

"In El Salvador," Rigo said, "you go to the beach with the children, Sunday, you stay all day. The sand is clean and white and the man, he comes with *las ostras* for you. *Limón,* tabasco, pepper: you go down like nothing."

"I can taste them now," Ramage said.

"Certainly," Rigo said. "Here, the beach is garbage. Everything wash up. Tonight, I find a door to the house. A door to the man's house, Ramish."

Rigo held his hands above the bar, staring into the empty space they created. He seemed to be picturing the thing his words had just described, trying to put his hands around the hallucination of it; they tensed with frustration; he could not hold the thing, and the picture in his mind floated away. Rigo grabbed his beer and finished it off. He ordered another.

"I no eat on the beach here," he said. "But the ocean, she is the ocean still."

They crossed the necks of their bottles together in a sloppy swashbuckling salute, and Ramage drank with the image of blue water, of open sea, before him. The soreness deep in his body had risen into a pleasant hum on the surface of his skin. He felt loose and shallow.

"I do not know what kind of movie this is," Rigo said.

"No," Ramage said. "I didn't tell you."

"Now I know," Rigo said.

Rigo drank his whiskey and spun the empty shot glass like a top on a tilted axis. The glass wobbled violently; it stopped and he spun it again. He seemed torn between maintaining dignity and getting trashed. Each word was the end of a very long journey. Every sentence jeopardized his loyalties.

"I am surprise how things are," Rigo said.

Ramage said, "It's only three days."

"Salvador," Rigo said, raising his bottle.

"Salvador," Ramage said.

They toasted each other, the bar, the empty tables, the juke-box that had fallen silent.

"Salvador," Rigo said again.

Another drink, and another after that: Ramage couldn't keep pace.

"I no choice. I must go away or die. I die, my family die. I come here. I don't know to what. To what, Ramish—*to what?*"

"You going back someday?" Ramage asked.

"They rape the women with rats," Rigo said. "A man from my town has a nail"—he pounded the air—"in his head, his—" and with a balled fist he knocked on his forehead.

"His skull," Ramage said.

Rigo shook his head. *"Su cerebro."*

"His brain?"

"Yes, he can no speak with a nail in his brain."

Rigo fashioned a gun out of his right hand; the hammer of his thumb slammed down rapid fire as he squinted and swept his aim along the glimmering funhouse row of bottles behind the bar.

"They kill my brother," he said. "But I go home, Ramish. One day I go home."

He slapped the bar and rose; Ramage watched him weave toward the door; it looked as though he was only taking a rough guess about the way out.

———

At different junctures, Ramage tried to recall what he and the blond woman were talking about, but he found the words were just falling out of the back of his head as they went along, and he was arriving in the present always empty. When last call was announced, she suggested they buy a bottle and stroll along the boardwalk and keep drinking.

"You're right," she was saying. "My name isn't Desiree Street—good God!—but we can just leave it at that anyway. I prefer it. Let's make up a name for you instead."

"Call me Payne, Payne with a 'y,' " Ramage said, "Payne Whitney."

"Payne's okay, Payne's a good porn name. Payne-with-a-y-Whitney. Okay Payne, where to?"

"You smell that?"

As they drifted up from the beach and further from the ocean the damp cloying odor of kelp and sea lettuce was replaced by the arid and spacious scent of oregano cooking in the spice factory. It was if they'd entered a new, fairer latitude. They walked through a back section of town where the sidewalks were cracked and slabs of concrete heaved up to make way for weeds and tree roots. A wooden boat listed in the dirt of a vacant lot; a cat with yellow eyes watched them from the glassless wheelhouse. A brick building dominated by a high square clock tower was just across the street. The clock had a white face and Roman numerals and the black hands were stuck at the pleasant hour of seven, a time of beginnings, of a new day, a new night. They leaned their heads through a window, canted open with a pull-chain; blue smoke rose from the ovens and spread and was sucked away by a whirring exhaust fan. Ramage shushed drunkenly with a warning finger to his lips. "Look," he whispered, "natives." Two men and a woman stood in front of a large spinning machine; they were dressed in white smocks and paper hats and surgical masks; behind them glass bottles filled with spice and were shunted down a metal chute and conveyed up a rubber ramp into waiting boxes; the clinking bottles made a cool Latin-flavored jazz in the cavernous factory; particles of oregano rained down in a fine green dust that settled over the cement floor; a faint trail of footprints was visible, the tread of sneakers stamped into the green spice, and the men and the woman were coated in green dust, too. Ramage leaned in and inhaled the warm fragrant air, and he started choking and hacking; the woman inside the factory, laughing at the conclusion of some joke or story, lightly touched the elbow of the man beside her. They stiffened and the laughter went out of them. They stared uncertainly at Ramage and Desiree in the window; they ventured a wave. Ramage waved back.

"Somebody got married," Desiree said, when they'd returned to the motel. She pointed to the neighbor's car.

"They're on their honeymoon," Ramage said. "That's why they came to this paradise."

"You are wasted."

"I'll tell you what."

"What?"

Ramage put a finger to his lips. He led her to his neighbor's room and tested the knob and it turned. Inside, the man and the woman slept naked on top of a tangle of sheets, the baby nestled between them like a puzzle piece. Whatever it was inside of Ramage that understood that he was outrageously drunk stifled the urge to scream. He quietly shut the door.

He put the key in the lock to his own room and then flopped over the threshold and crawled on his knees across the carpet to his canvas tool sack. He unzipped the bag and fumbled through an omnium-gatherum of plumb lines and box wrenches and pencil stubs and ratchets and tape measures until he found his gun. Further searching produced a plastic case of shells. "Look," he said. He lay on his back like a playing child, holding the gun in one hand, the shells in the other. He smashed the gun and the case against one another and shells rained down on his face.

"Hello, gun," he pantomimed. "Hi, bullet." The black polymer barrel waggled as the gun asked, "Will you marry me?"

"Is this like a kink or something?" Desiree asked.

"Let's have a baby," the bullet said.

"Fill me with your seed," the gun said.

Ramage loaded a shell in the gun. The bullet made a satisfying click in the chamber like a key turning in a lock.

"I'm pregnant," the gun announced.

"I'm out of here," Desiree said.

"They got a baby. The newlyweds have a child." Ramage jumped into bed and beckoned Desiree with the gun.

"Why don't you give me that gun?"

"I came here to kill myself."

"Why?"

"Why kill myself?"

"Why come here?"

She walked out, leaving the door open, and for a while Ramage lay on the bed, listening to the crashing of the ocean across the highway. His display had been grotesque. He had humiliated himself and now it disgusted him; he was mortified and filled with self-loathing and yet he watched the open door, hoping she might return. He had almost felt decent, standing with Desiree outside the spice factory, watching the quiet green dust spin through the cavernous room, but now he couldn't stop his black ruminations. His mind went round and round, churning pitifully, and finally he pictured himself crossing the highway and wading into the sea and pulling the trigger; if he lost nerve and flinched and only managed to blast off part of his head the ocean would drown him. It wasn't so unusual to consider these scruples; it was like a math problem one worked until there was no remainder. Regina, his friend from the hospital, had dressed ceremoniously in her grandfather's bathrobe and soaked the terry cloth in gasoline and then struck a match, immolating herself, and what she remembered was the noise, the horrid rushing sound, the wind howling inside the flames—that was what made her want to stop it. She'd rolled herself in the garden, digging into the dirt and desperately spinning, smothering the flames not to save her life, not to end the pain, but to stop the noise. She was hideously disfigured, her mouth a dry withered hole, her eyes drooping from their melted sockets, her graphed skin puckered and glossy, red and raw, as if she'd been flayed and turned inside out, but all she ever wanted to talk about, two years after striking the match, was the noise.

Ramage gulped a yawn to clear his head; tendrils of chalky saliva hinged his mouth and alcoholic tears welled in his eyes. Breeze from an open door did little to refresh him. When Greenfield cleared the set, Ramage went out onto the fire escape and found RB sitting on a metal step, furtively turning the crank on a hand drill and boring a hole in the plywood that blocked the window. When the half-inch bit punched through, he tested the peephole, then enlarged it, carving away at the wood with a pocketknife.

"Spooky," RB said. He stopped to pinch at a blood blister on his thumb. "You smell that smell?"

"Clove today," Ramage said.

"I been trying to figure it out."

"There's a spice factory," Ramage said.

"This town is ugly," RB said, "but it smells good."

"I'm all tore up," Ramage admitted. "I got drunk with Rigo last night."

"Harvard," RB said, with a laugh. "He don't like me kidding him, do he?"

"He might appreciate it if you laid off."

"Good. Then I'll keep on." RB finally popped the blister, wiping the spurt of blood away on his pant leg. "Guy doesn't know where he's at."

They could hear Greenfield calling for quiet as the filming was set to begin. RB peered through the hole he'd made in the plywood.

"This shit's tame," he said after a while. "I thought there'd be monkeys in it." He closed his pocketknife. "Still, there's boys and girls inside about to get their rocks off. And you out here sicker than a dog."

"I think I'll head home," Ramage said.

"Have a look."

Ramage pressed his eye to the peephole and saw Desiree naked on the bed. She was alone on the set and seemed not to know where to place her hands; she leaned forward, resting her elbows on her knees.

"You look bored," Greenfield was telling her. "You got a dick in your mouth but you got a face like a postal clerk."

"Scolding me doesn't put me in much of a mood," Desiree said.

"You're a professional," Greenfield said. "You get paid to be in the mood."

"No monkeys," Ramage said to RB. He looked out over the town. "I think I'll head home."

"You said that."

Ramage stood, steadying himself with the handrail. The gray overcast sky tumbled and spun and his stomach heaved. He buckled and was seated again, throwing up between his legs. He propped his arms on his knees and spat chunks through the grated metal landing. RB closed his hand over Ramage's, and Ramage slowly turned his palm up and clasped hold of RB, weaving their fingers together, holding on tighter as each new wave of nausea hit.

"Spooky?"

"Yeah?"

"I could give a rat's ass where you been. Crazy or whatever, locked up, I don't mind. It's nothing to me."

"Thanks."

"But you're different. You changed."

"Different?"

"You used to be somebody else."

He woke with a parched mouth and put his head under the faucet and desperately lapped at the water like a poisoned animal. He undressed and was asleep again when a knock on the door woke him. He wound a sheet over his shoulders and slipped the chain off and found Desiree standing under the walkway light. Night had fallen; he had to ask what time it was.

"Ten-thirty," she said.

"Man alive," Ramage said.

Desiree wore jeans and a white T-shirt. She'd let her hair loose from its usual hard, lapidary style, and an archaeology of treatments showed, strata of blond and silver, a bedrock of dark brown at the roots.

Ramage asked, "How was work?"

"Greenfield's got notions," she said.

"I heard him go off."

"There wasn't any call for him to humiliate me in front of everybody."

She slipped off her sandals and walked barefoot across the gold carpet. She poured rum into a plastic cup and sipped from her drink, then tipped out a little more rum and sat on the bed beside Ramage, her legs raised. Their knees touched. Ramage felt the faint pressure and in silence he ran his finger back and forth along her pants seam, tracing the outline of her leg as it rose and fell from her hip to her ankle. She primped the flat airless pillows beneath her head; she ran her tongue over her lips and her mouth settled into a pout as she stared at the ceiling. Ramage wished for ice but he was too tired to dress and search for some. Desiree balanced the plastic cup on her stomach, over her belly button. Ramage kissed her woodenly and touched her breasts; he faked the kiss a moment longer and slipped his hand under her shirt. Beneath her breasts, two faint surgical scars, like the twin curved lines of a cartoon bust, were clearly visible. He traced his finger along the pink welted tissue. The cakey foundation she had applied to cover the scars for the shoot came off on Ramage's finger in a kind of powdery dust the color of putty. He looked at his finger; he wiped it clean on the bedsheet. She reached for his crotch. His penis curled like a burnt match between his legs.

"I knew a guy killed himself," she said, sitting up. "I always wondered why."

"It's not that interesting."

"Come on, if we hung out tonight, and then you were dead tomorrow, you wouldn't want me to feel anything?"

"Nothing."

"Not even weird? You wouldn't want me to feel a little weird?"

"I don't know."

"That guy used to come to our shows. I had this rock band. I was sixteen. He was a fan. He shot himself in the parking lot. He had some kind of drama. I wrote a song about it but the song stank."

The light that had been leaking into the room was briefly eclipsed and someone knocked on the door. Ramage pulled the sheet around his shoulders and answered. Rigo held a six-pack in one hand and Ramage's tool sack in the other.

"You are not at the bar," he said. Without the past tense he could only protest pointlessly against the present; his eyes shifted, staring into the room. Nothing was happening but Ramage felt awkward and compelled to account for himself.

"I see," Rigo said. Red and black paint spotted his face and sand crystals flashed in his hair. He set Ramage's tools inside. "You forget, I bring." He opened one of the bottles from the six-pack and offered it to Desiree, who declined. Ramage turned down the offer, too, and Rigo drank the beer in one long hard swallow. When he was finished, he knocked the empty bottle against his knee, waiting. "I see," he said again.

There was nothing Ramage could do, and his guilt gave way to anger. "Thanks for the tools," he said. He abruptly said goodbye and shut the door. Turning back to face the room, he was conscious of the tableau from Rigo's vantage, the poisoned scene, tawdry and familiar: the twisted sheets, the tangle of clothes, the uncapped bottle of rum on the table.

"He gives me the creeps," Desiree said. "You know the way you can look at somebody just for a second, and that's one thing, but if you look longer, that's something else? That's him—he just keeps staring. He doesn't know when's enough."

She reached for Ramage again, but gave up quickly.

"I'm getting this feeling of familiarity around you," Desiree said. "I don't mean cozy. I mean like a past life, like we've been here before. Not way back in history or anything. We weren't

Roman emperors together. I mean a past life like maybe a couple weeks ago."

After the second day of shooting, Greenfield told Ramage to stay late and dismantle the sets, all except the black room. The weather had turned cooler; a light rain tapped against the plywood windows. Space heaters had been spread around the warehouse after some of the actors complained of cold. Ramage sent Rigo to the store for beer; he waited with RB, the warm air blowing over them.

RB looked out from the set to the tangle of equipment.

"All these people watching," he said. "You forget there's all these people looking on."

"This is some job," Ramage said.

"We've had lots worse."

"That we have, my friend."

Knocking down what they had only recently built hollowed their desire and didn't make either man inclined to work. When Rigo returned with the beer, they loafed on the bed and drank.

RB said, "What side were you on, Rigo?"

"Side?"

"A good guy? A bad guy?"

"He was in the military," Ramage said.

"No side," Rigo said.

"I seen you looking through my peephole," RB said. "I should charge admission. I'd make some money off you, boy. You like these bitches."

"I am married," Rigo said.

"You can look, Harvard," RB said. "It's okay. Looking don't hurt nobody."

Rigo flipped a bottle cap at RB, hitting him in the face.

"Lighten up," Ramage said.

"Spooky, he just threw a bottle cap at me."

"Wah wah, let's get back to work."

"Back to work, you niggers!" RB laughed, his dark lips rolling back, exposing a gate of white teeth. "That includes you, Rigoberto."

"Go get my claw hammer, RB."

"You know about black men, right, Rigo?" RB said, as he rose from the bed. He lifted a two-by-four off the floor and duckwalked the length of the warehouse with the stud crotched and angled up between his legs. "You're definitely some kind a nignog," he said. He stuffed the board in one of the galvanized cans they were using to haul refuse. He laughed to himself as he searched in Ramage's tool sack. He found the hammer and beneath it the gun. "Hey Spooky, man, what the hell?" He held the gun delicately like a small wounded bird in the palm of his hand.

"Put it back," Ramage said.

"Is it loaded?"

"No," Ramage said. "Are my smokes in there?"

The kerosene heaters burned orange and warmed the hue of Rigo's olive skin. His cheeks flared up and Ramage watched his wide black silent eyes track RB's movement across the room.

"You want a world where you have to choose sides?" RB said. "Go to prison, man."

He offered Ramage the handle end of the hammer.

"It's prison now, is it?" Ramage said.

"What?"

"First it was reform school, now it's prison. Which is it?"

"It's all the same," RB said. "You'd know that if you'd been where I've been."

"Let's strike these rooms."

Rigo walked over to the lockbox and grabbed a small sledge and began pounding away the supports that held the room together. Gypsum shook loose as the Sheetrock buckled and white dust sifted into the air. The back wall caved in and the others folded over like shuffled cards. A stud broke free and whacked against RB's leg. Ramage turned and calmly waited for things to surface. RB closed his hand around Rigo's neck and shoved his face to the floor.

RB said, "You got to be very careful. People get fucked up on jobs."

RB let go and picked up a pry bar and began to rip nails loose from the discarded studs. Each nail screeched like a gull. Rigo was still lying on the floor.

"Get up," Ramage said.

"Just act right," RB said. He slapped the pry bar in his palm. "Act right, you know what that means?"

"Enough," Ramage said.

"Fuck enough," RB said. "Little half-nigger almost fucked me up just being stupid."

"He's sorry," Ramage said.

"I didn't hear him say so," RB said.

For the rest of the night, Ramage worked with Rigo close by his side. His silence got on Ramage's nerves. After they'd hauled the last load of broken drywall outside, Ramage offered Rigo a cigarette.

"Don't get all quiet inside yourself," Ramage said. "It's a pain in the ass to everyone else."

Rigo said, "I quit."

"It's stupid to quit now. Hang in there, okay? Get paid." Rain swept through the blue light of a street lamp. Ramage squeezed Rigo's shoulder, giving it a pat. "The job's done," he said. "Gather up my tools and let's get out of here."

No one had arrived at the warehouse for the last day of shooting, and Ramage, after making coffee, sat alone in the black room; it was the only box still standing. The walls shone with the rich luster of ebony and his reflection floated as if submerged in dark water. Other than a bed, the room was empty of furniture. The floor was carpeted in orange shag and a pine box stood against one wall. Ramage opened the lid and found the day's drama: a braided bullwhip, handcuffs, black leather chokers studded with chrome spikes. He lifted the bullwhip and gave it a crack in the air.

When Greenfield showed up, he stood in the middle of the warehouse, silently taking in the scene. He scuffed his cowboy boots on the floor. A long blue cigarette hung from his lips.

"Don't put RB in the movie," Ramage said.

"Why not?" Greenfield said. He looked at Ramage, and then up at the skylight, washed with gray.

"I just prefer it."

"I was never going to anyway."

"He'll say you promised."

"I can't get caught up in all that," Greenfield said. "You're the foreman, you're in charge of the cheap seats. You tell him." Greenfield looked up at the skylight. "I still haven't quoted *Citizen Kane*," he said. "You know Rosebud was Hearst's pet name for his mistress's clit? You know that? Orson Welles knew that. Rosebud, Rosebud. It was an inside joke. It drove Hearst crazy." He shaded his eyes against the gray light. "I'd like to get at least one shot of all this from above."

RB was in back of the warehouse, dressed in slacks and a rayon shirt. The smell of pomade hung in the air around him, and he stood alone, rocking back and forth on the heels of his work boots, apparently the only shoes he'd brought with him. Ramage stepped next to RB, and for a full minute went unacknowledged.

Finally Ramage said, "I talked to Greenfield. There might not be time to get you in."

RB hesitated, then resumed his rocking.

"It's an orgy," he said. "Everybody climbing all over everybody else, can't tell one person from the next. I get in there, who cares? It's all equal."

"You can't just walk on."

"Won't nobody know the difference."

Four strands of rope were anchored to the corners of the room, and Desiree waited, shackled at the ankles and wrists, crouched quietly in the convergent center. Enough slack played in the rope for her to crawl a few feet in any direction. Her sunken reflection swam below the surface of the polished wall, surrounded by a vague wash of white faces. The wall did not reflect the crews' eyes or mouths; black hollows bloomed in their heads like the holes in a skull. An assistant took a powder puff and dabbed away the glare from Desiree's forehead. The chalky cloud caused her to sneeze.

The set was cleared, and Ramage left RB, who insisted on staying there on the sidelines until Greenfield called him in. Ramage went to sit on the fire escape. Rigo was planted in front of the peephole, peering through it as if it were a telescope, subdued and quiet, his open mouth pressed against the plywood. With RB out of the way, this was his chance, his opportunity. Then Ramage looked, too. Through a tangle of cameras and booms, he watched Desiree tug at one of the ropes binding her ankle. A hooded man cracked the bullwhip and the tasseled tip snapped against the back of her thigh. The contact was accidental, outside the choreography, and she lurched forward, trying with her bound wrist to protect herself. She howled, and then someone in the crew moved, standing in Ramage's line of sight.

Ramage left Rigo and climbed the fire escape, making his way up a ladder that curled over the parapet and onto the roof. The skylight was made of green tinted glass and reinforced with chicken wire. Ramage shaded his eyes against the dull glare. Twenty feet below, the full cast was assembled, the orgy well under way, a swarm of white bodies that gradually came apart as men and women, pairing up, crawled across the orange carpet. They moved silently, dividing like cells and then joining again, their skin pale and colorless under the burning lights. The hooded man loomed over Desiree from behind, holding on to her hair like it was the reins of a horse. It was hard to imagine what exhaustion, what wasting away of power, would bring the orgy to an end. Everything was eternally available, everything equal. Ramage sat up and looked out over the town. Nothing moved, not a car, not a pedestrian. It felt as if some vast Sunday had devoured the day. The sea was flat and the waves rolled evenly along the shore.

After an hour, a raucous cheer rose from the set, and Ramage went downstairs, entering the warehouse ahead of Rigo. Greenfield bowed first toward the cast and then toward the crew, sweeping his hand along the floor. "Thank you one and all."

Women wiped themselves off with towels. A few naked men stood nonchalantly in a huddle, asking one another about their itineraries, where they'd go next. Desiree's skin had a stung, hectic appearance, and one of her ankles was still bound, the rope trailing after her as she moved about the set, saying her goodbyes.

RB was partly undressed, standing foolishly in his stocking

feet and boxers and rayon shirt. He said to Ramage, "Greenwad fucked me."

Ramage didn't say anything.

"You get a bone on?" RB said, looking at Rigo. "You know what a bone is, right?" With a fist he feinted in the direction of Rigo's crotch. "Huh, Harvard? A bone? A woody? Huh? You like seeing women tied up? That what you do in your country?"

Rigo reached for RB's mouth as if to stop the flow of words, smashing it shut. An instant passed and then RB smiled, the gate of white teeth washed pink with blood. His lip was torn. RB slammed the butt of his palm against Rigo's chin, shoving back on his jaw as though pounding open a door. It was a moment before anyone noticed, but then a circle gathered, and the onlookers, by their steady gazes, seemed to freeze the fight in tableau: Rigo fallen on the floor, RB smiling down on him. Rigo rose once more and rushed RB, and again RB knocked him to the ground. This time Ramage bent over Rigo and told him to stay down. RB's hand filled with blood. He showed it to Ramage as if the substance puzzled him. "Fucking Harvard," he said, and then he slowly wiped the blood off his hand, painting Rigo's face with it.

After Greenfield paid him off, Ramage walked down to the pier, looking for Rigo. His encampment was on the lee side of a restroom; a picnic table tipped on its side formed a second wall of his shelter and he'd made a roof of the door he'd scrounged from the ocean. A small pit in the sand was filled with sticks of driftwood and wet ashes. Rigo was gone.

Desiree came by the motel later that evening, carrying her suitcase.

"Where to?" Ramage asked.

"Los Angeles," she said. "Another job. You?"

"RB's coming by," Ramage said. "I've got to pay him. Then it's over."

"I had a dream about me and you last night. Somebody was taking us somewhere, they wanted to show us something. We were riding in the back seat of a limousine. There was a baby in it, this dead baby."

Ramage waited. "And?"

"That's it," she said. "The baby was dead, but it wasn't ugly and rotten or anything. It was just still."

There was a hard rap on the door and Ramage answered.

"Oh boy, what do we have here?" RB said. He pointed to the bottle of rum. "Don't mind if I do."

Ramage found another plastic cup in the bathroom. He removed the safety seal and poured out a small measure of the rum and then watered it down. RB sat in the chair beside Desiree.

"I've got your money," Ramage said.

"There's no rush," RB said.

RB fingered the arm of his chair, running a nail back and forth through the fretted grooves, blindly retracing a rosette. In a minute, Ramage decided, he would give RB his money. The bills were crisply folded into a small manila pay envelope Ramage had slipped into his shirt pocket.

RB finished his drink and tapped the plastic cup against the armchair. He looked at Desiree. "I was wondering, how is it you get paid? You get your money by the hour, or you get a salary, or what?"

"By the scene," she said. She was looking at Ramage when she answered; her voice was barely audible.

"The scene? You mean what you do, how many times you do it, like that?"

"Will you call me a cab?" Desiree asked Ramage.

"Like two men—you do two men you get paid more?"

She nodded.

RB said, "I seen you in a movie with a midget. I figure a dwarf can do it, I can, too. You remember that guy, that midget?"

"Sure," Desiree said.

"That was sick."

She got up and went to the bathroom. RB and Ramage sat silently. Through the thin door, they could hear her peeing.

"Shouldn't hang no hollow-core doors in a small room like this," RB said. "No privacy."

Ramage handed RB the envelope. "Here's your money," he said. "There's a bonus."

RB set the envelope aside.

"You all laid-in, you taken care of. Desiree Street, huh?"

"Take your money, RB."

"Couldn't have no nigger in on that." RB counted his pay, tossing one of the bills to the floor. "I don't want your bonus."

Ramage dialed the phone and ordered a cab.

"Bitch taking a long-ass time in the bathroom," RB said.

"Don't make this a bad scene," Ramage said. He twirled his drink as though there were ice in it.

Desiree came out of the bathroom. She sat on the bed and worked the strap of her sandals, refastening the tiny brass buckles.

RB said, "Why don't we all make a movie?"

Desiree took a drink. Over the edge of her glass she said, "Where's your camera?"

"In my head," RB said.

"Oh, that's right," she said. "You all got cameras in your head."

"I'm not like all them."

"None of you are like all of them."

"In my movie," RB said, "I wouldn't tie you up and whip you or anything. I'd treat you right."

"Sure you would," Desiree said. "In your movie you'd send me flowers every day."

Ramage followed Desiree out the door and through the empty lot to a waiting cab. She settled in the back seat and he waited, expecting her to roll down the window and say good-bye, but she didn't. He went back to the room and gathered up his stuff, zipping his tool sack shut. RB had moved from the chair to the bed.

RB said, "I come here, I see you got your own little movie in progress. You didn't want me in on your thing. You cut me out."

"You're wrong," Ramage said. "There was no thing."

"Spooky, man, how dumb do you think I am?"

He put his sack down in the motel lobby. Behind the glass, through a beaded curtain, he could see the blue glow of a television, could hear the snappy rhythm of sitcom repartee and the spurts of canned laughter. On top of the television, between a potted cactus and a jar of pennies, was a photograph of a young man and woman, circa 1950, the woman laughing, her light hair blown by some long-ago breeze, the man with a cigarette in his mouth and a collar upturned against the same stiff wind. Ramage couldn't see where they were standing; the photo was overexposed and the background had bleached away. The desk clerk was asleep on the couch, her fat, heavy leg resting on a coffee table cluttered with magazines, a plastic bowl of popcorn, a can of diet soda, a spotless green ashtray. Ramage tapped the service bell.

"I'm checking out," he said.

The woman looked through her files; she shrugged, hopeless.

"I can't find your thing," she said. "How long've you been here?"

"Three days," Ramage said.

"Seems longer," she said. She started the itemized math on a receipt.

Ramage separated seventy-five dollars from his pay and set the money on the counter. Outside, the motel's blue vacancy sign was just beginning to glow in a halo of mist blowing up from the beach.

"Seventy-five," the woman announced.

Ramage slid the money forward. "Kind of dead this time of year," he said.

She gave him the receipt. "You know the others, that was next to you? They skipped out."

"You should make people pay in advance," Ramage said. They waited in an awkward frozen silence, staring at each other. Ramage rapped his knuckle on the counter, breaking the spell, and left.

He walked across the parking lot and dropped his tool sack at the foot of the palm tree. The brown fronds spread above him and the air smelled of cinnamon. Bruised and sore, he sat back against the trunk and unzipped his bag. He pulled out his clothes and groped along the bottom and then turned the sack over and emptied his tools into the sand. A car drove by, and in the wake of its passing everything was briefly quiet. The gun was gone. He considered the probable suspects and decided that RB had taken it. A moment later he was convinced that Rigo had stolen it. Then he wondered if it was Desiree. When his cab came, he repacked his things and stood to go. Behind him in the empty lot a string of tin cans his neighbors had cut

loose lay twisted on the asphalt—too much clatter, he supposed, as they made their getaway. The desk clerk sat at the
counter behind the sheet of bulletproof glass. He'd disturbed
her sleep and now she was awake. She'd turned on a lamp and
was reading, the white waste of her face set to the romance.

Blessing

My wife and I had been living in our house outside Mount Vernon, Washington, for just about a month. The land around there is alluvial and soft, and over the years the house had settled awkwardly and was so weather-beaten in places, yet so new and marvelously current in others, that it would have been hard for an outsider to guess whether it was an old house that was falling apart or a new house with many sly touches of distressed authenticity. The previous owner had been a tulip farmer with a large family, and we supposed that throughout the years market fluctuations had dictated improvements—how frail and precarious the futures in tulips must have been! In some years, obviously, this family had been flush, while in other leaner years, they'd simply made do—the house recorded and quietly testified to the course of their fortunes. Our kitchen came equipped with a dishwasher and a disposal, but the screened porch was rotting and lopsided, leaking not only rain but clouds of mosquitoes, one always following the other rapidly. Out back, beyond the porch, there was a fair yard, a seasonal pond choked with purple loosestrife, a gnarled gray apple tree, and a thorny brake of blackberry bushes that separated our property from the tulip fields, still farmed by the same family. The old man had simply moved to town after his wife died, perhaps feeling that an old, questionable house, without a wife or kids, was no longer worth the persistent effort it would take to restore and maintain.

No matter—it was our dream house. Two flat strips of black-top stretched away from it, falling off toward infinity, and we liked to imagine, in our private, silly moments alone, that the earth was our present, that the crossroads was the ribbon wrapping it, and that our house, shabby as it may have seemed, was the somewhat frilly bow atop this wonderful gift. Perhaps we'd lived as nomads in New York for too many years, and maybe the twin luxuries of space and ownership made us dizzy, but at times, during those first few weeks, we couldn't help ourselves. I'd lie awake at night and press my palms flat against the cool white spaces of the sheets and revel in the knowledge that tomorrow night I'd be able to do the exact same thing. That it wouldn't be taken away seemed a miracle. Those first giddy weeks, Meagan and I made love frequently and with renewed passion, exploring the different rooms and discover-ing each other at the same time, an intimacy that distance and the novel possibility of separation seemed to encourage. One night, however, just a few days after we'd celebrated our first month in the house, I woke and found myself alone—itself a rarity, after the cramped studios, the cheating one-bedrooms—and sprang up, startled and afraid. I searched the house upstairs and then down, and finally gathered the folds of my robe around my neck and went outside. The lawn glistened with mist, and a few high clouds scudded overhead in a clear-ing starlit sky. I could smell the wet dark soil all around me, and I could hear something too—something faint and far away that I couldn't quite place.

Meagan was standing out on the road. A balmy wind blew across the open fields and stirred the border of forsythia, and I watched her hand rise slowly to her face and briefly rest there. Although it made for a strange picture, seeing my wife out on the road, in her bedclothes, I wasn't alarmed. Her father and brother and her brother's wife and baby were to arrive the next day—it was her brother Jimmy's birthday—and I supposed that this visit, the first in our new house, in this new land we had decided to call home, had made Meagan both restless and thoughtful. To her the visit would in some way bestow official sanction on our choices, as a marriage is sanctioned by witnesses. This sudden convergence of her father and brother, as well as the absence of her mother, affected her outlook, I think, so that for several days, ever since the phone calls were made, the dates settled, then rearranged and settled again, she'd been seeing our house through their eyes and suddenly everything puzzled and depressed her. It was too much house, or not enough, too new or too old, and the landscape, of rivers and mountains and muddy fields, all sealed beneath a lid of gray and black and white February clouds, was too foreign, or too monotonously familiar.

"I just wanted to look at it," she said, when I came up beside her. "It's big, isn't it?"

In fact, it was—far more house than was needed for two people who'd agreed, early on, that children probably wouldn't be part of the picture. There was a huge attic with a row of dormer windows, out of which no one ever looked; they were an odd, decorative flourish without function. I wasn't even sure how to get up there, although I assumed some sort of hatch-and-ladder contraption existed, perhaps a boarded passage hidden away in the back of a closet. In the house proper, aside from the master bedroom, there were two other bedrooms upstairs, and a third downstairs. The rooms upstairs were papered with Grecian pastoral scenes, and the downstairs room, obviously a young boy's, was done up in a Western motif, with horses hitched to cacti and men gathered around a campfire. In a fit of rebellious mischief, someone had drawn crayon stick figures along the lower reaches of the wall—ambuscading stick figures aiming bows and wearing Indian headdresses, no less. The drawings were the primitive dreams, like the ancient petroglyphs of a hungry tribe, of a boy sent to bed without his dinner. Upstairs and down, the wallpaper was old, yellowed by age and sunlight, mapped with brown water stains, and in many places it fell off in big clumps to reveal the soft, flaking plaster beneath it.

"Hear that?" Meagan asked.

"I did before. What is it?"

"Somebody out there is playing the piano."

"It's beautiful."

"It's lonely."

To the west, across the road and below the levee, a ragged wisp of gray smoke rose in the wind. Our closest neighbor, Mr. George, lived down there in a one-room cabin along the banks of the Skagit River. The Skagit Valley is a flat stretch of fertile land that lies between the sea and the mountains, and at times, when the fog is low and rolling, or at night, in the dark, when the small, sad lights of some distant house glow like portholes, you can still imagine what it was like twenty thousand years ago—a cold, silent world buried in glacial ice, and then deep under water. At times the air is so damp and dense with fog you feel as if the waters had just yesterday receded; other times, the feeling is antediluvian and expectant, especially in late winter or early spring, when the rains fall and the Skagit floods. The winding network of levees generally holds the floodwater in check, and most houses, like ours, are protected— we carry flood insurance just in case. Yet there are remnants along the river of the days when people contended more openly with nature, and fearless or defiant men, or men who are simply too old and too poor and too proud, like Mr. George, still live in some of the ramshackle houses on the banks of the river. When the floods come, they simply take to their roofs, or hop in an aluminum pram, plying the oars against the current, and wait.

When I'd first come out, I thought the sky was clearing. It wasn't. The wind had died out and in the stillness the fog was thickening around us. My robe was damp, the absorbent flannel heavy with sea air.

"Let's go back inside now," I said.

Early the next morning, Meagan shopped for Jimmy's favorite foods (he was a fussy eater), purchased three sets of new sheets, emptied our modest liquor cabinet into a mop bucket and hid it beneath the sink, and in the bedrooms set vases of fresh flowers, each with half an aspirin dissolved in the water. It didn't seem to me that family should be a source of so much anxiety, especially in our own house, and I was slightly annoyed at the elaborate, endless preparations, as Megan ran from room to room, wiping a fingerprint from a mirror, or restacking books on a night table. Perhaps because my own father died when I was young, and I, as the only child, was absorbed into a larger and more casual clan of aunts and uncles and cousins, my sense of family, and of love and loyalty, too, had always been friendly and equable rather than fierce and divided. The weight of my expectations, and therefore the burden of my disappointments, was spread evenly among many people, so that a typical Saturday in my childhood might find me baking a cake with a cousin in the morning and then drinking Roy Rogerses in a bar while my uncle shot pool until the Old Style beer sign in the window began to warm in the night air and it was time to return home for a dinner cooked by my mother.

The sky had turned a deep, dull pewter, and rain fell as I pushed the mower back and forth over the dandelions and puffballs that make up our lawn. Across the road I could hear Mr. George pounding with a hammer, the racket echoing above the river like rifle shots and then fading across the fields. With all the noise I hadn't heard the car pull in the drive. Meagan and Mr. Boyd came running across the lawn with sections of newspaper held over their heads. Never a thin man, Joe Boyd had gained weight without seeming any fatter, just bulkier and more imperial, and he called my name in his rolling stentorian voice as he struggled across the yard.

"Tony, my boy!" he called, slipping.

I offered my hand to Joe.

"Good to see you," he said. He held my hand in his grip as he looked around. "So this is it, huh?"

Meagan tugged my sleeve.

"Daddy has some bags in the trunk," she said. She looked at me, and then out across the road. The rain fell in pellets that bounced and exploded over the asphalt. "God, it's raining. I wish it wasn't raining."

"You're known for your shitty weather out here," Mr. Boyd said, "but it keeps everything green, I guess."

Just then Jimmy and his gang pulled into the gravel drive.

"Hey, monsoon season," he said, huddling around the woman I presumed was Naga, holding a coat over her and a dark-skinned, squalling baby.

"Jimmy, Jimmy!" Meagan screamed, hugging him, then stepping back. "Let me look," she said, then collapsed toward him again.

Jimmy was a sweet-looking kid with reddish hair and the sort of sparse moustache I've always associated with young guys in the military—just a little disturbance above his lip. He

was twenty-five, soon to be twenty-six. Joey, the baby, was
wrapped in a bundle of blankets, his bawling face pinched
tight. "He's hungry, " Jimmy said, taking the baby from Naga.
His wife was young, eighteen I guessed, though she might have
been younger than that, and her skin was as smooth and brown
and lustrous as a chestnut—darker than the average Filipino
woman. Her hair was long and coal black. Her lips were wide
and kind of flat, purplish in color, with the distant sensual
pout of a child still in a daze, just waking from a dream. I won't
try to mimic the way she spoke, but her manner was polite
and formal, peppered with odd Americanisms. Throughout the
visit she called me Anthony, and when she called Mr. Boyd
"Father" it sounded honorific. She didn't talk much, but she
liked to say "honey" a lot, as in "Jimmy, honey" or "Good
morning, honey," so that I wondered if the word "honey"
had some twittering musical similarity to a word or sound in
Tagalog.

We pushed into the entryway and I gathered an armload of
wet coats.

"Jimmy," Mr. Boyd called.

"Joe," Jimmy said. "Dad."

The two men shook hands, and kept shaking them, like
strangers with little to say, strangers who cling to each other
in an oddly intimate manner, trying to remember an old
connection.

Everything lapsed awkwardly into silence.

"This is Naga," I said. "Jimmy's wife."

"And this is Joey," Jimmy said. "Joe Junior."

I'm not sure he or anyone else caught his slipup, and I was
happy to let it ride, a nervously misplayed note at a recital.
Jimmy pulled the blanket away from his son's face, and our little group huddled closer, gathering in a circle, but it was hard

to adore such a disconsolate, wailing baby, and after a moment of embarrassed stammering Jimmy sent Naga off to the kitchen to warm a bottle of formula. The rest of us sat in the living room, and I thought how pleasant it was to hear other voices in the house. So far, it had only been Meagan and I and the mute voices of the past, those little evidences, like the crayon stick figures, that someone had lived here before us. I'd never owned a house and was a little mystified, surprised that anyone could manage. I tended to read these traces of the past as if there were affidavits from the previous owner, affirming, under oath, that he'd actually made it. I found myself listening to these new voices for reassurance, too, and although, at the moment, I couldn't really hear what anyone was saying, the music of the conversation was more than enough: Mr. Boyd's booming bass, Meagan's rising melody, Jimmy's percussive babbling to the baby, and the din of the rain outside, thrumming against the windows. I offered to light a fire and Meagan said that would be nice. I brought in logs from the tarp-covered rick in back of the house and chopped kindling and got a rip-roaring fire started. "How about music?" I asked. And when no one answered I put on a Brahms sonata that was a little mournful, Germanic and dirgelike. I worried that Mr. Boyd or Jimmy might find my choice pretentious, but as the first heavy strains lifted into the room, it seemed to fit the weather and the fact that I was there, in my own house, with my wife and these guests, sitting before a big fire. The flames licked up into the flue, the logs crackled, the rain fell and tapped against the roof, the cello and piano approached each other tentatively, and I felt warm and enclosed.

"So," Joe said. "Theater arts?"

"It's a job for now," Meagan said.

"You still acting?" Jimmy said, chucking the baby under

the chin. He said to Naga, "Meagan's an actress—or used to be, sounds like."

"She still is," I said.

"Those who can't do, teach," Jimmy said.

"And those who can't teach . . . ," Joe said.

"Teach gym, ha ha," Meagan said, playing her part in the routine like a seasoned trouper.

"That's what they say," Jimmy said.

Meagan smiled, then frowned, then looked at her brother. "If you'd write to me every once in a while you'd know what's going on."

"What do you teach them?" Mr. Boyd said.

"I do write," Jimmy said. "Just I don't ever have stamps."

"The college puts on two big productions a year," I said.

Mr. Boyd pressed his palms together and then touched the tips of his fingers to his lips.

"I'll send you stamps," Meagan said. And then, to her father, she said, "Well, come on, what do you think of the house?"

Joe said, "Nice."

"It's really old," Jimmy said. "Makes me want to hear a ghost story. I'm surprised a couple yuppies like you would buy such a beater."

"We'll fix it up," Meagan said.

"It's like a pioneer house or something."

"Slowly."

"Good luck," Jimmy said. "I can't imagine Tony using a hammer."

"How's the commercial and film market?" Joe asked.

"I haven't really looked into it," Meagan said. "I'm sure its the usual small-market stuff."

"Auto dealers and carpet sales," Joe said, "and that kind of thing."

The conversation at dinner had a similar broken flow, full of a casual bickering that, along with the Bordeaux I'd bought for the occasion, gave me a headache. The constant quarreling made every topic seem trivial, and although the Boyd clan, including Meagan, seemed comfortable enough, I found it impossible to orient myself within their universe of disputed claims. By the end of dinner I had no idea what was true or false, important or petty. Fortunately, everyone was tired from their respective trips, and we went to bed early. We got Jimmy and Naga and the baby settled upstairs and then showed Mr. Boyd to our room, which Meagan decided we should relinquish because it had a private bath. Meagan and I slept downstairs.

At some point in the night I became convinced that I'd forgotten to lock the front door and that it had blown open in the wind. I could feel the leak of draft at my ankles like a cold hand. I got up and put on my bathrobe and slippers. The door was open wide. I shut it and went into the kitchen for a glass of water and found Mr. Boyd standing at the sink. The mop bucket sat on the counter and he had fixed himself a cocktail. I think if Meagan had caught him he might have tried to hide the glass, and if Jimmy had found him he would have challenged his son by taking a drink, but with me, and whatever my reactions were, it didn't seem to matter. It was as if I made no impression. The tumbler of Scotch remained on the counter.

"Meagan always hides the booze under the sink," he said. "She must have seen it in a movie."

"She was only trying to do right by you," I said.

"It's Jimmy she's worried about," he corrected me. "Apparently I'm a little *harsh* on the boy after I've tipped a few."

He shrugged and took a drink and licked his lips. The rain-beaded window cast shadowy streaks on his sober gray face. "Join me?" he said.

I questioned whether or not I should be party to this, and then I said yes, not all that sure what string I was yanking, and what would unravel, if I accepted a nightcap. It struck me that it was my house, my kitchen, and I could drink Drano in it if I so chose. We sat across from each other at the kitchen table.

"You like it here," he said.

"Love it."

"Driving up from the airport this afternoon, I was surprised how far it is from everything. Meagan led me to believe it was closer to Seattle. You're pretty isolated."

Often when I talk to Meagan I have the feeling I'm answering to Mr. Boyd, and then, as I spoke to her father, I felt that I was responding to my wife. This elusive layering made me tongue-tied.

"It's only two and a half hours to Seattle," I said.

"And two and a half hours back," Mr. Boyd said. "So five hours, in good weather, with no traffic. Have you made the trip since you moved here?"

"We've been busy."

"Who goes to the theater around here?" Mr. Boyd said. "Farmers? Lumberjacks?"

"There's the school."

"Don't kid me," he said. "That school is nothing, and you know it."

I said, "This is a bit of a compromise, I guess."

"Ambition that's compromised," he said, "isn't ambition."

I knew that Joe Boyd had played two seasons of minor league ball, and that on a road trip to Appleton, Wisconsin, he'd met Meagan's mom, but I suspected that the sense of

sacrifice and halfness came later, only after his marriage began to deteriorate. One of the bigger gyps in Joe Boyd's life
was that the lovely farmgirl he'd married turned out to be a
manic-depressive.

Mr. Boyd wet the tip of his finger and ran it slowly around
the rim of his glass until he coaxed a high, clear note out of it.
The sound was like the song of a whale, and with the water
washing against the windows it was easy to imagine the
beseeching cry of the leviathan, mysteriously astray in the
fields.

"We had to get out of New York," I said. "New York was
depressing."

Toward the end of our time in New York, Meagan would come
home from a round of auditions and collapse in a fit of crying.
After a while she'd just stop herself. She'd wipe her eyes and
say, "Everything's always going to be like this." And I'd tell her
no, things were going to change, although, honestly, I never
understood these attacks of despair—I never really got their
profundity—and felt nothing but a rising panic whenever they
came up. Myself, I drifted widely and affably from job to job
until insurance took me in; it was Meagan who had the passion
and depth of a single ambition. My ideal life is a quiet one. I
like to read, to sit still in the same chair, with the lampshade at
a certain angle, alone, or with Meagan nearby, and now and
then, if I'm lucky, I'll come across a lovely phrase or fine
sentiment, look up from my book, and feel the harmony of
some notion, the justice of it, and know that everything is
there. That's life to me, those privately discovered moments. I
wouldn't settle for less, yet I don't expect a whole lot more,
either.

But Meagan does, and because of that, those moments of harmony are elusive, if they come at all. She's always nervous, a little frantic, looking back at what she's done, wondering what lies ahead, what comes next. That night, after I shared a drink with Mr. Boyd and returned to bed, she said what she had always said when New York was coming to an end for us.

"I love you," she said. "At least there's that."

The floorboards above us sagged as someone—Jimmy or Naga—paced the room, trying to put the baby down. Meagan turned, staring at the ceiling.

"I don't know how people do it," she said.

I ran my finger back and forth behind Meagan's ear. The vein in her neck throbbed.

"You get used to it after a while," I said. "You don't hear."

"Jimmy's never going to get what he wants."

"What does he want?"

"I guess that's the problem," Meagan said. "What does that boy want? He told me he has a new great idea for a business. He says it's all lined up." Meagan was quiet, and then she laughed. "Every loser in the world at some point decides the future is in janitorial services. Have you ever noticed that?"

I told her that I hadn't, but that it made sense to me.

"You know why it makes sense?" Meagan said. "It makes sense because all you need to get started is a sponge. His idea is he'll keep his job at the convenience store but then clean shitters all the way home. That'll be his route." Meagan looked at me. "Dad's in top form. Why couldn't he say he liked the house?"

"It was a little awkward," I said. "It's been awhile. As soon as he relaxes he'll feel more at home and everything will be fine."

"Boy, you're naive."

Once I overheard Meagan tell a girlfriend that the reason she loves me is because I'm simple. I think she meant it in a good way—I'm solid and reliable, I can be predicted—but it was wounding nonetheless. I spent several days weighing the comment, and in the end I didn't say anything to her.

"Dad kept asking if 'Naga' was short for 'Nagasaki.' "

"So?"

"Something's not right with that baby."

Upstairs I could hear Mr. Boyd coughing, the baby crying. Something about all these people in our house excited me, and I wanted to make love, perhaps to regain possession of my wife, but Meagan said, "Will you pet me?"

I petted her forehead, soothing her toward sleep, while she talked in a dreamy, disjointed way.

"The last time we saw Mom, all of us together, was just before Jimmy went into the Marines. He was seventeen—Dad signed him in, gladly. She was back in the hospital; she couldn't manage the group home we had her in. We sat in the game room. People were playing Ping-Pong—I remember one guy had a rubber paddle, the other guy had a hard sandpaper paddle. Mom was shaking in her chair, staring away. She didn't, or wouldn't, recognize us—I don't know if she was pretending or what. There was always that blurry line with her. Finally she stood up and said, 'You're not mine, and neither is that dirty little boy!' She blew us kisses as we left, like some movie star."

I've never known what to say to Meagan about her mother. My own father passed away before I was two, and I have no evocative memory of the man, so that my sense of him has always been a little like that of a child who believes that a brightly colored ball, when hidden from sight, never existed. I've never longed for him in the abstract or made a crazed, mistaken search after his substitutes. In an old Te-Amo cigar box tucked in the bottom drawer of my dresser I keep some pictures and other mementos—his Phi Beta Kappa key, a pocket watch, a few random mateless cuff links—that aren't significantly more curious to me than the stuff that haunts the thrift stores in town.

In my business, I deal in collisions, mostly, and people make claims, redressing the world's suddenly revealed bias—for the scene of an accident is always a cruel, unusual, lonely, but somehow plotted injustice. I suppose that's what insurance is all about, hedging bets. You expect a normal life, but wager against it. When some guy's just been T-boned at an intersection, he thinks his whole life's been one long, inexorable drive toward that terrible moment. But it's hard for me to find the workings of fate in most auto accidents. They happen, stupidly. Not to be overly philosophical about a job that is, after all, notoriously dull, even to those of us who work in the field every day, but history doesn't offer the average person the consolation of being interesting.

When I look at the photographs—old black-and-whites, with deckle edges and the date printed along the bottom border—I understand that my father was topping off the tank of his car at a filling station (in Tucson, my mother says) and I see that he was, apparently, quite a handsome man. My mother stands beside him, wearing a neat white scarf and squinting into the same harsh sun, but other than that, the photo yields nothing in the way of memories, nothing I might attach myself to, and my perspective on the scene, those rare, bemused times when I open the box and linger over its contents, is that of the anonymous man who, strolling down a sidewalk sometime in AUG 1961, was stopped by a young couple, handed a camera, and asked to press the button—a stranger on his way elsewhere.

Jimmy's car was nearly out of gas, so we took mine to town the next morning. The birthday party wasn't until later that night. Jimmy figured we had some time to kill, and he wanted to see the sights, so we drove a back route, winding along the levee. There wasn't much to see, the mountains were gone, the landscape blurred. The rain beat down hard and ragged shreds of mist and fog rose off the dark strips of harrowed earth. A dirt road ran along the top of the levee and here and there as we drove we saw men unloading sandbags off the back of flatbeds.

"I did that before," Jimmy said. He wiped a clearing in the windshield and leaned forward. "Those bags are nothing but deadweight, nothing but sand. In the Philippines, half of the bags would be rotten from storage. There'd be sand spilling out everywhere when you tried to lift 'em."

"How long were you overseas?"

"Two tours," Jimmy said. "A year total."

When we left the levee, Jimmy turned to watch it vanish. "You want to see some tired-ass people, talk to those guys tonight."

The talk in town was of the flood, whether it would come or not, and, after that seemed beyond all reasonable doubt, when it would come, and how bad it would be. Comparisons were made to past floods, floods in memory, floods in history. We heard the news like we heard the rain, rumorous talk falling all around us, filling the air. We walked to Melvin's and I fixed Jimmy up with a decent fly rod and a reel; I bought him a tackle box, too, and loaded that up with everything he'd need to get started—tapered leaders, flotant, flies, knife. Jimmy was like a kid, happy to be indulged. At the register, he picked up a net, and then at the last minute, already headed out the door, he added a duck-cloth cap to the inventory. Jimmy wore the cap, stretching it on as we left. "Gotta have my top," he said. He hooked a fly in the crown, for the proper look.

"Happy birthday," I said.

"Thanks," he said.

We walked to a bar called The Usual, a dark room with a jukebox of corny standards and stools fashioned from old tractor seats. It was empty except for a few older men. Jimmy seemed pensive and distant, as if slowly and vividly picturing to himself everything he said. As he spoke he rattled a fistful of peanuts in his hand like dice, stopping now and then to pop one in his mouth and wash it down with a swallow of beer. His upper arm flexed tightly each time. He had a tattoo of a blue dagger on it. A snake was wreathed around the shaft, a drop of red blood falling from its forked tongue, and the Marine motto, *Semper fi,* was etched across the hilt.

In conversation, he went back to the Philippines.

"I've never seen such a fucked-up place," Jimmy said. "They do this thing, they get a young girl in a boat and dress her in white. Like a wedding dress. And she stands in the boat, spreading her arms out, like an angel. There's boys in the boat, too, and you throw coins in the water, this canal, this dirty fucking canal with dead dogs and stinking fish, oil slicks, all this floating shit." He pushed a peanut along the bar with the lid of a matchbook, then flipped the peanut into an ashtray. "The boys dive down in all that shit for the coins."

I listened, letting him go on. He seemed to want to draw a picture for me.

"They all want to come to America," he said. "But for twenty-five dollars a month you can get a straw hut and a whore to clean it. She cooks for you, washes your shit, fucks you. Then tour's up, and it's goodbye."

"Where'd you meet Naga?" I asked.

Jimmy looked at me.

"Her people are different," he said. "They're sugar people. From the mountains. I met her at church."

I said she was beautiful.

"She's perfect," Jimmy said. "The women over there are great, the good ones, at least. The man's everything to them. When they get married, they get married, and that's it. They know what it means. They don't make you dive in a shit river, that's for sure."

I felt a sort of tender condescension toward Jimmy and his need for this purity. In Naga he'd found a girl too young for corruption, whose language was that of a child. She would never call him a dirty little boy.

"Meagan's happy for you," I said.

"You mean she's happy things aren't worse," Jimmy said. He pushed his glass forward for another beer. "I'm trying to get this business started."

"The janitor thing."

"She probably had a good laugh about it."

"She wouldn't do that," I said.

"I need to borrow some money to get started."

"You could get a small-business loan," I suggested.

"Says who? I don't even have gas money to get back to California. I was hoping you guys could help."

"We're stretched pretty thin, Jimmy."

"You just bought a house," he said. Jimmy looked down the dark length of the bar and out the window, a bleached gray square in the wall. Rain washed over the canvas awning; the streets were empty. "You must have some money."

I didn't know what to say, and I held my hands up, to show they were empty. Jimmy shrugged.

"Can I have the receipt?" he asked.

"The receipt?"

"For the fishing stuff. Just in case I have to return it."

"We can return it now," I said. "I'll give you the cash."

"Maybe Dad will give me a birthday check," Jimmy said. "I don't think he likes Naga."

"He'll come around."

"I doubt it," Jimmy said. "But who knows? It's like with Joey. He cries all the time, and it's a real pain in the ass. At first I thought to myself, Shit, man, I don't want that! But now I look at him and think, That's mine. All mine. I'm just as proud as any father. I'll play ball with him. We'll fish. We'll do those things."

We finished our beers. Jimmy stood slowly and made a show of fumbling for his wallet but I paid our tab and left a generous tip. The old bartender shuffled over as we left, saw the tip, and said, "Stay dry, fellas."

Jimmy grabbed his tackle and went inside, and I ran up to the road on the levee for a quick look at the river. Normally an easy emerald green, the Skagit churned muddy brown, sweeping small uprooted trees and bone-gray logs away from its collapsing clay shores. The water was certainly rising. Mr. George's dog, an old grizzled retriever, stood on the roof of the cabin, soaked and barking, and Mr. George himself, stumbling around under an oppressive olive-drab raincoat, loaded a spare dinghy with supplies and furniture from inside. The dinghy was tethered by a long slack rope to the roof of his house; in it he'd crammed a chair, a stool, a box of books, a lamp, an axe, a fruit crate stuffed with papers, a stack of wooden bowls, a chandelier and silverware and what looked like a toaster, several knotted plastic sacks, a golden trophy of some sort. I watched him lash a blue tarp over the boat. Anything that could be secured was tied down, covered in canvas or caught in fishnet, hung from the eaves of his tiny shack; things that wouldn't fit in the net or float were left to fend for themselves. I yelled to Mr. George but my voice instantly vanished, lost in the pounding rain, and when he finally saw me on the levee he could only pantomime his helplessness, pointing to the river, and then raising both hands to the sky. I waved farewell and went back across the road to my house.

Meagan and Mr. Boyd were in the midst of making dinner and Jimmy stood under the apple tree, whipping his new fly rod back and forth. He hadn't loaded it up, so I took his reel out to him, fastened it, ran the line, and snipped the barb along the shank of a fly so he wouldn't impale himself while he practiced. I watched him work a few tentative and mechanical casts, thrashing his arms in the air, and went inside. Meagan and Mr. Boyd had stopped to watch him through the window. His motions were spastic, but he was smiling.

"How long do you think it'll be before he quits?" Mr. Boyd asked.

Meagan took up an onion and moved to the cutting board.

"Let's bet." Mr. Boyd winked at me, as if he'd found a crony, a sporting collaborator. "Just a friendly wager, huh, Tony?"

"He quits everything," Meagan said. "That's not a fun bet."

"You guys are tough."

"I say he'll never catch a fish," Joe said. "In fact, I'll lay odds he won't even get the thing wet."

"Give him a chance," I said.

Meagan sliced the onion cleanly in half, peeling the brittle outer skin away. From the living room, we could hear Naga calling to her husband. "Jimmy honey. Honey?" The baby was crying again. "Look, Joey. Look." She rapped on the window and Jimmy stopped casting and waved to his wife and child. He jerked another feeble cast out onto the wet lawn. Behind him were the field and the far-off lights of a house, the lights low to the horizon and dim against the darkening gray sky. Right then, it looked like Jimmy might stay out there forever. It was raining like hell, and I felt the urge to bet on him.

"Daddy's got an old friend in LA, a casting agent I should meet with," Meagan said. She kept chopping, staring down at the cutting board, although her eyes were blurred and glassy.

"You want me to chop for a minute?" I asked.

"No," she said. "I'm alright." She wiped her eyes. "I think I'll go next month, during Spring Break."

I looked at Mr. Boyd.

"I'm contributing airfare," he said. "I bought a couple round-trips to help out."

"It can't hurt, I suppose."

Mr. Boyd turned to Meagan and said, "See?" He reached for his shirt pocket, then patted the place above his heart; he'd given up cigarettes, yet still searched for them now and then—an old reflex—always surprised to find nothing there.

Jimmy came in. "D'you see me out there?"

Mr. Boyd smiled. "Catch anything?"

"I lost my leader," Jimmy said. "Got it tangled up in the tree."

He went to find Naga.

Moving, we had made our lives smaller, and I didn't want to talk about careers. I went outside and untangled Jimmy's fly line from the tree. He'd just left the new rod on the ground. It pissed me off. I went back in and groused to Meagan but she only shrugged and then we worked in silence. Slicing a neat circle from the other half of the onion, Meagan nipped the tip of her finger, one of those clean, shallow cuts that bleed and

bleed. I went to find a Band-Aid and when I came back Meagan
was crying and sucking her finger.

"God damn it, I shouldn't have done this."

"Yeah, well," I said, "next time we won't."

She pushed me away, wiped her eyes, and left. A deep purple stain seeped through the ringed layers in the remaining half
of the onion. I cut that part out and finished the dicing. Naga
came into the kitchen, asking me to hold the baby while she
fixed a bottle of formula. He was the tiniest little thing, with
hardly any weight to him, and his red puffy eyes and thatch of
thin black hair gave him the look of an old man. His entire
body clenched like a fist with each cry; his small, astonishing
baby hands flailed around blindly until he found my finger and
latched on, sticking the tip in his mouth and suckling. Naga
took the bottle from the pan and then filled it to the top with
water from the tap.

"You can't dilute the formula," I said. "No water."

"Lasts longer," Naga said.

"That's why he's crying," I said. "He's hungry."

"Very expensive, Anthony."

"But you can't do that. Do you understand? He's starving."

Late in the afternoon, needing a little quiet, I found a way into
the attic through a hatch in the upstairs hall closet. I stayed
up there to investigate and linger over the odd bits and pieces
the previous owner had left behind. He'd jettisoned half a lifetime, throwing out what I, at least, considered collectables: old
clothes Meagan could tailor and wear or donate to the costume
shop at the community college, blue and yellow medicine bottles for curing ailments I'd never heard of, and enough dusty
old cookbooks to stock an entire shelf in the kitchen. Among

them was *The Boston Cooking-School Cook Book,* by Fannie Mer-
ritt Farmer. I knew Miss Farmer's work from my mother's
kitchen and felt, to a certain extent—like a loving aunt or resident muse—that she'd helped raise me. She was listed on the
title page as the author of *A New Book of Cookery, Chafing Dish
Possibilities,* and *Food and Cookery for the Sick and Convales-
cent.* The book was dedicated to Mrs. William B. Sewall, "in
appreciation of her helpful encouragement and untiring efforts
in promoting the work of scientific cookery, which means the
elevation of the human race." Hardly scientific, it was more like
a work of witchcraft or alchemy, and it actually began with
an arcane discussion of the elements, air, water, and fire—
progress had antiquated Miss Farmer, as it had my mother and,
for that matter, my childhood. No one I knew ate like this
anymore.

In addition to the cookbooks, I found a learned work on
playing cards, a dour gray volume explaining the evolution
of the pack from its outlaw Gypsy days in the fourteenth century to its increasing acceptance in modern times. Apparently
the Jack, or Knave, was based on a rogue who at one time
rode beside Joan of Arc—not too far, wisely enough. That was
interesting, but leafing through its molding pages made me
a bit melancholy. It seemed like such an eccentric effort, an
orphaned, unloved book, authored by a man who doggedly
persisted in penning it, I supposed, by shoving aside the disturbing questions of doom and oblivion at every turn. He was
authoritative, insistent, and priggish, perhaps overly conscious
and somewhat resentful of the world's silence and the loneli-
ness of his pursuit. The writer's name was W. Gurney Benham,
F.S.A., F.R.Hist.S. I had no idea what those initials stood for or
what weight they carried as credentials, but I imagined an elderly bachelor before a dying fire, a damp stone cottage, slugs

crawling toward the door on the flagstone walkway outside. I could almost hear Mr. Benham's pen scratch across the sheaf of paper, could almost see the ink fade and run dry in mid-sentence; I thought of him pausing to moisten the nib with his tongue, and pressing on, and I decided right then to give the book a final home on the coffee table.

I came across many other things, too many to list, but I'd like to mention one more. In a plain white envelope, folded neatly, once, I found a Christmas card. In one corner was written "Christmas, 1947," and then in the middle of the page, scrib-bled in terse black strokes, was the forlorn message "I hope these help. Love, Milt." There was no indication on the card about what "these" were, or who or what, exactly, was in need of "help," or how all of this was to connect up and suceed, but something about the message, along with the signature, and the lack of specific reference, gave the note a timelessness by accident that neither Farmer nor Benham had achieved by effort. But I couldn't quite finger what really distinguished Milt from Farmer and Benham, and it puzzled me. They shared a similar degree of anonymity, although I supposed Milt's was deeper, and I felt equally responsible for each of them, as if entrusted and obligated by an almost filial bond. This was my house, I thought, ghosts and all. At last I decided the differ-ence had to do with the hint of uncertainty in Milt's note. Whereas Farmer and Benham presumed absolute knowledge and final clarity in their respective works, Milt was tentative and doubtful, perhaps rootedly skeptical about the efficacy and outcome of his gift. Yet in the note "love" stood firm, like a con-stant in an equation full of variables and unknowns. I tucked the mute, prayerful note away in my shirt pocket. I liked Milt, who, by the way, was not the previous owner of our house. I had no idea who he was.

Mr. George was knocking on our door as I came down from the attic. When I answered I could see behind him a flatbed, parked on the levee and loaded with sandbags. It was obvious he wanted help. He wore a green sou'wester smashed down on his little fissured appleface, and his blue eyes, nested in folds of wrinkled flesh, seemed like a kind of natural extravagance, like the brilliant spawning colors of a salmon. I like to think that I know what's right, that I've got a fairly resonant sense of my obligations, but when Mr. George showed up on our porch I was hesitant and confused. We had the party, and everything already seemed so calamitous to me, so tense and tentative, that I could only think like a child whose good manners are memorized, going through the motions without feeling the spirit. In fact, I felt oppressed by his need, and didn't know what to say. But Jimmy, who'd come to the door, said he'd go help, and then Mr. Boyd, never one to be left out, or to be upstaged by his son, put on a pair of my hip boots and clomped off across the street, the very spectacle of authority, immediately taking charge. I went upstairs to tell Meagan what was going on and she hurried downstairs, switched off the oven so the ham wouldn't burn, and ran across the road to Mr. George's. When I arrived, Mr. George was rubbing grease into the shoulders of an oilcloth jacket.

"That'll hold you," he said, offering the coat to Meagan. He looked doubtfully at the sky. "I hope you weren't in the middle of something. I know it's almost supper time."

"Not at all," Jimmy said.

The river had risen to a foot below its natural bank and carried odd things in its current. A chair floated by, and then a realtor's sign. Mr. Boyd marked with a stick the line the wall of sandbags should follow, and then Jimmy retraced it, adding slightly more curve where the downstream force of the river would likely hit the wall. We formed a small chain from the truck to the line gouged into the grass. Mr. George offloaded the sandbags and passed them to Mr. Boyd, who handed them to Meagan, who handed them to me, and I passed them on to Jimmy, who, slipping and sliding, stacked them. Jimmy, with something to do, was a muddy ball of joy. His historical spot at the end of the line now seemed a place of privilege. In no time his face was flecked with wet clay, his jeans were soaked, and the new cap we'd bought that afternoon looked like a seasoned hat he'd been wearing for years.

The bags were dead weight, and after the first course my arms were leaden and numb. As I looked at the water, lapping at the bank, our job seemed impossible. I'd never seen the river so blown out. I was exhausted, wet and cold, and certain every bag I cradled during the second course was the last I could manage; still they kept coming, and I kept passing them to Jimmy, feeling weirdly condemned—not entirely myself, but a little bit of what was behind me, and a little bit of what was ahead of me. When I asked Meagan how she was doing, she said fine. "Really?" I asked. Meagan just frowned, picked a daub of mud from her eye, and passed me another wet bag of sand.

We were on the sixth or seventh course, the wall of staggered bags about hip level, and I was still feeling the same way, like I couldn't move another bag, and still I was taking them, pivoting, and passing them, when suddenly Jimmy, who'd gone to the other side of the wall to inspect the rising river, launched into a berserk dance, flailing his arms and kicking his feet. "Goddamn! Goddamn!" he shouted. The chain of sandbags stopped and we all watched. Jimmy kicked and splashed, waving his arms crazily, and then dove out of sight. When he stood again he seemed to be holding up a section of the river, hoisting a piece of the flowing silver water victoriously over his head. In fact, he was clutching a bright salmon by the gills. It thrashed mightily, slapping its tail back and forth, but Jimmy, grinning, kept a tight grip on his trophy.

"Son, you got yourself a king," Mr. George said.

"I thought it was a log at first," Jimmy said.

Mr. George grabbed a sawed-off section of stout dowel from his porch and gave the king a firm rap on the head and the life shivered out of it.

"I can't count the fish I've taken out of this river," Mr. George said. "But I've never seen any man land one with his feet."

"Let's finish here," Mr. Boyd said.

We added two more courses, then admired our work.

Mr. George said, "I'll cook this for you all, if you want."

"Oh man," Jimmy said, "I'm dead. I'm gonna run and go get Naga and Joey."

Meagan went with her brother, and the rest of us went inside. Mr. George's cabin was small but shipshape. One long room, a kitchen in back, sleeping loft above it, a wood-burning stove out front, a table and two chairs, and, curiously, a small upright piano. The west wall of the house had a big window and a view of the river. Opposite was a rack filled with fishing rods, and above that, taxidermied fish—pink, king, silver, and dog salmon, sea-run cutthroat, steelhead.

"You aren't prohibitionists, are you?" Mr. George asked.

Mr. Boyd smiled. "I've been known to take a drink now and then."

"This is a jug of blackberry wine," our host said, pouring out three glasses. "It's not as bad as you'd imagine."

The wine was actually perfect for the day—thick as brandy, with a haphazard, homemade taste, a hint of soil in it.

"Hey, hear that?" Mr. George asked.

I listened and didn't hear anything. Mr. Boyd, sipping his wine, looked out the window. "Rain's slowing," he said.

"Music to my ears," Mr. George said. We went outside and saw the others approaching. "Now if I can only get that pooch off the roof. Hey Pepper!"

Far to the west the sun lowered beneath the solid black slab of the squall. The river washed over the bank, but was turned back by the wall of sandbags.

"Are we out of trouble yet?" I asked.

"We're probably just between storms." Mr. George shook his head and led us back inside. "But I think there's call for a blessing. You don't mind a blessing before we eat, do you?"

"I'll do it," Jimmy said.

"Be my guest," Mr. George said.

"Bless us our Lord, and these your gifts," Jimmy said, the shy mumble barely taking shape as words, "which we're about to receive, from your bounty, through Christ our Lord. Amen."

"Dear God, Holy Ghost," Mr. Boyd said, "whoever eats the fastest, gets the most!"

We ate salmon steaks with corn and coleslaw. I noticed a water stain zigzagging along the walls and Mr. George told us about the sixty years of floods in his personal memory. He insisted, proudly, that he never lost anything. "I chased a few sticks of furniture way down river and had to fish a lawn mower out of a pool, but that's about the worst of it." In fact, he said, he'd found far more than he'd ever lost. "Half the stuff here come to me from the river," he said. He'd seen everything in the skajit, at one time or another. Drowned cows, dogs floating like Snoopy atop their doghouses, a half-sunk johnboat with chickens and a cat riding the current.

"And a whale," he said. "A cruddy little gray, all covered in barnacles and mud, that no one's ever been able to explain to my complete satisfaction."

"And now this," Jimmy said, hoisting a forkful of salmon.

"That was truly something," Mr. George agreed.

"Do you play the piano?" I asked.

"I do, by God," he said. "Just some old songs I learned in Sunday school."

When dinner was finished Meagan invited Mr. George to join us later for cake and coffee. Then we headed home. I sat out on our screened porch. It began to rain again, and across the field, along a rutted mud road, I could see a flatbed rumbling away toward town. It was late February, one of those cool wet nights when I could imagine the glacier that once covered this valley, imagine the ice and all the things that once moved across it, and then the sea that slowly formed and eventually receded, leaving dry land and the rich deposits of silt and low floodplain so perfect for raising tulips. A month from now, for three brilliant weeks, the tulips would bloom and a sea of red and yellow would sweep toward our house, rolling our way like a wave; the huge field was planted in staggered intervals to assist with the delicate, precious, timely business of harvesting tulips. I tried to imagine Meagan moving across the field in sunlight, a clutch of red tulips in her hand, but I couldn't really sustain it: somewhere along the way my mood had slipped into a minor key.

A light came on inside the house, and then all I could see was the dull mesh of screen. I drank my coffee, listening to the falling rain and feeling the mist on my face as it edged in from the dark fields. It was the first time I'd felt anything but a rising elation since we'd moved. In this damp old house, surrounded

by these soggy fields, a vivid sense of the people who'd sat on
the porch before me came unbidden, without invitation, and as
palpable to me as Meagan or Mr. Boyd or Jimmy. My own presence felt vaguely intrusive, and it occurred to me, as I listened
to the water run over the roof and puddle in the yard, that the
rains in this part of the country seemed to fall from clouds that
were a thousand years old. You always felt just slightly out of
joint, or a little bit canceled. I gave my shirt pocket a pat. My
legs were stiff and there was a cold in my bones no coat would
fix, a raw chill radiating from within; I could feel my wet toes
bloat in my boots. I tried to chase my mood down, rummaging
through thoughts and memories of New York, of the life we'd
lived there, of the work we'd done and what we'd abandoned,
of the people we'd left behind. I found nothing, nothing worth
saving, and finally told myself it was atmospheric negative ions
from the squall.

Behind me, somewhere in the house, I heard Naga calling
for her husband: "Jimmy? Honey? Honey?" And then I heard
Meagan, from upstairs, perhaps in Mr. Boyd's room, calling for
her father: "Daddy?"

Both men were outside, under the apple tree. I was aware of
their voices but couldn't quite see them, and something about
the disembodied conversation gave it a strange sound, as if
father and son were reading from a script.

"What can I say?"

"I don't know, Jimmy."

"I'm sorry. I'm desperate, or I wouldn't ask."

"You're what now, twenty-seven?"

"Twenty-six. It's my birthday today."

"You got a wife and a kid to support."

"I know. Don't you think I know?"

"Take this. That's the best I can do right now."

"Just till I get back home."

"Yeah."

"Just a loan. Okay? I'll pay you back."

"It's a gift. Just take it. Happy birthday."

"You don't understand. I want to pay you back."

"Okay, you want to. We'll see."

Meagan came out onto the porch. "Have you seen Daddy?"

"He's out there," I said. "With Jimmy."

Meagan walked quickly into the yard. I heard the familiar timbre of their voices weaving faintly through the rain, Meagan mollifying, Mr. Boyd staunch and bullying, Jimmy eager for whatever scraps of attention fell his way.

When all the Boyds came in sometime later, they were drenched; Meagan seemed especially small, her hair darkened and lying flat around the oval frame of her face. I ran out to the car and grabbed my Polaroid from a box in the trunk. Mr. George came down the road, cradling a second bottle of blackberry wine. "They're all inside," I said, and he went on to the house ahead of me, while I fished through my supplies for extra film and flashbulbs. By the time I came back inside and loaded the camera the candles were already lit and Meagan was carrying the cake onto the porch. Mr. George shut off the light. Jimmy sat there, staring at the swirls of blue frosting that looped across the cake: *Happy Birthday Jimmy!* He looked around, then at the cake again. Shadows from the candle flames danced on the rotting roof above us. We sang "Happy Birthday"; and then Mr. Boyd continued to sing, his voice deep and bold and bad, forcefully off-key. Meagan joined in, and when she put a reassuring hand on Jimmy's shoulder, he sang, too. The baby gave a cry, and Naga moved in closer to her husband. When Mr. George joined them, humming along, I stepped back, expanding the frame by just enough to include everyone. Jimmy gazed up at his father, his sister, his wife and his baby, and then, with his eyes shut, made a wish, and blew the candles out—while I, futzing with the Polaroid, caught the moment just before the wish, which we watched develop, all of them huddled together, faces pressed cheek to cheek, singing the words to a song I'd never learned.

The Bone Game

They'd only taken a simple wrong turn somewhere—taken a wrong exit off the freeway, then got caught downtown in a maze of one-way streets—but to D'Angelo it was as if they'd traveled back in time to the nineteenth century. He looked out the Caddy's tinted window and saw, through a haze of watery green, a few Chinese men in loose slacks struggling up the steep hillclimb, old coolie stock, it seemed to him, stooped over as if still shouldering the weight of a maul. "Look at those chinks," he said. "I bet they laid some track in their day." Kype found the street he wanted and steered the car north through Pioneer Square. An Indian sat on the curb with his head in his hands, tying back two slick wings of crow-black hair with a faded blue bandana. A pair of broken-heeled cowboy boots lay in the gutter while he aired his bare feet. D'Angelo rolled down his window, waved a gun in the air, took a bead, and dry-fired. The hammer struck three times against empty chambers, but in his mind D'Angelo had dropped the Indian, right there on the sidewalk. He raised the barrel to his lips and blew away an imaginary wisp of smoke.

"What if that had been loaded?" Kype said.

D'Angelo grinned, and fired the gun at Kype's face. "It isn't, is it?"

"Jesus." Kype said, grabbing the gun. He tossed it in the back seat. "Cut the cowboy crap."

D'Angelo just smiled and watched a couple of Filipino hookers shuffle under the awning of an expedition outfitter and guide service. Behind them, in the display window, a stuffed grizzly bear reared up on its hind legs. Kype palmed the steering wheel into another sharp turn, the Cadillac's tires squealing rubber on the warm asphalt. A container of ashes rocked in the seat. D'Angelo picked up the decorative urn and unscrewed the lid. Caught in a gust of wind, a cloud of gray ash eddied through the car. Kype coughed and fanned the air as some of the powdery remains of his grandfather drifted under his nose and blew into the street. He ran his tongue over his lips, tasting ash.

"Damn, man," Kype said, spitting.

"Ashes to ashes," D'Angelo said. He screwed down the lid and gave the urn a shake. Something inside rattled. "Bones," he said. "Teeth."

Kype snatched the urn from D'Angelo and set it in the back seat with the gun. He wiped the sweat from his forehead. It was hot, and he hadn't bathed in more than a week.

"How old was he?" D'Angelo asked.

"Ninety-nine," Kype said.

"I hope I don't live that long."

"Grandpa lived a good life."

"Some of those old boys just spend the golden years fouling their drawers."

"Grandpa maintained his dignity," Kype said.

"I can't get into old people," D'Angelo said. "I never seen my grandparents."

"They still alive?"

"Somewhere. Maybe. I don't know."

D'Angelo took a quick pull off the bourbon and eased back in his seat. He was wearing a red Western shirt with pearlish plastic snaps and a turquoise bolo tie, an outfit he'd bought in a tack shop in Tonasket, near the Canadian border. He'd hoped the shirt and tie would give him a Western look, but he was chubby and short and he still wore the baggy pin-striped slacks and red hi-top sneakers he'd left Brooklyn in six months ago. To Kype he looked like one of those midget clowns that rode Shetland ponies at rodeo intermissions.

"A century," Kype said, thinking of his grandfather. "He almost lived a century. Washington wasn't even a state when he was born. It was just a territory."

"You live that long," D'Angelo said, "there just aren't many people left to bury you. That's why you're out here, driving around like the Buddha, looking for the spot."

Kype let the conversation die and navigated the old Cadillac Eldorado along the waterfront. The car had belonged to his grandfather, a tall, lean white-haired patriarch who had remained vigorous—still splitting and stacking his own cordwood, still fishing at dawn for kings and silvers off Camano Head—until one evening two weeks ago when he said, "I'm awfully goddamn tired," and then sat down on the davenport, shut his eyes, and died. Later that night, sharply missing the old man, Kype had looked through his grandfather's address book and seen something that resembled the score sheet of a high-200 bowler—all spares and strikes, thick black diagonal slashes and X's drawn through name after name, as one by one all his friends had passed away.

The Eldorado was the last car let on the ferry. Kype and D'Angelo stood up front, gripping the gate chains, the stiff onshore wind whipping their faces.

"Maybe it's this way," Kype said. He gestured expansively, sweeping his hand west, the sky a wash of leached red as the sun began to set.

D'Angelo drew a dented Marine Band harmonica from his

shirt pocket and tried desperately to turn "Home on the Range" into an upbeat blues number. It was the only song he knew, and it sounded awful. He played it incessantly, but Kype, in the two days since he'd picked up D'Angelo, hadn't heard much improvement.

When the ferry's horn blasted, Kype tossed a penny into the Sound, something he'd done for luck on every crossing since he was a kid.

D'Angelo said, "He couldn't have been much of a dad to you."

"You don't know," said Kype.

"You guys never played catch, I know that."

"Yes we did," Kype said.

"You got a fem throw," D'Angelo said. "You got sissy muscles. Nobody ever showed you, I can tell."

Kype futzed with the zipper of his thin yellow windbreaker, and said, "Throwing isn't everything."

"We'll find the spot."

The "spot" was the exact right place to cast loose the old man's ashes. Kype didn't know where it was exactly, not on any map at least, but he knew he'd recapture a certain feeling when he got there. He'd been traveling back and forth across the state for a week, retracing his grandfather's steps, visiting his birthplace, his old haunts, looking for that feeling, that spot. Now Kype was headed for the ocean.

The funeral service—a society gala, a rather garish cross between the stilted air of a museum fund-raiser and the drunken sloppiness of a send-off—had seemed ludicrous to Kype—with everyone from old family friends to business cronies to newspaper reporters speculating about the life and times of ancient Henry Kype Green. His grandfather's wealth came from sources deep in the history and raw materials of the region—trees and fish, mostly—and the old man had been something of a legend, a legend the local newspapers had been rehashing with sycophantic abandon for the past week. The last of the pioneers, the papers were calling him. True enough, during the Volstead days he'd run booze down the Strait of Haro, he'd been big in timber, the fisheries, he'd served a stint or two in the state legislature. Of his generation, he was certainly the last. Now that he was incinerated and resting in an ash urn, suddenly everyone was an authority. In several hectic days a substantial body of myth had collected around those pale gray ashes.

Kype sat beside his drunken mother in the front pew and listened to the encomiums with the same anxiety he'd felt all week when poring over the accounts that had washed up in the wake of what one journalist rather regally called his grandfather's "demise." The reverend mounted the pulpit and announced that for a man as great as Henry Kype Green death was a simple passage, a great reward for service rendered: old Kype, having done so much to improve the earthly garden, had long ago earned a providential seat in Paradise. It seemed to Kype a measure of his grandfather's eminence in the community that the key passages for the sermon and eulogy were taken from the Book of Revelation—*the Alpha and the Omega, the beginning and the ending, the twenty of this, the seven of that, the angels, the trumpets!*—but then, too, the memorial service had been noisy with senile rumblings, old men and women muttering to themselves, calling out like dreamers, and the whole affair had been a little dotty and obscure and ultimately incomprehensible.

Following the service there was a lavish spread: crustless

Walla Walla sweet onion sandwiches, poached sockeye salmon, Dungeness crab, Willapa Bay oysters shucked and bedded in a glacier of shaved ice, mountains of red Delicious apples, all gifts from friends delivered—half in homage, half in throwback to Roman taxation—from the various corners of the state. Kype gave several interviews, but he had the uneasy feeling his words were being reshaped and slotted into a story that had already been written. "My grandfather started out," he told a reporter from the *Times,* "as a whistle punk in a donkey show." The woman asking him questions brightened at the prospect of an unseemly revelation about old Kype's obscure origins, but grew disappointed, then bored, when she learned that a whistle punk and donkey show had nothing to do with sex. Others were interested in Kype himself, the grandson rumored to be the primary beneficiary named in the will. Kype had never known his father, who'd drowned in a boating accident—waterskiing drunk, he'd neglected to let go of the rope and smashed into a dock—shortly before Kype was born. Kype had been raised in his grandfather's house in the Highlands. With the reading of the will, he'd be filthy rich. The legacy he'd been raised to expect was about to arrive. This made people want to gawk at him, to see the mechanics of money, or wealth, grinding away inside.

Kype slipped out of the hall and walked next door to the church, where his grandfather's ashes still rested in the urn. He tucked the urn under his arm like a football and quickly made his way out of the church, down the steps, to the corner where the old man's car was parked. His mother planned to set the urn on a marble shelf in the family mausoleum, but Kype had other ideas, or thought he did, as he turned the key and started up the ancient Eldorado.

The big car's headlights bored a tunnel through the dense over-hang of cedar and blue spruce, a tunnel that opened briefly before them in a shaft of white light and closed immediately behind them in a darkness tinged red from the taillights. It was the dry season near the end of August and there hadn't been any rain in weeks. In a few of the gypo outfits, makeshift mills set back from the road, they could see wheels of blue sparks spin from the saws and smell fresh-cut wood as the blades bit pulp. Every now and then they passed a crop of white crosses that marked the location of a deadly wreck. The Eldorado sailed along, its generous suspension floating around the bends and curves so that, although he was driving, Kype managed to give himself a touch of seasickness.

At a fork in the highway, a young woman appeared, holding her thumb out. She was wearing tight white shorts, ankle-strap sandals, and a man's shirt with the tails knotted together high on her waist. She was leaning against a huge searock, an erratic scrawled over with Day-Glo declarations of love.

"Slow down, slow down," D'Angelo said. "Let's get a look."

Kype eased the car onto the shoulder. The woman picked up a woven basket and hopped into the back seat. She didn't even ask where they were going. She seemed to know.

"Well," said D'Angelo, "I guess you'll take a ride. I guess you're game for going wherever the hell we go, huh? Want a drink?"

"Sure," she said. She slugged from the bottle and wiped her lips. A rhinestone clip in the shape of a horse sparkled in her hair. "If you're on this road, there's only one place to go. You got no choice. Nothing but reservation up ahead." She took another drink before passing the bottle back to D'Angelo. "And the ocean," she said. "There's a big ocean at the end of this road."

"You from around here?" Kype asked. He tried to catch a

glimpse of her in the rearview mirror, but she had sprawled out in the big back seat, out of sight.

"Yep," she said. "Name's Nell, Nella Ides."

"Well, Nella Ides," D'Angelo said, "this guy's grandpa died. He was very fucking old, a real big shot. You may have heard of him. Kype, his name was Kype. Just like this guy. His name's Kype, too. Anyway, me and my friend Kype here, we're drinking the old man's bourbon, and we got his old gun, and we're going to catch the biggest, wildest fish in the ocean with his old fishing pole."

"Putting the fun back in funeral," Nell said.

"That's right, "D'Angelo said. "And since you're from around here, and you know the lie of the land, you're invited."

"Suits me fine," Nell said. "I got a cousin might be interested, too. For your friend there."

"My grandfather knew Mungo Martin," Kype said, looking in the rearview mirror.

"Who's Mungo Martin?" Nell asked.

"Mungo Martin? Mungo Martin was a tyee, a chief—Satsop or Haida, Bella Coola, maybe Makah."

"He wasn't no Makah," Nell said.

"Some chief, anyway. I don't really know. Supposedly a great artist or something. He carved totem poles, if that's art. Grandfather met him negotiating a timber contract after the war."

"See what I was saying," D'Angelo said. "This guy's granddad, old Kype, he was a high-ass muck-a-muck. A very big deal who knew Mungo, another very big deal. It was a high old time in town when old Kype and old Mungo got together."

"I'd know if he was a Makah. That I'd know."

"How old are you, Nella Ides?"

"Old," she said.

Nell's skin was dark and smelled richly of sweat, smoke, and coconut oil. On her purple lips was the fiery taste of bourbon and deep in her mouth was the sour smell of the beer she'd been drinking earlier that day, in Port Angeles. She'd been starting to sober, standing against that rock, smelling the sea, the dry cedar, and, she'd thought, the stars. The man from PA had dropped her off on his way out to Forks. Before that she'd blacked out, and before that she recollected going to a pink motel with the man, where a suspicious night clerk had forced her to sign the registry. She'd used her Makah name, the long English translation that took up three spaces in the guest book: What-you-get-you-can't-store-up-because-it-is-so-much.

D'Angelo climbed into the back seat and sat beside her. "Your eyes are green," he said, kissing her.

"Get us that bottle back here," Nell said.

Kype handed the bottle over, feeling jilted, suddenly the hired chauffeur for his hitching passengers. A convoy of logging trucks boomed by, their wake a vacuum that made the big Cadillac shudder. Kype couldn't see Nell or D'Angelo, but he listened to the sounds they made, to their voices.

"Don't look back," he heard D'Angelo say.

In Neah Bay the road ran out, dissolving into a patch of packed dirt and windblown sand, the Makah Indian Reservation. A few white shacks lined either side of the street. One of the houses looked like the site of a massive collision. Smashed, junked vehicles surrounded it. Axles, tires, doors, bumpers, bucket seats, and radiators were strewn in the dirt. A few intact cars that—powered by prayers—had probably seen the open road for the last time when Eisenhower was president seemed to be under repair. A beat DeSoto with a broken windshield and sun-hardened tires, the rusted rims sunk deep in white sand, was parked beneath a shade tree. Above it, a half-stripped engine dangled from a winch, rocking back and forth as the branches swayed in the breeze. An open toolbox and a coffee cup sat on the fender.

"That must be the chief's house," D'Angelo said.

When Nell sat up, one of her small breasts showed, the nipple dark brown like a knot in wood. It glistened with saliva. She tied the tails of her shirt together.

"Salmon season closes today, fellas."

"How about that?" Kype said. "The ocean must be the spot. My grandfather's spirit guides us."

"Here's to Grandpa," Nell said, taking a long drink from the bottle.

"Here *is* Grandpa," D'Angelo said, holding up the urn. He unscrewed the cap, poked his fingers in, and marked a cross on Nell's forehead. "Ashes to ashes," he said. "And dust to dust."

"Please don't fuck around with that," Kype said.

Grains of sand blew across the street, needling the sides of the car. At the far end of the dirt plaza, a motel sign sputtered, the red neon bleeding into the fog.

"I'm going to check on my baby," Nell said. She pulled back her hair and adjusted the clip. "I'll be right back."

"Don't forget your cousin," D'Angelo said. He slapped Kype on the back. "For my friend here."

The first pale cast of light shone inland, a faint silver rim, like a lid ajar, in the world they'd left behind. Slowly the street wakened to life. A few lamps went on, glowing a cold yellow in the salt-whitened windows of the shacks. A young girl walked toward the water, watching the sun rise, and a hesitant old man left a trail of footprints in the dust as he crossed the road. A boy with a net began scooping bait from a blue plastic pool. Kype stood beside him. In the pool, hundreds of small dark fish swam in circles, darting ahead of the sweeping net. The boy flicked his wrist and twisted the net into the air, and the silver scales of the struggling fish flashed like coins.

The boy emptied the net into a clear plastic bag and tied it shut. The herring flipped around inside, thrashing against each other. In Kype's hand, the bag squirmed with life, beating like a heart, and then slowly stilled to a few last fitful flickers as the herring suffocated.

"Got our bait?" D'Angelo said.

Kype showed him the dead herring.

When he saw Nell, D'Angelo asked, "Where's your cousin?"

"She's sick of fish," Nell said.

Inside the bait shop, a steel coffee urn percolated, bubbling with the first brew of the day. A plume of steam rose from beneath the rattling lid. A few operators sat on a bench, waiting for customers.

"We need a boat," Kype said.

A man named Porter stood, rising stiffly on arthritic knees, his joints thickly crusted from a lifetime at sea. He looked at Kype and immediately disliked his smooth white skin, his blue eyes, the easy loose movement of his arms and legs as he approached the counter. He was a kid but wore the fussy clothes of an old man, a thin yellow coat, a pink oxford shirt, khakis with an elastic waistband, a pair of leather boat shoes. Porter guessed the young man was drunk and he didn't like taking drunks out on his boat. All they did was barf and moan.

"And I want it exclusive," Kype said. "There's three of us."

"Can't give it to you exclusive," Porter said.

Kype unfolded his wallet. "I'll buy up the other spots."

Porter looked at the neat square edge of new bills crowding the wallet.

"You'll pay for twelve?" he asked. Porter's boat would only accommodate six, but what did this kid know?

"No problem," Kype said.

He spread a fan of bills across the counter, paying for the phantom spots, paying for their tackle and bait, their lunches and their fishing licenses, too.

"Slip five," Porter said. "She's called *Kingdom Come*."

Cabin lights had come on in some of the pleasure craft. A few men huddled on the docks, sipping coffee.

Kype loosened the bowline from a wooden cleat. D'Angelo and Nell kissed under the blue light of an arc lamp.

"That girl your friend's with," Porter said, "she's not right in the head. She's the res punch, you know what I mean? You can charter her easy as you can charter me. She's got a kid, and herself only a kid. They live with the great-grandmother. I hate to see it."

Porter ran the bilge and checked the radio.

"This old can seaworthy, Captain?" D'Angelo said.

"Was yesterday," Porter said. He looked at Nell. "You go on home."

She got in the boat.

Porter ran the throttle full-open, watching from the wheelhouse as Kype and D'Angelo and Nell stood in the bow. When they were three miles out, he idled back and headed south along the coast.

He shouted over the droning engine, "It's now or never."

Kype assembled his salmon rod, sliding the ferrules together, and then Porter baited his hook. The herring had been kept on ice and were cold and firm. Porter double-hooked the bait, run-

ning one snelled hook through the head and the other through
the tail, snugging them together so the herring curled and
would then spin and twist beneath the water, turning with a
wounded motion. When he was finished, scales flecked his
fingertips, each like a sunrise at sea, a pearlescent swirl of pink
and blue rolling across a pale silver sky. It was the last day of
the season, an okay season, he'd winter over without much side
work, and Porter decided to set up a rod for himself in the
downrigger. Normally he wouldn't do that, but this was the
end. He'd always moved around a lot, working seasonally, and
the end of anything saddened him.

Nell had fallen asleep on the hatch, her long skirt bunched
up around her thighs, her brown face turning soft and shapeless as putty in the warm sun. D'Angelo sat in the bow, nervously tightening the straps on a bright orange life preserver.
He'd never learned to swim, and each swell terrified him. His
queasy stomach felt lined with fur. Kype held his grandfather's
rod as if it were a golden staff and he a sentry assigned
guardianship of the sea.

"Reading the will's going to be something," Kype said. "You
know what my program is, from now on? Exhaustion. That's it,
exhaustion. That's my ambition. I'm just going to go everywhere and do everything and then get totally sick and tired of
it all."

"Thataboy, Kypester," D'Angelo said. "You'll be like Ecclesi-
astes Jr., all fucking worn out and shit." D'Angelo slid closer
to Nell. "Hey Nell, Miss Ides, you want to hear about his
inheritance?"

"You're blocking my sun," she said.

Kype had never fished much—his grandfather liked to go
alone—and each tug of the bait and spin of the spoon lure felt
like a strike to him. Twice he reeled in, and twice found noth-

ing. He stripped out line in two-foot lengths, measuring as Porter had showed him, until he reached seventy feet. He traced the white thread of monofilament from his rod tip into the sea and then followed it below the surface until the line disappeared in the green water, beyond the reach of light. He felt a strange resignation, his floating on the surface separating him from the dark sea, not knowing a thing about salmon. Given over to the rise and fall of the boat, he was lulled into a forgetfulness, the heave of the ocean now working beneath his bones, softening them. He eased the cork butt of the rod against his navel and shut his eyes and allowed the rhythm of the sea to sway his body. He felt the ocean in his stomach, calmly rolling on. He imagined the bait beneath the surface, gently turning over, swimming back and forth in slow undulations like a kite in the sky.

The strike called Kype back to himself. In panic he jerked the rod and started reeling in, watching the line cut wildly across the surface. The pole curled over like a scythe. He reeled as fast as he could, instinctively afraid the life on the other end of the line would escape him. And it was life, life struggling so mightily that the rod seemed to Kype like a sensitive instrument measuring the fight not only of the salmon but also of the entire ocean. He was so beside himself with excitement he made a promise—to God, it seemed—that if he was lucky enough to land this fish he would commemorate the event by spreading his grandfather's ashes over the water. Life! Kype kept thinking. Life! And then for a moment the priority of things reversed, and he felt that he'd been caught and could not let go, that whatever was fighting on the other end of the line had suddenly engaged a tug-of-war and was trying to haul him overboard into the sea.

Then the rod snapped straight, and the life in the line was gone.

Kype reeled in quickly, hoping that perhaps the salmon had simply given up the ghost.

But it wasn't so: whatever it was had spit the hook. The herring was stripped to the bone, just a head with eyes trailed by a white comb of cartilage and vertebrae.

He set his rod aside.

Porter had also gotten a strike. He played it leisurely, allowing the fish to exhaust itself in several long streaking runs, and then brought it up against the boat and scooped it with the landing net. He lifted the net high, the salmon thrashing the air, throwing off a spray of water with each spasm. Porter grabbed a gaff hook and raised the butt end over his shoulder and then hesitated—he looked at Kype and said, "You want it?"

"Yeah, sure," Kype said. "I lost mine."

Porter clubbed the silver in back of the head. He did it once, hard, mercifully. Blood trickled from its eyes, its caudal fin twitched and a shiver uncoiled along the length of its body, and it was done.

Nell's house was entirely embosked in blackberry. A thorny tangled patch of brambles, a grotesque confusion of growth, twenty feet high, rolled like a rogue wave over the unseen roof. A hole in the vines was worn and maintained by use like a rabbit warren, and that gave way to a set of gray weathered planks, each board slanted and wobbling, which led to a gated entry. Beyond the gate was a teak door with layers of dry varnish peeling away, a small door, cockeyed in its frame, the upper hinge broken and replaced by a strap of leather. Dusty beams of sunlight filtered down through the dome of stickers and a few bees, humming in the last warmth of the day, moved lazily among the delicate white flowers. Berries hung everywhere, black and ripe, redolent and sweet, weighing the branches down. The house listed to one side, and Kype realized why when he looked up a narrow set of steps and saw the flying bridge. The house was not a house; it was a boat. An old woman sat in the dark cool galley with a blanket on her lap. Nell touched the woman's shoulder and continued on toward the bow of the boat, into the forecastle. D'Angelo followed and soon Kype heard them giggling and wrestling on the bunk. Kype stared at the old woman, whose face flowed smoothly, like rock eroded by waves. Her eyes were a silverish silt-green and sat in their sockets like marquetry. Kype stood with his fish in one hand and the urn of ashes in the other and didn't know what to say. A lattice of light and shadow entwined her face and around her forehead she wore an odd red crown of wicker, woven from cedar. She seemed possessed of a patience so vast this moment's discomfort didn't register, or perhaps she was only indifferent. She didn't move or acknowledge Kype in any manner. The ancient smell of fish rose from a hold that hadn't seen a salmon in decades. Kype listened to the stupefying murmur of the bees, a drowsy dusty buzz that now resided as an itch in his ear. He stuck his finger in, deep as it would go, digging and scratching at the irritation, then pulled at the lobe. He looked out the larboard porthole at the enmeshed vines and saw an old snub-fingered baseball mitt snared in the stickers.

We didn't know what on earth it was when the ship came into the harbor. So the chief, he sent out some warriors in a couple of canoes to see what it was. They were taking a good look at those white people on the deck there.

Kype raised his salmon by the gill and stared into its face as if it had spoken.

One white man had a real hooked nose, you know. And one of

the men was saying to this other guy," "See, see. He must have been
a dog salmon, that guy there. He's got a hooked nose." The other
guy was looking at him, and a man came out of the galley and he
was a hunchback. And the other one said, "Yes! We're right, we're
right. Look at that one. He's a humpback. He's a humpback
salmon."

Kype shook the urn at his ear but only heard the dice-like
rattle of bones and teeth.

So they went ashore and they told the big chief, "You know
what we saw? They've got white skin. But we're pretty sure that
those people on the floating thing there, they must have been fish.
But they've come here as people."

Kype looked at the old wooden woman, whose silver eyes
had closed, the leather of her lids lowered like shades. He
was still hearing the story, a steady somewhat distant drone of
words, like the sound of an alarm in another room that's heard
from inside a dream. He swallowed hard to clear the pressure in
his ears and reached for a lamp stand, trying to steady himself,
but his hand clutched empty air as the house yawed and his
rubbery legs buckled. He turned and bolted aft, up the steps to
deck level, down the crooked gangway, through the cavernous
tunnel and out. He ran into the middle of the road and waited
in the white dusty light until Nell and D'Angelo emerged from
the boat, blinking like tired children.

Nell led them to a corrugated-tin shed, where they found, in
a walk-in refrigerator, cases of milk in pint cartons, stacked to
the ceiling. D'Angelo hoisted one of the cases onto his shoulder
and they marched off along a path spongy with duff and down
a steep crooked slope with worn steps of rocks and exposed
roots until they came to a tiny inlet. A small stream, not ten feet
wide, spilled into an estuarial flat choked with eelgrass and
then into the ocean. They forded the stream and came to a

campsite. A bleached stick, pitted like old bone, had been jabbed in the sand. Bird feathers, clamshells, and the pinnate fronds of a sword fern, dried brown, were strung together, dangling from the stick and fluttering in the wind. Nell sat down and hitched her skirt up over her knees, gathering the loose folds in her hands.

"You can light a fire there," she said.

Kype and D'Angelo stared at one another.

"Are you men or what?" Nell asked. "Gather wood and light a fire or we're gonna freeze our asses when the sun goes down."

They stripped moss and bark from the trees and hauled several loads of driftwood and then stopped by the stream for a drink. It was a beautiful little stream, the water pure and clear as crystal, shining with light, but the banks were stacked with dead fish. They were drying in the sand and swarming with flies, their skin baked a golden bronze by the sun, or they were caught up in the weeds along shore, rotting in the shallow water. Their eye sockets were ghostly accusing hollows like the gaze of a vacant mask and their long ragged teeth were bared as if to scare away scavengers. "I guess I'm not thirsty," D'Angelo said. "What the fuck's wrong with these fish?" The living didn't look any better than the dead. They were thin and weak and mutilated, their flesh ripped and trailing from their bodies like rags. Their scales had coarsened, rough and crude as chain mail, and their gaunt skeletal faces were filled with sharp canine teeth. Some of these haunted fish were hardly motile, finning drowsily in the shallow stream, while others fought for position over the redds, weaving in and out, and others still, ravaged by parasites, were alive but so near death they were already decomposing.

"You gonna cook that salmon?" Nell asked, when the fire caught and began to bank up.

"Sure he is," D'Angelo said.

Kype asked, "Who was that old woman?"

"That's my great-grandma," Nell said. "I bet she's older 'n your grandpa and she ain't in no jewelry box either."

"She wasn't what you'd call friendly." Kype hadn't brought a knife but he patted his pockets anyway.

"She probably didn't even know you were there. She's blind."

"Bullshit," Kype said.

"Bullshit you," Nell said.

"She looked right at me. She knew I was there alright. She talked to me. She told me a story."

"You maybe heard something, but you didn't hear her. She doesn't talk. She stopped a while back."

"I'm telling you, she spoke to me."

"Cut up that fish," Nell said.

"I didn't bring a knife."

D'Angelo hopped to, arranging a row of the square pint cartons along the top of a gray driftlog. Empty shotgun shells and spent casings marked the location of an earlier milk massacre. Old cartons sat in the sand, bled dry but still giving off a soured reek.

"Gummerment milk," Nell explained. "We don't know what to do with it all. We drink a little and shoot the rest."

D'Angelo said, "I can't wait."

"My grandfather got that gun out of the Everett morgue," Kype said. "From a friend who worked there. He had a bucket of guns just laying around."

D'Angelo said, "That musta been way back yonder in nineteen aught something or other, wasn't it?"

"I don't know," Kype said glumly.

He removed his boat shoes and burrowed his pale pink feet

in the sand. He stepped into the stream and started walking through the throng of dead and dying salmon toward the beach. A glassy wet margin of sand where the waves of a rising tide turned back left a wrack of sea lettuce and sand dollars and long whiplike ropes of kelp. Out to sea the lowering sun brought the craggy silhouettes of rocks into relief. Kype stood in the churning white froth, waves collapsing around him, growing cold; a blueness had crept into the light. Cormorants gathered on the rocks and dried their wings, a strange apostolate with their heads turned aside and their black wings outspread, like robed priests offering a benediction.

When Kype returned, Nell was gutting their salmon with the shell of a razor clam she'd whetted against a rock. He stood behind her and saw how the firelight brought the red in her hair to the surface. She'd been singing to herself and then she stopped and turned and said, "Hey, asshole." He moved out of her light and her song resumed. Nell skewered the salmon with sticks, interlacing several deft sutures through the meat, and then she cantilevered the whole fish over the fire with a tree branch staked in the sand. The unadorned fillets began sizzling, the skin dripping gobbets of crackling fat on the coals.

"Kype." D'Angelo's voice echoed off the wet rock walls of the tiny cove and, reverberating, seemed to call Kype's name from out at sea. "I'd say this is your spot."

"I'm not feeling it."

"You're running out of choices, Buddha-boy."

"I think I'll head back," Kype said. "It's been a long day."

"You can't leave me out here."

"You can't leave period," Nell said.

"Three's a crowd. You guys enjoy the salmon."

"The trail's under water," Nell said. "You have to wait for the tide to change."

"Under water?"

"Not forever. It goes back out, dontcha know? All you have to do is wait."

Kype pulled at the salmon with his fingers. The pink flesh was fatty and moist, with a smoky wood flavor. He folded the crisp skin in half and ate that, too. Finished, he picked his teeth with a white bone and said, "The old woman told me we were fish."

Nell said, "You were hearing things."

"I know what I heard," Kype said.

"She don't talk."

"She talked to me."

"Well, I'm just a dumb injun," Nell said. "Maybe it's me that's gone deaf."

Kype remembered how his own grandfather had gone selectively deaf in his last years, dialing down his hearing aid at dinner to cut out the highs, the yammering treble of his drunken daughter and Kype's own adolescent screech, or blasting the volume on the television when the conversation bored him. In truth, he'd been a nasty old man most of Kype's life, except in the early days. Then, briefly, out of pity for the fatherless boy, he'd mounted an effort, teaching him the sort of folksy wisdom and woodlore that was supposed to build character—in 1937 or whatever. Out camping, the vast gap in age between his grandfather and himself had left Kype with deep feelings of incompetence. Back home, the ancient objects in the house—the dim dusty lampshades, the brass doorknobs that had blackened with time, the monumental rolltop desk where the old man kept his leather-bound ledgers, even the quiver of sharpened pencils in their hammered pewter cup—filled him with a pervasive sorrow, as if the future itself were a legendary relic. He'd been raised to revere a forgotten, disappearing world, a tomorrow so filled with the glories of yesterday that he was forbidden to touch any of it. Nothing in that old house in the Highlands ever changed; in Kype's memory, even the shadows seemed to have been nailed to the walls.

"How long until the tide changes?" he asked.

"Quit whining," Nell said. "But, uh, you only bring that one bottle?"

"Let's do some shooting," D'Angelo said.

They left Nell by the fire, walking off thirty paces, arguing ballistics as they searched for an angle where they weren't likely to get themselves killed by ricocheting bullets.

Kype loaded the gun. "Let's wager," he said.

"Oh, a wager, how delightful," D'Angelo said, in a mocking hifalutin accent. "Well okay, old chap, old sport, let's see—my harmonica against your Cadillac."

"That's not fair."

"Fuck fair, Kype. You're about to inherit a fortune. You're done with fair." He ran a hand through his greasy hair and said, "I'll throw in my bolo."

"I want Nell."

"Oh," D'Angelo said. "Okay."

Kype shot first and missed. He'd never used a gun before, and he had expected something monumental, a big bang and some kick, but the pistol was tiny, nearly a toy, and it only made a faint, insignificant pop against the waves resounding in the cove.

"My turn," D'Angelo said.

"I only get one shot?"

"If you miss it's not your turn anymore." D'Angelo frowned, shaking his head. "Everybody knows that." He steadied the pistol at his side and then yanked it from an imaginary holster, popping off a shot that managed to plug the carton cleanly. "Oh yeah," he said, stopping to watch the stream of milk bleed into the sand. "That's the way you do it." The next shot exploded in a spray of white. The tattered box fell into the river, spilling milk, and drifted away.

"Never thought I'd be shooting milk when I left Brooklyn," D'Angelo said.

"Why'd you leave?" Kype asked.

"I always had that dream, to hitchhike out west."

"I never did."

"Where the hell would you go?" D'Angelo said, sweeping the barrel of the gun across the horizon. "Swimming, I guess."

"Let me see the gun."

"I haven't missed yet, Kype. It's still my turn. Why don't you get us some of that –what did you say your grandfather called it, that hootch? This shooting is giving me a thirst."

Kype went for the bottle but Nell refused to give it up and he returned empty-handed.

"But this isn't the West anymore," D'Angelo said. "It's like west of the West or something."

"Let me take a shot."

"Kype, if I have to tell you one more time, I'm going to shoot *you*."

Kype wondered if the new life awaiting him after probate would be like this, lived among strangers. He would inherit a fortune but never feel entirely at home—it was like a rider in his grandfather's will.

"I thought there'd be something else," D'Angelo said. "It's disappointing. It's making me lonesome. Nothing but stinking fish and the ocean. It's no wonder you can't find your spot, Kype. From out here, you have to go east to get to the West."

"What are you talking about?"

"We need to reload." D'Angelo handed him the pistol. "But it's still my turn."

"Why do you get the girl?"

"Her pussy smells like fish," D'Angelo said. "Just like everything else around here."

Kype fed a shell into each chamber and closed the cylinder and gave it a spin. Then he made a break for it. D'Angelo lunged for him, but Kype juked across the beach, and when he reached the log he shoved the barrel of the gun against the belly of the first carton and shot it. He shot the one next to it; and he shot the one next to that. He tossed one of the milks in the air and tried to shoot it on the wing, missing wildly as the carton zoomed out of the sky, but after it caromed off his head and came to rest in the sand, plopping at his feet, he shot it twice for good measure. He mowed them down, picking off carton after carton, and when he ran out of bullets he grabbed the hot barrel and beat the last few milks with the butt of the gun, hammering away until the seams burst and the waxed cardboard turned to pulp. He caught his breath, looking over the carnage. The milks were slaughtered, and his shirt was soaked. Downstream the dark humped backs of the migrating salmon stirred indifferently in water that had turned cloudy white.

"Happy, Buddha-man?" D'Angelo brushed sand off his pleated pants and shook out the cuffs. "Now give me the gun."

"We're out of milk, my friend," Kype said. "I shot the last milk. They're all dead."

"Some sport you are."

"There's nothing left," Kype said, handing over the gun and the crumpled box of ammo.

"There's you," D'Angelo said. He cinched up his bolo tie,

flexed the fingers of his right hand, and squinted at Kype. "And there's these fucking fish."

His first shot pierced the eye of an old buck with a bony face and a long, grim snout that curled like a brass coat hook. It had been holding in some quiet water behind a rock, and when the bullet entered its brain, it merely gave up and let go and was borne gently downstream. D'Angelo knelt near the bank and bumped off two more of the weary, spent fish. They flopped in the shallows, their blood pouring out pink as it mixed with the milk. The stream was small, its narrow channel choked with salmon, and D'Angelo hardly bothered to aim. Every blind shot killed. He blasted the adipose fin off of a hen. He popped another fish in the belly. He shot one that was already dead, and the salmon dissolved, drifting away like a cloud. He stopped to reload, slipping the last shell into the chamber while eying Kype, who turned away and watched the stream flow by. The remaining fish, undisturbed, went about their business. The dying ones swam with a pathetic list, twisting in the current as if blown by the wind. Others were still fighting to make it home to their spawning ground. Upriver a mating pair wove in the current above a redd, braiding the water with their bodies, releasing eggs and milt as if pollinating a flower. The hen eventually dropped back to fan gravel over the nest and cover her fertilized eggs and D'Angelo raised the gun and fired and she died without much agony, just a shiver and then her slowly gaping mouth, faintly protesting, as the current drew her down to the sea.

"I oughta make you fuckers eat those dead fish!" Nell said. She was holding the urn and the bottle of bourbon hostage in her lap. "Those are my ancestors, you know. You killed my people!"

"I'm sorry about your fish," D'Angelo said. "And I'm sorry about your ancestors, too, but I think we're just gonna have to let bygones be bygones. I don't see any other solution. Be reasonable."

"You be reasonable!" Nell shouted.

"We're just going around in circles here," D'Angelo said. "Young Kype wants old Kype's ashes back, and Nell, honey-bunch, what is it you want?"

"I told you already." She was sick of repeating herself. She scooped out a handful of ashes and broadcast them into the river as if sowing seed.

"Please don't throw any more of those ashes," Kype said.

"Those fish were all sick," D'Angelo said.

She shook the urn in their faces. "And this guy is dead! You want him back, this burned-up old Ashtray Man!"

They had been fighting forever, shouting over the waves, screaming to be heard, as the cove filled like a bowl, first with shadows, then with night. Now the moon was directly above them, a nimbus floating in the fog, as vague as a coin at the bottom of a well. Kype was cold and shivering in his clammy shirt.

"I'm thirsty," he said.

"Have some milk," Nell said.

D'Angelo coaxed heat from the fire, stirring the coals, and then drew the harmonica from his shirt pocket. He tapped spit from the blowholes and then twisted his gummy lips over the instrument, flapping his hands as if he were wailing the most homesick blues ever, but the miserable honking was no match for the sound of the crashing surf, and his song drowned. He threw the harmonica at Nell. "Might as well have that, too," he said.

"They come here so we can eat," Nell said. "What if they don't come back next year?" She looked at both men, waiting for an answer. "That old woman, my great-grandmother, came here to bathe and pray every morning of her life."

"I can't swim," D'Angelo said.

Under cover of dark, Kype stared promiscuously at Nell. She had flat wide cheekbones like the Sphinx and he imagined that for a kiss all he would do was hold those bones, tip her head forward, and drink from her face.

"Okay," he said, "I'll do it."

"Smart man," Nell said. "Otherwise bad spooky shit was gonna follow you everywhere and forever."

Nell muddled ash and bourbon in the palm of her hand and then dipped her finger in the paste and painted a thick line down the middle of Kype's forehead. "After this," she said, "we'll play the bone game." She traced two circles around his eyes, enlarging them, and then brushed a black streak across each temple, giving him pointed ears. "You can win back the rest of these ashes," she said. "I'm giving you that chance." She drew fangs on either side of his mouth and whiskers that dashed away from his nose. "And then you got to go in that stream and clean yourself up," she said, unbuttoning Kype's shirt, "because you stink real bad. The spirits won't come near you." On his belly she made a school of crude fish, each like a lopsided Möbius strip. They swam out of his navel toward his heart and then migrated across his collarbone and up his throat to his mouth.

Kype lay still, hoping Nell would draw more fish on him.

She said, "You got to get your soul back in your head. Somebody stole it, that's my guess. Maybe it happened while you were sleeping. Or maybe you got a bad scare and it just jumped out of you. You ever feel the top of your head moving?"

And just then, he did, as if the top of his skull had been opened like a jar. Calmed by the flutter of Nell's fingers at his throat, Kype closed his eyes and heard her voice from a distance and strangely saw his grandfather slip a hand in his and lead him into the lobby of a home for retired sailors. It was the dark lobby of what had once been a very fine hotel where old mariners now sat day and night in stuffed chairs and dusty couches and a row of splintering church pews. That there were no more high-seas adventures in the offing, that the distant horizon had finally drawn near, seemed to drive the retired sailors toward extreme solutions—lunacy or silence. Collectively, there wasn't a corner of the world these men hadn't visited, not an ocean, a sea, or a river foreign to them, but now they rarely moved from the lobby. A single lamp was lit low beneath a torn shade and an ashtray of cut green glass held a smoldering cigarette from which smoke rose heavenward as slowly as a prayer. But only the rising smoke stirred; it was so quiet and deadstill in the lobby Kype suspected that even the hearts beating beneath the men's soup-stained shirts pumped like old leather bellows and blew nothing but soft gray ash. No one conversed; no one spoke a word. A silence reigned as if these sailors had been drawn back through time and a private darkness were once again upon the face of the deep. All the waters of the world had retreated and finally gathered in their eyes, deep pools of black or blue or pearl white, glassy reflections that floated like mirages on the surface of their dry and deserted faces.

Kype was led by the hand up a set of stairs and down a long corridor and somehow he felt that he'd been promised this moment all his life. The hotel's glory days still hung in the air, still haunted the rooms and halls. The velveteen wallpaper suggested a gay opulence gone seedy, empty linen closets lined the dark hallways, dumbwaiters rose from a kitchen full of cold stoves, and the rooms all had long braided cords, thick gold ropes that once rang service bells but now summoned nothing. A door to one of the rooms opened, and Kype stood outside where he watched an old sailor twist his service rope into a noose and hang himself. Had the bells been working, the old man might have lived, inadvertently calling for help as he swayed back and forth, but long ago the tongues had been clipped, and in the silence of that hotel the hoisted sailor strangled. Kype looked on hopelessly. In the mute corridors of the hotel he alone had a voice, but when he screamed for help a dove flushed from his mouth, crying *alas, alas,* and all Kype could do was stand in the hall and watch. This was a man who had circumnavigated the globe, who had seen the sun set in every hemisphere, and yet he died swinging, as if by a lanyard, in the empty air above his bed. The silence that settled in the room was like the moral at the end of a fable. Kype now felt that he knew what all the sailors in the lobby knew. And what they knew, because they had circled the world, was that the end is pretty much everywhere.

When Kype opened his eyes, Nell was breaking a stick in half, marking one of the pieces with a band of black ash and leaving the other plain. He understood the rules even before she explained them, as if he'd played the bone game in a past life. Nell would shuffle the sticks behind her back and then all Kype had to do was point left or right and pick the one without the ash. For the first round, just to be fair, Nell agreed to put up her rhinestone hair clip against Kype's Cadillac.

"John Wayne gave it to my great-grandmother," she said.

"He just came up here and gave it to her?" D'Angelo said.

"It used to belong to Pilar."

"Just pulled in and said, Hi ya, Grannie, I'm John Wayne, here's a hair clip?"

"All those guys used to sail up from Hollywood in their

yachts. John Wayne, Bing Crosby, Clark Gable. They came here to fish for salmon and they didn't use no guns, either."

Nell hid her hands behind her back, shuffling the sticks, moving in tune to a song that seemed to have no real words and therefore, to Kype, at least, no beginning and no end. Over and over she sang *he ha ya ho ho ha ya ho he*, a loop of sound that made no more sense to Kype than the surf or the wind. He looked long and hard at her face, trying to see the truth, but his first guess was wrong and so was his second, and in a matter of a few minutes he'd lost his car and his boat shoes. She shuffled and sang and Kype pointed to Nell's right hand, and she showed him, once again, the unmarked stick. Between rounds Nell drummed, beating Kype's boat shoes against a log, but the cadence was off; it seemed crazy and disruptive, working against the heart's rhythm. The jumbled pounding made Kype tense and excited, it confused and deranged him, and then Nell started weaving taunts into her song. "You're blind, *he ha ya ho*," Nell sang, "you can't see, *ho ha ya ho he*." As a game it seemed no more complicated than a coin toss, and Kype kept playing, believing the odds would naturally swing in his favor. All he needed was time. "*He ha ya ho,* your head's got no top." Nell now had the urn of ashes, the keys to the Eldorado, the bottle of bourbon, the dented harmonica, the gun, and the fishing pole. Kype had never won games or awards or prizes, although his life had always been vaguely presented to him as a kind of victory. He unbuckled his wristwatch. He lost his pants and the contents of his pockets. He discovered that losing didn't really bother him. It wasn't nearly the disaster he would have imagined. When his wallet was emptied of cash, he started writing IOUs on old credit card receipts. He pledged his collection of baseball cards, his Mickey Mantle, his Willie Mays, even pawning his autographed Don Mincher from the

1969 Seattle Pilots. Nell's drumming drove time out of his
mind. Unable to stop himself, he began to gamble away little
pieces of his inheritance —an antique dining set and a muffineer
and a box of costume jewelry that would complement Nell's
hair clip. He stood before her in his forlorn saggy white briefs
but didn't feel cold. He had nothing, like all the great men—
like Gandhi. Nothing, like Jesus. Nothing, like the Buddha!
Nothing! he thought. Nothing!

"Now you've got to swim," Nell said.

It was a shallow stream, but the current was strong, the
water cold. Kype clawed the streambed, his belly scraping over
rocks, his ribs jabbed by snags that jutted from the banks. The
slither of salmon passing over his back or brushing by his face
gave Kype the feeling that he was running a gauntlet and
that hands were grabbing for him. He tried to fight his way
upstream, but was tugged by his feet toward the sea. He took a
deep breath and dunked below the surface. It was noisy, turbu-
lent, not the quiet he had expected, and the water tasted like
dirt. That surprised him, the faint scent, the trace of earth in
the water, and it filled him with longing. As a lonely, disconsolate boy he would watch container ships and tankers turn with
the tide, watch them all day long, out his grandfather's window, as if in their slow turning they were the hands of a large
clock, a clock madly trying to mark time on a face of water.
Behind the ships, further west, he could see the headlands of
an island. The island was privately owned and it appeared only
in detailed nautical maps, but as a child Kype had believed it
was his: everything that fell away, everything that died, all the
broken promises and routine disappointments and lost hopes
of his boyhood eventually washed up out there, or so he imagined. For him it was a kind of afterworld across the water, a
combination of sacred ground and junkyard. The idea started

when he reached the age where he understood that he had no father, and for weeks he'd consoled himself, imagining that his dad was a desperado who had lammed it across the bay to that island. Later he believed that all the cowboys and Indians had gone to that island, too. Lost marbles, broken toasters, snapped shoelaces, discarded razors, odd socks, old TVs, shopping carts, and an endless series of small pets found a final home out on the island. The words to the bedtime prayers he no longer said were out there. Anything he couldn't explain was out there. People sang lyrics to forgotten songs and rediscovered the steps to old dances on that island. The good friends of his father's who he called Uncle and one he called Druncle, men who came around for a while and then all of sudden didn't, they'd all left for the island. Sometimes if he stared long enough he believed he saw bonfires burning above the headlands, flickering on the high, forested banks. The island was a new and an old world, it was always full and it was always empty, and it could accommodate everything. He hadn't thought about it in years, but now, as he fought the current, it came back to him with all the vivid romance of his childhood, and he imagined that his grandfather, old Kype, had set sail for that island. And young Kype's soul was out there, too, he was sure of it, and so he kept swimming.

Early the next morning, Kype stood in the dirt plaza outside the bait shop, picking blackberry thorns from his palm. His hands were bleeding and his arms were covered in fish scales, each hair holding a shimmering blue-and-pink sequin. The stink on his skin reminded him of the old jars of fertilizer his grandfather used in the rose garden. His stomach was scraped and scarred and a deep bruising beneath his ribs made it hard to breathe. Nell had been asleep, curled in the sand, and D'Angelo had been snoring next to a log, clinging to it, perhaps afraid that he'd be swept out to sea. Kype had left them there, dressing quickly, grabbing the gun and what remained of his grandfather's ashes and his car keys, wading quietly into the teeming river, through the crowd of spawning salmon. He knelt in the water and held one of the battered fish by the belly and looked into its eye, wondering what it might be thinking. The gills worked lethargically, opening and closing like the wings of a butterfly, and he leaned in close, as if the fish might whisper to him. The stream was full, the dying still dying, the living continuing their run, while yesterday's dead had been washed out to sea, making room for today's. A couple of milk cartons hung in the reeds, but the water had cleared and was once again bright as crystal and shining with light. Kype bowed his head and placed a kiss on the salmon's cold lips, and then he eased the fish back into the river, letting it slip through his fingers. It couldn't find a quiet hold, and the stream carried it away, its exhausted body wholly given over to the current, its final rhythm on earth the rhythm of water flowing past.

Climbing out of the cove, winding his way up the crooked path, Kype got banged up pretty good, but he had his ashes and his gun, and over there, parked in front of the chief's yard, was the Eldorado. He felt in his pocket for his car keys and found a couple of the hasty IOUs he'd written. In the light of a new day he was no longer able to imagine how Nell could possibly have believed that the bone game was for real. The whole fantastic ordeal seemed like a fevered dream, and as the remnants of last night's hour of faith faded he felt strangely deserted. The sun rose over the water and the wind came up, blowing sand and dust across the plaza. The small white shacks started to glow. The old woman came outside and sat with her blanket and wicker hat, warming her face in the sun. The scene was as stubborn and enduring as a monument, and to Kype it seemed as if the dust rising in whorls off the road had claimed these people, all of them overtaken and turned to stone and standing around like statues, arranged just as they had been the day before. The little girl stood in the street, looking east, shielding her eyes against the rising sun. The old man walked by with the same hesitant shuffle, his feet dragging through the dust as he stooped forward and followed his shadow across the road. The engine swayed above the old DeSoto and the open toolbox and the coffee cup still rested on the fender, as if work might begin at any moment. Salmon season was over, but otherwise nothing had changed.

Acknowledgments

I would like to thank Carin Besser for her invaluable work on so many of these stories. Thanks as well to my longtime readers Mary Evans, Tom Grimes, and Jordan Pavlin. The italicized passage on page 219 is taken from an oral account of the first Native American encounter with Captain Cook and is fairly well known to people who grew up in the Northwest. It can be found in many sources, but acknowledgment is owed to Mrs. Winnifred David, a Nuu-chah-nulth elder, who originally told the story. I stripped the historical references from the passage and slightly rewrote the sentences to suit my needs.

Charles D'Ambrosio is the author of *The Point,* and *Orphans,* a collection of essays. His fiction has appeared in *The New Yorker, The Paris Review, Zoetrope All-Story,* and *A Public Space.*

A NOTE ON THE TYPE

The text of this book was composed in Apollo, the first typeface ever originated specifically for film composition. Designed by Adrian Frutiger and issued by the Monotype Corporation of London in 1964, Apollo is not only a versatile typeface but also pleasant to read in all of its sizes.

Composed by Creative Graphics, Allentown, Pennsylvania
Printed and bound by R. R. Donnelley & Sons,
Harrisonburg, Virginia
Design by M. Kristen Bearse